B

BERMONDSEY TRIFLE

Chris Ward

ISBN-10: 1494442167
ISBN-13: 978-1494442163

CHAPTER 1

"You're just a fucking cunt aren't you?" Tony was in a terrifying mood and was actually frothing at the mouth. Physically, he was a frightening sight, tall and muscular. But the thing people really didn't like about him was his eyes. They were always shining as though he was permanently on something. "You're such a clever cunt, aren't you?" he snarled.

The man was tied to a chair while Tony walked around him. "Did you really think we would not find out? You didn't want to steal a few hundred quid, no, you stole hundreds of thousands! Are you fucking insane? We gave you a good, well paid job, you shag all the girls in the club, eat and drink what you want, but that's still not enough!" Tony was incensed and pushed his face right up to his, just touching his nose. "Take my fucking money." He drew back and head-butted the man on the bridge of his nose. The two other men in the room heard the crunch of shattering bone and saw blood flying in all directions.

"Jesus!" shouted Tony, looking at his blood splattered suit. "Do you know how much this fucking cost?"

"What the fuck are we going to do with you, eh?" Tony was brushing the blood off his jacket, making it worse. "You're just a complete fucking cunt." He turned to his two heavies and repeated again slowly, "What are we going to do with him?"

One of the heavies, Sid, did a hand motion across his neck, signifying he should have his throat cut.

Tony turned back to the man who was shaking uncontrolledly, and to all intents and purposes, was completely out of it. He then managed to mumble something, "Go to fucking ... hell, Tony."

"That's where you're fucking going, you cunt!" shouted Tony. Tony was still stalking round him, thinking of what to do with him. He kept glancing at Sid and Steve for some sort of reassurance he was doing the right thing. Tony really wanted to kill him, cut him up into tiny pieces and make sausages out of him, but what would Paul, his brother say? Tony again pushed his face close to the man, "Paul will be here in a minute, and then we'll decide what we're going to do with you."

The man lifted his battered head as best he could. “Always doing what your brother tells you, can’t do anything on your own, can you!” He sniggered painfully, spat a mouthful of blood onto the floor and laughed as he added, “Either Paul or Marie is always babysitting you, you’re pathetic, do you know that? Fucking pathetic.”

Tony was getting more and more psychotic as he listened to the man drone on. Marie was Tony’s wife and Tony did not like her being brought into the conversation.

“You better shut your fucking mouth! I mean it, shut your fucking mouth!" Tony was screaming at the man, saliver was hitting his face, not that he could feel it with his smashed nose causing so much pain.

The guy looked hard at Tony. “Nice lady, your Marie; I’ve been there Tony, very nice it was, a fucking great shag, mind she’s been with all your so-called mates, she knows how to dish it out alright.”

Tony was shaking his hands in the air and shouting, “Don’t say another word, not one word, not one fucking word!”

The man just couldn’t resist, “Your mother was a fucking whore, seems to run in the family.” That was it. Tony pulled his 357 magnum out of his trouser belt and smashed it over the man’s head, knocking him unconscious.

“Shit Tony! I hope he’s not dead!” said Sid anxiously as he walked towards the prone body lying on the floor, with blood forming a puddle around his head.

CHAPTER 2

Paul thought that going to see Millwall wasn't so much fun these days.

"What do you reckon on the score tonight then Tony?"

"Got to be two fucking nil, don't you think?" Tony was smiling and in good humour, he was in his element, a few pints at the Globe pub and now striding down Cold Blow Lane to watch Millwall verses Leeds at the den.

"I fucking hate Leeds, a bunch of northern cunts."

"Yes, we know you don't like them Tony!" said Paul.

"Don't like them, they should all be fucking gassed!" spat Tony.

Paul and Tony Bolton had been football thugs for many years. Many were the times they had preyed on away supporters and attacked them without compunction or provocation. That had all changed in 1993 when the new den was built; a walkway for away fans had been built to take them directly into the stadium and back to the station after the game; all that was a few years ago now.

Paul was the older brother at 29, and Tony was 27. Paul and Tony made their way into the stadium and nodded at various menacing looking men, who they obviously knew. Leeds games always had a bit more of an edge, as the fans hated each other with a passion. They found their seats and looked round the stadium.

"Looks like a decent crowd," said Paul.

"Always are, when those cunts come down," replied Tony, looking around the milling fans.

The Leeds fans started singing obscenities at the Millwall contingent and they replied in kind.

“Great!” said Tony. "It’s warming up now." Tony stood up and screamed a mouthful of abuse at the Leeds fans. It was highly unlikely they could actually hear him but it made him feel better!

“Not like the good old days, is it Paul?” said Tony. “We have more important things to deal with now than beating up away supporters.”

“Yea, I know that Paul, you know best. You know you’re the boss and I’m the hired help,” said Tony laughing.

“Don’t talk crap, Tony. You’re far more than the hired help. You’re my brother and my partner.” The crowd bayed for blood as the two sets of fans sang abusive and disgusting chants at each other. The whistle went and Leeds kicked off.

Tony was again off his seat, screaming abuse at the Leeds fans. “Go back up north, you load of cunts, fuck off.” He then joined in with the famous football anthem aimed at the Leeds fans. “Who are ya, who are ya, who are ya!"

It never ceased to amaze Paul that Tony had changed so little over the years. They had grown up in a really tough part of South East London and had now made their mark. Nobody messed with the Bolton brothers, particularly Tony who had the nickname "Mad Tony." Paul still enjoyed going to the den to see matches but his life had changed dramatically over the years. He now had a posh totty girlfriend called Emma, a fabulous apartment in Chelsea Harbour overlooking the river Thames, a superb range rover, a love of fine wines and he even liked opera music. Yes, things had changed and he wanted it to stay that way. Tony still lived in Bermondsey, albeit in a very nice property and he still loved the area he knew as a child and grew up in. Tony would never change. Paul had tried to introduce him to the finer things in life, like eating in Michelin-starred restaurants, but Tony still loved Kentucky Fried Chicken, McDonalds and best of all, pie and mash, with plenty of green liquor in Manze’s on Tower Bridge Road or Deptford High Street.

The game was turning into a boring draw when Leeds made a break from the half way line; the winger was away and bore down on the Millwall goal. The blue and white lions were scattering in all directions except towards the man with the ball!

Tony was on his feet. “Break his fucking legs!” He was screaming at the players. “Somebody fucking tackle him!” He was now losing all control, jumping up and down and hurling abuse at Leeds and Millwall players. The Leeds winger centred the ball. Tony stopped shouting and time froze. The ball glided as if in slow motion towards the far post, the Leeds centre forward rose majestically above the defenders and headed powerfully into the net. Tony collapsed into his seat. “Fuck, Fuck, Fuck” he screamed. He started to pull at his hair and Paul could see he was getting close to the state of mind which got him the nick name Mad Tony.

Half time came and the two brothers joined the crowd heading towards the bar and toilets. Paul hated queuing and there were literally hundreds trying to get a pint.

“Fucking shit game,” said Tony.

“There’s still time,” Paul said, looking at the bar queue. He was looking for anyone he knew who was near the front and he was in luck.

“Duke!" he shouted. "Get us two pints, will you!” A huge bald-headed hard looking man at the bar turned round, looked for who had shouted, saw it was Paul and nodded.

“Good, we’re in luck,” said Paul, rubbing his hands together.

Tony grimaced, “Yea good, but doesn’t change the fucking score.”

Jesus, thought Paul. He never stops swearing or moaning, no wonder Emma doesn’t like having him round to the Flat. “For God’s sake Tony, get a life.”

Tony stared at Paul. “Yea well, OK sorry, Paul. I’m just, you know, up for the game and we’re losing.”

Paul suddenly shouted a greeting to a big guy in the middle of the bar queue, “Hey Bob you alright?”

A thumbs up came as a reply “Who’s that Paul?”

“Bob Crowe the union bloke, big Millwall fan.”

Duke turned up with the beers, Paul gave him a tenner and said, “Thanks Duke; long time. What are you up to at the moment?”

Duke was a huge man and must have been 6"6 at least. He looked down at Paul. "I'm resting Paul."

Paul looked surprised, thinking that's what actors say when there out of work. "Resting from what, exactly?"

Duke had to think about this and after a couple of seconds said, "Work." He stood there looking at Paul, waiting for him to say something.

"What sort of work?" asked Paul.

"Security guard," said Duke.

Paul was looking thoughtfully at Duke. "You mean bouncer on the door"

"Yea," said Duke.

"I might have something for you, you interested?" Paul said between sips of his pint.

Duke perked up. "Yea definitely"

"Come and see us at the Club tomorrow night about eleven, OK?" Said Paul, taking another sip of his pint.

"Yea, thanks Paul," said Duke smiling. "Look forward to it." He fumbled in his pocket for the change, but Paul put his hand up quickly. "Don't worry Duke, keep the change."

Tony and Paul quickly finished their pints and rushed back to their seats. The match had already started as they sat down. Tony turned to the guy sitting next to him. "What's happening mate?"

"Nothing."

"Shit, we need to get a grip of this game," Tony said to no one in particular.

The game became more and more boring and the 2, 000 Leeds fans up in the top tier of the North Stand continued to bait the Millwall faithful. Paul could see the pressure building in Tony and desperately wanted to keep him as calm as possible.

"I'm telling you Tony, don't worry, it'll be alright," soothed Paul. The game continued and Paul started to think he would soon be made to eat his words of comfort to Tony.

Tony had given up. “One fucking minute to go, those bastards will be laughing all the way back up north, cunts.” He turned away and was trying to act all cool. Paul suddenly grabbed his shoulder. “Corner!”

The whole crowd were on their feet. “Come on you lions!” rang out throughout the stadium, making an incredible noise. Tony was back, alert and singing his heart out. “Come on you lions!” roared the Millwall faithful. The ball swung in, it bounced across the penalty area. Steve Morison, the Millwall number 9, dived to head the ball towards goal. The whole crowd were raising their hands to acclaim a goal. Suddenly, a Leeds player appeared and blocked the forward from getting to the ball.

“Penalty!” roared the crowd. Everyone looked at the referee. He raised his arm, play on. The ball was cleared, the whistle went. Millwall had lost.

“Shit! Fuck and bollocks!” Tony was glowering over at the celebrating Leeds fans who were cheering wildly.

The last thing Tony heard from the other end of the ground was “No one likes us, we don’t care” the Millwall chant.

"Let’s get out of here,” Paul said, grabbing Tony’s arm. Soon they were outside the stadium.

“I’m going down the Angel for a pint. You coming?” asked Tony.

“No, not tonight,” said Paul. The only thing Paul was interested in was getting back to Emma and having a relaxing glass of decent wine. Going out with Tony now was a nightmare. You never knew what sort of mood he would be in. Jesus, let me get out of here, he thought.

“I’ll see you at the club then,” said Paul.

“OK,” said Tony and they parted company. Tony stood still for a second and quickly turned the pages of the match program. He was looking for a particular page. He found the right page, ‘Referee Profile.’ He scanned the page until he saw what he was after, the ref’s name, Cyril Jones, from Hatfield. Tony closed the program; the name would be remembered, just in case. Tony then set off at a brisk pace to the pub.

CHAPTER 3

"I'm telling you, Jack, the Bolton brothers are getting too fucking big for their boots! We need to teach them a fucking lesson and as soon as possible." Richard Philips was knocking back whiskeys in the Green Man down the Old Kent Road. Richard was 6' 3, well-built and had a sort of face that looked like it had been punched more than a few times.

"Jack, you're not listening. They need sorting." Richard was well pissed off with the Bolton's, they had started encroaching on his business and Jack seemed not to care.

"Richard, you are worrying about nothing," said Jack reassuringly. "They are two young punks trying to make a few quid."

"Are you serious?" asked Richard impatiently. "They were in two of my pubs last week, offering cheap door security. My fucking pubs!" Richard was glaring at Jack, daring him to say that was not serious.

"Nobody told me that, why wasn't I told?" Asked Jack.

"Well, I'm telling you now," said Richard angrily.

"OK, let's call a meet and warn these boys off," Jack said quickly and raised his empty glass at the barman for a refill. If Jack had been aware of the ambition of the Bolton brothers, he might well have looked at the so called little problem more closely.

Jack Coombs and Richard Philips went back a long way, in fact they lived in the same road as kids, went to the same school and got expelled at the same time.

They were brought, or some said, dragged up in Bermondsey and had built up a nice little business supplying doormen to clubs and pubs. From that they branched out into prostitution, drugs and supplying guns. It was what you would call a 'thriving business.'

Although successful and making bucket loads of cash, they were always on the lookout for new ways to make some easy money. This usually led them into conflict, but they dealt ruthlessly with anyone who got in their way.

"Where do you want the meet?" Richard asked Jack.

"Let's make it somewhere safe for all concerned. The Frog, Friday night, 8pm. Tell Gary to make sure he's there on time."

"Consider it done," said Richard.

Gary was one of the heavies Jack and Richard relied on to visit anyone who was messing them about. Richard was more than pissed off with the Bolton's. He was beside himself

With hatred for the two of them; it was really Mad Tony who upset him more than Paul. One day, that mouthy cunt will get what's coming to him, that's for sure, he thought.

Jack and Richard now controlled the doors on 87 pubs in South East London. It had turned into a multimillion pound business with huge profits. They also owned ten brothels in London, from Peckham to Fulham to Mayfair. This involved 125 girls working shifts, so they could offer a service twenty four hours a day, seven days a week. This brought in millions as well. They only really dabbled in drugs. Jack wasn't very keen, and they were useful in controlling the girls, so it made sense to sell some as well.

Their latest business was hiring out guns. This had only recently started but was going well. It had cost a fair bit to get a stock of twelve gauge shot guns, AK 47 assault rifles, 9mm automatic pistols and Uzi sub machine guns, but the two grand for a hire was a good return. All the weapons were kept hidden at a secret address in Basildon, Essex, only known to Jack, Richard and Phil, one of their top men.

Jack and Richard were very wealthy men; they were both multi-millionaires and had an incredible lifestyle. Both lived in huge mansions in Essex and their families lived the life most people only dream about.

Richard finished his drink and made for the door. It was still early and he needed some excitement. He knew just where to go. He got in his top of the range Jaguar and set off for Peckham. Well, there's no point having loads of girls available and not taking advantage of that occasionally yourself, he thought.

"Ted, its Richard. I'll be there in about twenty minutes."

"OK," replied Ted. "You want anyone special?"

"Yea, that new girl, the black one, what's her name?"

"Julie," said Ted.

"Yea, Julie will do nicely, and Ted, I want Trudy as well, in the blue room, OK?"

"Sure thing, boss, I'll arrange it." Ted clicked off his mobile. "Fuck" he said, "that's all I need, Richard coming down and taking two of the girls for a couple of hours. Jesus, how am I meant to run this fucking place?"

Richard arrived and breezed into the modern five bedroom house that was hidden away from view by a high wall and electronic gates.

Ted met him in the reception. "The girls are upstairs in the blue room, all ready and waiting."

"Great," said Richard and he bounded up the stairs, two at a time. He pushed the door open and went into the blue room. It had always been his favourite room. The colours relaxed him and he now always used it. He saw Julie and Trudy immediately. Julie was lying on the bed while Trudy was in one of the arm chairs. Both of the girls looked incredible, Julie was wearing white and Trudy black.

"Hi girls, how you doing?" he asked. The girls squealed and said in unison, in sexy voices: "We've been waiting for you."

"Well, I'm here now," said Richard. "All ready for a good time?" he asked.

"You bet we are, baby," said Trudy. "Shall we have some champagne?" she made towards the small bar in the corner of the room.

"Love some," Richard said. "But first of all, I'm going to take a shower." Richard moved to the en suite bathroom, he turned and looked at the girls. "Open the champagne. I won't be long."

Richard undressed and got in the shower. He reached up and turned the water on, adjusted the temperature so it was just right. He started to wash and was feeling more and more relaxed. He then felt a movement behind him and he jumped in surprise. He turned his head to see Julie the black girl, she pressed herself against him, and he could feel her ample breasts rubbing against his back. He closed his eyes and felt his cock hardening. Julie's hand came round his side and clasped his cock and started moving it up and down. Oh shit, he thought, this is soooo good. He was getting too excited too quickly. He grabbed Julie's hand and stopped the motion.

"It's great, but better slow down, eh." Julie understood.

She took a fresh bar of scented soap and started washing Richard's back, her hand then made its way down to his arse and she rubbed the bar gently and then hard between his cheeks, he groaned in pleasure.

"That's good, really good," He groaned. She continued to wash him spending a long time smothering his cock in soap and then rinsing it off. She then bent down and took his huge hard cock in her mouth, she pushed her mouth right to the end of his cock and then quickly released.

Julie then took a step back and said, "All done."

Richard laughed. "Not yet but it's a good start!" he then patted Julie's very rounded bottom as they moved out of the shower. Trudy had poured some champagne and offered Richard and Julie a glass each.

"Fabulous, thanks Trudy." Richard took his glass and sipped at the champagne. "This champagne has not been chilled. We charge people a fucking fortune to get first class service and then give them fucking warm champagne, fucking hell!" He threw the glass against the wall, it smashed and showered glass and champagne over the carpet.

"Trudy, go and get some beers and make sure they're bloody cold!" He didn't want to ruin the atmosphere so laughed and said "Good job there's no broken glass on the bed!" The girls laughed as well and Trudy went off.

Richard turned to Julie. “How long have you been here now, Julie?”

“Six months," said Julie. "I wasn’t sure I would like it, but you know, it’s OK.”

Richard was looking and admiring Julie's beautiful body. “Come here.” He held out his arms. She came towards him and placed her hands on his shoulders. Richard bent and took one of Julie’s nipples in his mouth and sucked whilst moving his tongue in a licking motion. “Hmmm.” Julie moaned. He moved to the other nipple which was now erect like his cock. Richard was really enjoying this. He moved to the bed and Julie followed. Richard lay lengthways and Julie climbed on top; Richard moved her round so that they were in the sixty nine position. Julie took him full in her mouth and started to move up and down. Richard Couldn’t resist grabbing Julie's arse with both hands and then started licking her. Julie was going up and down, up and down, continually, speeding up. Richard knew this was it. He would have to finish, there was no going back. He was so excited; he was licking furiously at Julie's arse and pussy. He started to buck and lift his arse to push his cock into Julie’s mouth; he couldn’t last much longer.

He heard the door. Trudy came in and her eyes opened wide at the scene in front of her. She could see this was going to end soon and quickly knelt down to suck Richards balls. This was too much for him, he was bucking and groaning ever louder. He tensed, and then he was there. "Ahhhhhhhhh!" He shot his load all over Julie, Trudy and the bed. He felt like he came about three times. The girls were lying back.

Julie was breathing hard and licking her lips. “Wow that was good, real good!”

“What about me?” said Trudy, looking really hard done by.

“Don’t worry," said Richard soothingly. "There'll definitely be a next time and you will be in the lead.” He momentarily thought of his wife. He loved his wife and she had given him three wonderful children but sex at home was a complete waste of time. His wife had no idea how to make a man happy in bed. Perhaps I should base myself here, he thought. Oh God, I don’t think so. I would never get any work done.

He had another quick shower, got dressed and went downstairs. He went to the back office to find Ted. “Ted, you gave me warm champagne, are you fucking mad?”

Ted withered under the broadside. “I’m really sorry Richard. We had a new delivery in and just didn’t have time to chill it enough.”

“How much are we charging for the champagne?”

“Err... a ton,” replied Ted.

Richard was speechless. “A hundred quid for warm champagne? Don’t ever let it happen again.”

Ted was sweating. “Yes, don’t worry Richard, it won’t happen again.”

“Good, as long as we understand each other,” said Richard, giving Ted a steely stare. Richard walked towards the door. He put his arm out and held the handle and turned. “Ted?”

“Yes, Sir.” said Ted,

“Look after Julie, she’s special to me, you understand?”

"Yes Richard, I’ll look after her.” Ted was still nodding his head as Richard walked out. Richard went towards his car and had a brainwave. Why not? He thought. I’ll set Julie up in a flat and then she will be mine and mine alone. He smiled and started whistling. Life is good, he thought.

“What the fuck do they want?” Tony was asking Paul in a concerned voice. “I don’t like it.” “You worry too much” said Paul, looking very thoughtful. “They want a chat about business so we’ll go and see exactly what they want.”

“That Richard is a hard cunt. I’m telling you, I don’t fucking like it!” Ever since they had been contacted by one of Richard Philip’s boys, they had been trying to work out why Jack Coombs and Richard wanted to see them.

“They can’t know about how much business we now have, can they, Tony?” asked Paul.

“We’ve kept really quiet about the clubs, Paul, so no, I don’t think so.”

“Hmm.” Paul was thinking. He'd always been the brains with Tony providing the muscle.

What Jack and Richard didn’t know was that the Bolton brothers now had a sizable business, they had control of 20 odd local pub doors, but their real business was owning five drinking and sex clubs in Soho, London. The profits from the clubs were incredible and it was mostly cash, so they didn’t pay much tax. It had been tough to get the first club open, but after that, they kept ploughing the profits into opening more and it had proven to work really well. Apart from those businesses, Paul did not know about Tony’s other activities which included protection, burglary, and armed robbery. Roddy was their accountant and was now one of the top men they relied on to run the business. He knew every dodgy scam there was to know, and he was based at the Den, their biggest and favourite club.

The day of the meeting arrived and Paul and Tony were at the Den in Soho. Tony was his usual worried self. “We should have told them to fuck off; they fucking tell us to jump and we ask how fucking high, I don’t fucking like it Paul.”

“Have you ever spoken a sentence without swearing?” asked Paul, frowning.

“Oh great, now your living with that Emma tart, you suddenly think your above me. So I fucking well swear a bit, it’s where I come from same as you.” Tony had spoken exactly as he felt.

“You call Emma a tart again and we will fall out big time, do you hear me Tony?”

“Yea, sorry Paul, I didn’t mean it. I’m just worried about the meet tonight.”

Paul looked thoughtful again. “Now we have Duke on the payroll, he can come with us tonight. I’ll feel better with him at our back.”

“Good idea,” said Tony, brightening up a bit.

“Better have a couple of extra guys outside, just in case. Organise it Tony.”

“Now, you’re talking.” said Tony. Tony was happy when they went somewhere mob-handed. He seemed to think the more heavies you had with you, the more respect you got from people. Times were changing, it was now more about off shore accounts, tax evasion schemes and keeping the peace.

“OK, quiet please,” said Paul. He was looking at the crew going down to the Frog. Tony and Duke were sitting sipping whiskies. Rob and Steve were two heavies brought in from one of the other clubs.

“Right guys, listen up, this is a business meeting at the Frog, but I want to be prepared for any eventuality.” He glanced round to make sure everybody was paying attention. “Duke, you will come into the club with me and Tony.”

Duke looked at Paul. “Tooled up?”

“No,” answered Paul.

“He should be carrying,” interrupted Tony.

“This is a friendly meet to discuss business, they’ll check us for weapons, same as we would if they came here; better we don’t”

“OK,” said Tony. “But Rob and Steve can carry just in case.”

“Agreed,” said Paul. “But pistols should be enough, yea?” Everything was agreed. They were to get to the Frog dead on eight o' clock. No point being disrespectful and arriving late.

CHAPTER 4

Dunton Road nick in Bermondsey had been closed for years and the local station was now at Rotherhithe. Jeff Collins was in his five year old Ford Mondeo, just coming out of the Rotherhithe Tunnel. He would be at the nick in five minutes. He glanced at the Albion Primary School on his left. It seemed a lifetime ago that he was kicking a ball about in the playground, down past the enemy (in those days St. Joseph's Roman Catholic Primary School) and then Bermondsey station. He took a left into lower road and he was quickly pulling into the nick's car park. He was as depressed as usual. Driving round Bermondsey, Rotherhithe and Deptford, just really pissed him off these days.

Bermondsey, historically, had been the most densely-settled, slum-ridden borough of London. Over the years, high-rise developments had been built, but had done little to change the lives of the ordinary Bermondsey working class people.

Jeff was fifty three and was tired, tired of dealing with low life scum who plagued his patch with petty crime, tired of dealing with the gangs that made life for poor housing estate residents even worse than it had to be, tired of seeing good people who had been destroyed by drugs, and worst of all, really tired of the kingpin gangsters who owned mansions and drove round in flashy cars when they hadn't done a proper day's work in their lives.

He walked into the reception. "Here we go again," he thought to himself. "Another day, another dollar."

"Morning Jim," he proffered to the reception sergeant on duty.

"Well, thank goodness, the CID have arrived. We can all sleep soundly in our beds tonight!" Jim was old school, same as him. He laughed.

“Anything happening?” Jeff asked.

Jim looked thoughtful for a second, “urmmmm, no. We’ve got a couple of drunks in the cells but other than that it’s been pretty quiet.”

“Good, let’s hope it stays that way,” said Jeff as he moved through reception into the offices. Shit, he thought, I need a fag already. He started to cough as he went to the side door and opened it quickly; the cigarette smoke was choking.

“Jesus! Don’t you lot know smoking is bad for your health?”

Jeff looked around to see who was there. Taffy the Welsh sheep shagger and Karen his partner in CID. He looked at the two of them. “You should both know better!” Karen and Taffy both laughed.

“Morning Jeff, what’s happening?” asked Karen.

Jeff took a long drag on his fag. “Well according to Jim, absolutely zero, which is the way I like it!” Jeff’s aim in life was to just do enough, after all he only had a couple of years left till retirement. Karen was still young, thirty two, to be precise and still keen to make a difference.

Karen had worked her way up through the normal channels, done her time on the beat and then moved into CID. Someone had told her CID was where it all happened. Maybe it was, but not in Rotherhithe. The door opened and a young man stuck his head out the door. "Jeff and Karen are to see Michael at eleven am," he shut the door. Jeff looked at his watch, it was nine am. A couple of hours to go till then.

Jeff looked at Karen. “Let’s grab a coffee and have an update.” What Jeff really wanted to do was find out why Michael Green, head of CID, wanted to see them.

“OK,” said Karen. “Let’s go.”

They made their way back into the offices and ended up in the open plan CID unit at the back of the building.

“So what’s happening?” Jeff said to Karen.

“Let’s get some coffee and we can talk,” said Karen quietly.

Jeff suspected Karen knew something. Jeff and Michael didn’t really get on. Michael got the job Jeff thought he should have had. Since then, their relationship had gone downhill. Michael was a little like Jeff, he didn't want to be the best cop in the Met but he did want to keep law and order to a degree on his manor. Things had been getting out of hand recently; shootings, and a couple of murders, even a kidnapping, which was unheard of in Bermondsey.

"So Karen, what do you hear?" Jeff asked as he sipped his scolding hot coffee.

"I've heard whispers we are going after one or two big fish, but any more than that I don't know"

"Any idea who?"

"No idea," said Karen.

"Ok, I'm sure Michael will tell us more," replied Jeff. He didn't believe Karen at all. She always knew what was going on; perhaps she was even shagging Michael, who knows. He thought it was possible. Jeff looked at Karen. "I'm going to chase up a few leads on the Filbert case. I'll see you in Michael's office at eleven am."

"Yea, OK," replied Karen.

Jeff made a couple of calls but couldn't quite get out of his mind that they might be going after a couple of big fish. Who exactly?

At 10.50 am, Jeff made his way to Michael's office. He noticed that Karen was already inside and she and Michael were laughing at something obviously hilarious. He knocked on the door and without waiting for an answer walked in.

"Hello Michael." He nodded at Karen. "So, what's happening then?" He sat down and made himself comfortable for what could be a very interesting meeting. There was an uneasy silence for a few seconds and Jeff looked around the room as though he was used to all this cloak and dagger stuff.

At last, Michael stood up and faced the two of them. "Right, let's get on, shall we? Today is the beginning of an investigation that can change Bermondsey and the surrounding area. This briefing is top secret and is the start of a campaign to get to grips with one or two of our, shall we say, more shady Bermondsey residents. The good news is that we have an informer on the inside." Michael was quiet for a second to let this sink in. Fucking good luck to him, thought Jeff. All this informer stuff was beyond him, but the fact was you needed serious evidence to send criminals down nowadays, and this was one way of getting it.

"Don't keep us in suspense any longer please, Michael, who are we going after?" asked Jeff. Michael looked at him then Karen and finally the names came out. "Jack Coombs and Richard Philips."

Jeff was shaking his head. "Michael, we have tried before, in fact the whole bloody Met have tried before!"

Michael's face was stern. "That's right, Jeff but now we have some help from inside."

"Oh, and what might that be?" asked Jeff. Michael tapped his nose. "All in good time but what I can tell you is that, we have some intelligence guys coming to give us some help from the National Crime Squad." Well, thought Jeff, this is serious; NCS secret squirrels coming to Rotherhithe, it's unheard of in the annals of the Met. Jeff was getting more interested by the minute "So what do the NCS have on these guys?"

Michael looked thoughtful. "Well, as far as I know, there's all the normal stuff ... bank accounts, tax records, company records, all sorts of stuff, but something has come up to enable us to really have a go at getting these two bastards, not only in court, but the strong possibility of a conviction." Karen was smiling at this, and Jeff suspected she had been told all this before he had, and I'm meant to be her boss, he thought. He began to wonder if Michael and Karen could be an item.

He looked at Karen and thought, yea, I would, she had good legs, nice-sized firm breasts and a pretty face. He suddenly had a vision of her sucking his cock but swiftly got back on track in case he missed anything.

Jeff's thoughts were interrupted by Karen. "Is this investigation starting straight away, boss?"

"The NCS guys will be here tomorrow," said Michael. "There'll be a briefing from them, probably about 6pm and then we'll all be wiser as to exactly what we have." Jeff could feel the meeting coming to an end.

“Jeff, you and Karen, review all you have on those slippery toe rags so you’re ready for the meet tomorrow.”

“Will do,” Jeff said crisply as he left the office, closely followed by Karen.

CHAPTER 5

Paul and Tony pulled up outside the Frog. Tony had been his usual self on the ride down, 'fuck this, cunt that, I'm going to shoot every fucker!' But he had gone quiet as they got out the car and headed for the door. Paul turned to Tony with a serious expression. "Let's just listen to what they have to say and no trouble eh? Let me do the talking."

"Yea, OK," agreed Tony. "Duke, watch our back."

The three of them crossed the road. Tony was not happy he was entering enemy territory without a weapon and he felt naked. Out of habit, he kept moving his right hand to his trouser belt, but this time there was no weapon.

They opened the door and strolled in. One of the bouncers immediately pulled them over to the side and asked, "You carrying?"

"No," said Paul quickly."

"OK, but a quick check, you don't mind?"

"Carry on please," said Paul. That was very civil, thought Paul. The heavy then slid his hands quickly and expertly over his suit, front and back. The heavy then turned to Tony. Paul shot Tony a-behave-yourself look and then relaxed. Tony looked the heavy in the eye and dared him to carry on.

"This won't take a second," the heavy said as he ran his hands down Tony's suit. He was nowhere near as thorough with Tony as he was with Paul. The heavy didn't like the look of Tony one bit and he'd heard some stories about what a nasty piece of work he was. He then checked Duke.

"Good, that's done," said the heavy. "Follow me." He headed to the back of the pub and opened a door marked 'Private Staff Only.' They went up a flight of stairs and the heavy stopped at a door and knocked. "Come," said a voice. The heavy opened the door and motioned for Paul, Tony and Duke to go in.

It was a lovely room, spacious with huge windows right across the width of it, overlooking the Old Kent Road. Paul glanced round and saw three men, Jack Coombs, Richard Philips and at the back of the room, some muscle.

"Paul," Jack held out his hand and Paul took it. "You know Richard of course." Richard and Paul shook hands. Jack turned to Tony. "Tony, how are you?"

Tony looked him hard in the eyes. "Fine Jack."

Richard held out his hand to Tony. "Hey Tony, how are you?" Two faced cunt, thought Tony. One day, mate ... "Good, thanks Richard," he answered as he shook hands. Duke had

Settled into a chair at the side of the room. He looked at Gary and they nodded to each other.

"So, it's been a long time," said Jack. "What's your poison?"

Paul had told Tony not to drink too much, but bollocks, he thought. "Large single malt for me, thanks, Jack."

"Paul?"

"I'll have a beer please, Jack."

"Great." Jack looked at Gary who got up to fix the drinks at the small bar in the corner.

"Let's sit down and relax." Jack waved to a sofa where Paul and Tony sat down. "It must be all of twelve months since we last met, where was it now?" said Jack.

"I remember it well," said Paul. "Tom Farmer's Funeral."

"Oh, Jesus yes," said Jack. "In the bar afterwards, now I remember." There was a silence for what could have only been three seconds but it seemed like minutes; it was broken by Gary bringing the drinks over. Gary was very precise and placed the correct drinks in front of the four men. They all nodded at him and he went back to his seat.

"Tom was a good man," said Richard. "He worked for Nat down in Southend, and did you hear if they got the shooter?"

Jack laughed. "Tony had heard alright, yea they got him, he was buried in cement and is holding up the Dartford Bridge."

"Well at least he's doing something helpful!" he added.

They all took sips of their drinks and as Paul expected, Jack at last got down to business. "So how's business?" Jack asked, looking at Paul and Tony.

"Business is OK," said Paul. "But you know what, it's getting harder and harder to make a decent living."

"Tell me about it," replied Jack. "Everybody wants a cut of the pie till there's nothing left." They all laughed and agreed.

"So, Jack, you invited us for a drink. Was there a specific reason for that?" Asked Paul. "Straight to the point, I like that, Paul," Jack replied. "Not really Paul, we're neighbours and in a similar line of business, so I just thought it would be good for us to meet up occasionally to see if we can help each other in any way." What a load of bollocks, thought Tony. I wonder what the fucker really wants.

"Jack, we're not in the same league as you guys," said Paul. "Hell, we have a tiny business compared to you."

"Apparently, you were looking for business in a couple of Richard's pubs the other day," said Jack.

Paul didn't know that and could have swung for Tony. "We had a couple of guys out knocking on doors," said Paul. "But as soon as we knew they were Richard's, we backed off."

Jack looked at Paul and Tony. "Look, we do the pubs, you know that. Why don't you just leave them to us? We don't want any disagreements." Richard was very happy. He could see Paul and Tony were not happy being told off like a couple of school kids. Ha, ha, keep going Jack, he thought.

Richard looked after the pub business and it was his baby, it also gave him a standard of living he could have only dreamt about when he left school. Tony was fuming. Who does this fucking wanker think he's talking to? He glanced at Paul.

Paul was sitting, sipping his beer as though he hadn't a care in the world. "No problem Jack. Look, why don't you pay us a small consideration for the twenty odd pubs we have, we don't make much money from running the doors. You might as well have them."

Richard was now listening intently, another twenty pubs would be nice, thank you very much, but he was wondering why Paul was willing to give them up so easily.

Jack turned to Paul. "That would seem to make sense but what do you want in return?" Before Paul could answer, Jack held up his glass. "Refills all round please, Gary." Gary came over to collect glasses.

"Not for me thanks," said Paul. He wanted to keep a very clear head.

"Yea, thanks," said Tony giving Gary his glass. Jack and Richard held up there glasses and Gary took them to the bar.

"Jack, as you know, we have the Den club and we see that as the way forward for us." Jack was listening with interest, his view that Paul and Tony were small time had been confirmed.

"Paul, is that your only club?"

Paul hesitated for a second. He would have to tell the truth or a downright lie. "That's right Jack."

"So, carry on Paul." Jack was looking forward to this. "OK, look, your business is mainly in pubs and girls."

"Yes, mainly," replied Jack.

"I heard somewhere you've got a couple of clubs in town, we would like to buy them off you."

Jack turned to Richard. "Have we still got those clubs Richard?"

"Well, there's the three clubs we got from Tilley about eight years ago, there in the west end. Ryder runs them."

Jack looked surprised. But what Richard didn't say was that the clubs were run down and not making any money. They had left Ryder to manage them and all he did was drink the profits, which was why there weren't any. Ryder was a complete tosser thought Richard. That's what happens when you do relatives favours. Ryder was his cousin and because of that, had got away with murder.

"OK Paul, I think we can look at that." Although Jack did not know the figures off the top of his head, he did know the three clubs were old, not making any money and were in the wrong location.

Paul dived in quickly without wanting to appear too eager. "Great, Jack, I'll get my man Roddy to call. Who does he need to speak to?"

Jack turned to Richard. "You better handle this Richard," he laughed as he added, "Don't give them away, eh!" Everybody laughed and were suddenly best friends.

Richard and Jack had twenty extra pubs and had a deal to sell the three clubs they didn't really want. Paul and Tony had agreed to pass over the pubs, which was unfortunate, but Paul was ecstatic to get the three clubs. What Jack and Richard didn't know was that Paul had visited the clubs over the past three months and was sure he could turn them round. Paul knew how to run clubs. The five clubs they had were grossing eight million a year with a net profit of two and a half a million. Paul's recipe for success was simple: nice décor, good quality girls, live music and reasonably priced drinks, security and confidentiality. Paul knew that a guy called Ryder was running the clubs, the prices were extortionate, the girls were old hags and the clubs hadn't seen a lick of paint in years. Unlike the other clubs, the three of them would be lap dancing clubs. Yes, he could turn them round. Paul was also in the process of opening one new club and had just agreed to buy another, so all in all, they could have ten clubs up and running in six months' time. The money they would be making would be incredible. The only issue was that the three clubs would need huge investment, but Roddy can sort that.

"Great, let's have some more drinks." Tony was getting drunk and speaking loudly. Paul could see Jack and Richard looking at Tony out of the corner of their eyes. I better get him out of here, he thought.

"Time we were off, Tony," said Paul loudly. "I'm sure Jack and Richard have got plenty of things to do." Paul looked at the two of them. Tony was pissed off, he wanted to celebrate and was in the mood for a good drink. Paul decided quickly and made to move out of his seat. Everybody suddenly got up out of their chairs.

“Richard, Roddy will call you to tie up the club deal and Tony will give you the info on the pubs.” Paul turned to Jack, “Jack, it’s been a pleasure.” Everybody shook hands and Paul, Tony and Duke left.

The door shut. Jack looked at Richard. “What do you think?”

Richard thought for a second. “Paul's obviously the clever one and Tony’s just a complete wanker.”

“What about the clubs? Asked Jack.

“Well, Ryder won’t be happy, but it’s probably a good time to get rid of them.”

“I wonder if we could make it part of the deal that Ryder goes with them,” said Jack.

“Jesus, Jack, they would be mad to take him, plus Ryder won’t be happy."

“I know he’s your cousin but he’s useless, see what you can do.” said Jack.

“OK, it all depends. How much do they want for the clubs?” Jack was interested “Could they turn them round?"

“With a huge investment, maybe.” Richard was keen to get rid of them and the sooner the better. If he could also get Ryder off the payroll, even better. “Look into their business. I want to know the works," said Jack as he headed towards the door. "If they're planning on turning those clubs round, that will cost, I want to know how they can afford it, and if they can’t, where they will get the money from.”

CHAPTER 6

"Did you see her?" Paul was slapping Tony on the shoulder. "Did you fucking well see her?" Tony had had a few drinks and was not that interested but eventually, he spoke "Who are we talking about now? That's the fifth time you've said that to me tonight!"

"The blonde, did you see her? Jesus, what a looker, fantastic tits and what an arse!"

Paul liked to give some of the staff a treat now and then. Roddy, the accountant, was out with them, plus two of the club managers, Dave and Angus, who had achieved record months. They were doing a pub crawl down the Old Kent Road and it was proving to be a good night. It was also good because they knew all the owners and managers of the pubs; so got good service. They were in the Thomas A. Becket, having already downed a few in the Lord Nelson.

"This is the one, Tony, shit I'm in love!" he was looking round and she seemed to have disappeared. "Oh God, where is she?" Then he saw her. He was transfixed. Slim, pretty with a gorgeous smile, she kept flicking her long blond mane back and running her fingers through it, she turned round and they made eye contact. He was looking straight at her, then she smiled and turned back to talk to her two friends. Did she just smile at me? She just smiled at me. Yes, yes, yes, he muttered to himself.

He turned away and touched Dave's elbow. "Dave, I need your help."

"I'm sure you don't really," said Dave.

"Can you see the blonde behind me talking with her two mates, the one in the sexy short black dress?"

Dave took a quick look without making it too obvious. “Nice, Paul, very nice indeed. Is she really your type, though?”

“My type? My type? 'cause she’s my fucking type! Have you seen her arse? It's beautiful!” “Well, I was just checking cos if you’re not that interested, I’ll have a go.”

“You fucking toe rag. I'm going to marry that girl, just see if I don’t.”

“Yes, Paul, but first you’ve got to speak to her!” laughed Dave.

Paul was becoming more and more successful; he had money, and they had the clubs in London. Things were going well. He was a confident, successful, young and good looking guy but he still found it difficult to chat up girls. His brother Tony was a pig, he liked birds that would put it out, any port in a storm for him. He would go and talk to a girl, and if she told him to get lost he would call her a frigid cunt and walk off. Paul could never do that, never.

“Emma, isn’t it about time we left, this place is such a dump.” Mel was not happy; Emma had suggested they forgo the west end for a change, and head south east for a laugh. They ended up in the Old Kent Road. Emma, Mel and Sophie did everything together. They were out on the town every Friday and Saturday night at classy west end nightclubs. Money was no object. All their parents were successful business people and they all lived in the Kingswood, Epsom and Ashtead areas, in expensive leafy Surrey.

“We can’t go yet,” said Emma. “We haven’t met any real life gangsters.” They all laughed. “This load of losers, I don’t think so," chipped in Sophie as she looked round. Although, there’s a group over there that don’t look too bad.” Sophie was looking at Paul, Tony Dave, Angus and Roddy.

Emma had already seen them and that’s why she didn’t want to leave just yet. One of them particularly interested her, the tall good looking dark-haired one who for some unknown reason, she thought, was in charge.

“Are you two serious?” asked Mel.

“Humour us, Mel,” said Emma, who had already given the good looking one the come on but like most men, he hadn’t even noticed. Or if he had, he was too scared to come over. Al Capone he was not. Emma turned to Sophie. “That group of blokes, how are we going to get to talk to them?” As it happened something was about to happen that would help that come about.

The three drunks at the bar were well pissed and had been on the lash all day. They’d been chatting girls up all day and got nowhere with any of them. They were in good humour, apart from the fact that there were no girls. The truth was, all three were drunk, unattractive big lumps, who, most girls would run a mile from. Steve, the biggest lump who must have been six feet five and about eighteen stone, was looking round the pub for likely targets and he set his gaze on Emma, Sophie and Mel.

“Guys, we’re in luck, look at those three.” Steve was pointing at the girls. “They’re gagging for it!” The two other men looked and both said at the same time: “You’re not serious.”

“I am totally serious," said Steve. "Look, if you don’t try, you won’t know.” He was looking at his two mates and then clasped them round the shoulders. “Are you with me lads?” The two did not look very supportive and they thought the three girls Steve was interested in were well out of there league.

“OK, we’re with you," said Fred, one of the other two guys “but, you do all the talking and we’ll be right behind you.”

“Great. Get three large shots in and we’ll be on our way to heaven. By the way, I want the one with the long dark hair.” They knocked back the shots and made their way over to where the girls were standing.

Paul had seen the three men moving towards the girls and he was beside himself. “Guys, look, some one's trying to muscle in on our girls.”

Tony looked at him. “What do you mean, 'our girls?” We haven’t even spoken to them!”

“Yea but ...” Paul trailed off as he saw the huge one, Steve, start talking to the girls.

Mel looked at her two friends and muttered, “Don’t look now but three creeps are coming this way and I think they’re going to talk to us."

Sophie discreetly looked up in the direction of the three men approaching. "Shit! These guys are ugly, fat losers."

"Say what you think then, Soph!" said Emma.

"Hi girls, how's it going, do you come here often?" Steve was right next to them with the other two on each side of him.

Emma looked Steve straight in the eye. "We're not looking for any company, thanks." She rudely turned her back on him and started to speak to Sophie and Mel.

"There's no need to be fucking rude," said Steve.

Paul was watching what was happening very closely and was overjoyed to see the men got, from what he could see, the brush off.

"Tony, are you ready?" asked Paul.

"Ready for what?" Tony asked, looking confused.

"Could be some trouble, get ready."

Tony was looking round the pub and couldn't see anything untoward. "I'm always ready but what the fuck are you talking about?"

"Watch those punks with the three girls," said Paul, looking tensed.

Steve put his hand on Sophie's shoulder. "Listen, you ugly shit. There was no need to turn your back like that." He started to pull Sophie round so she was facing him. Emma was incensed and grabbed Steve's arm shouting. "Get your hands off her, you bastard!" Steve swung his arm and sent Emma flying to the floor.

Everything then happened very quickly. Steve, Tony and the guys had been watching and sprang into action.

Tony was striding over to the girls. "Paul check the girls are alright, I'll deal with this."

Paul knelt down next to Emma and took her arm. "Are you OK?" He was so close and even though she was on her back, she looked stunning. He could smell her perfume which was so intoxicating.

"Are you going to help me up then?" asked Emma.

“Yes, Yes of course, sorry.” Paul helped her up. They both glanced over to where the others were.

“You fucking great lump! What the fuck are you doing? The three of you fuck off out the pub, now!” Tony was always in the mood for a bit of agro, he thrived on it. He was right up close to Steve and was ready for anything.

“Who the fuck are you?” asked Steve, angrily.

“Don’t even go there mate. Now fuck off before there’s trouble!”

“Trouble! And who’s going to give me trouble?” Steve rose to his full height and gave Tony a hard stare. The first punch hit Steve in the kidney, as his head went down Tony hit him on the jaw with an uppercut. It was all over in two seconds. Steve was sprawled on the floor groaning, his two mates put their hands up as if to say, it’s over, we’re not getting involved.

“Take your mate and fuck off home,” said Tony to the two men. The two men grabbed hold of Steve and helped him towards the door.

Paul and Emma joined the group. “Thanks Tony,” said Paul.

“Yes, thank you for helping us,” chorused all the girls.

Emma was now OK and looked at Paul and Tony. “The least we can do is buy you guys a drink.”

Sophie gasped a warning. “More trouble on the way.”

Tony and Paul turned quickly to see what Sophie was looking at: three more huge men were approaching the group. Emma was ready to move quickly if more fighting started. Mel took her arm “Let’s go” said Mel, taking Emma's arm.

“No, wait,” said Emma.

“Paul, is everything OK? Sorry we missed the action or we would have sorted it for you” Andy was in charge of the door and overall security at the pub.

“No problem Andy, it’s over. Just a small misunderstanding.”

Andy looked round at the group. "Paul, perhaps you and your guests would like to move into the private bar." Paul looked at Emma who smiled and nodded her head. "Love to, thanks Andy, appreciate that."

Andy led the group through a side door and they entered a very plush bar.

"This is better!" tweeted the girls, heading towards the bar. Andy called the barman over. "Champagne for the ladies, whatever these gentlemen would like and as much as they want."

The girls could not believe this. Champagne and free drinks all night! This was getting better by the minute, they thought. Emma noticed Andy speaking to Paul. She could just hear what was being said.

"If there is anything you need, please just ask for me."

"Will do, thanks Andy, I appreciate your help." said Paul.

The champagne was opened and glasses filled.

"Before the toasts, I want to introduce the heroes of the night," said Paul. "My brother, Tony." He took Tony's hand and raised it like a boxer's who has just been declared winner of a fight. A cheer rose up from the girls.

"Next, the two best club managers in London, Dave and Angus!" More cheers from the girls. So Paul's involved in London clubs, Emma was thinking to herself. Wow, he could actually be a real life East London gangster, maybe they had met some gangster types after all. And last but not least Roddy the financial whiz kid, the girls all booed in a very friendly way!

"It's my turn to speak," said Emma. "We were three damsels in distress and the five musketeers rescued us."

Sophie and Mel cheered wildly, they held up their glasses and drained them. Angus went round, topping up all the glasses.

Angus and Roddy soon went home to their wives so there was now the three girls, Paul Tony and Dave. The drinks had flowed and everybody was getting very happy. Paul had been chatting to Emma and felt like he had known her all his life. He was about to really shock her. "Emma you won't believe this but in twelve months' time we are going to get married."

Emma looked him in the eye and could see he was deadly serious. "Maybe we will," she giggled. The drink continued to flow. Soon, it was 11pm.

Paul called for quiet. "I suggest we go for a curry. All those in favour say I!" there was a loud resounding "I" from the whole gang.

The party of six spilled out of the pub and jumped into a taxi. Paul sat in front. "The Tower Tandoori, Tower Bridge Road." They sped off. They got to the restaurant and piled out of the car. Paul took a huge wedge of cash from his inside pocket and paid the cab driver with a twenty quid note.

"Keep the change." Paul felt this was an historic night and was in an incredibly good mood. They took a window table and all sat down. Paul and Emma were sitting together and kept touching each other's arms, it was all very touchy-feely. Masses of food arrived and more drinks.

Suddenly, an empty wine bottle smashed into pieces on Dave's head. Before Tony or Paul could even move, it was over. They saw the big guy from the pub run straight out the door and into a waiting car. There was no way they could have caught him. Dave had been sitting on the inside chair, which was why he got hit. The meal was over, the girls were shocked at the violence and just wanted to get home. Paul organised a cab and sent them on their way. Dave had some concussion but miraculously, was alright. Paul had made sure he did one thing before the girls left and that was to get Emma's phone number.

When Paul and his party had arrived at the Tandoori, they hadn't noticed the three guys from the pub incident, who were sitting in a booth at the far end of the restaurant.

Steve told his two mates to go out the back, get the car and drive it over five yards to the side of the front door. He then finished the bottle of wine they had been drinking. He was pissed off because he would have liked to have smashed the bottle over the bastard who had thumped him but he was sitting right by the window. So Dave got it instead. He had sauntered down the side of the restaurant then cut over to walk past their table. He lifted the bottle up and smashed it onto the nearest guy's head. He would have a serious headache for some time. As for the others, he hoped to see them again.

Paul and Tony had sworn revenge and put the word out that they would like to know where these three men could be found.

The next morning, the three girls woke with severe hangovers. It had been a good night, but they were shocked that, in one night, there had been two acts of serious, well, serious to them, violence, one in the pub and the attack in the Indian restaurant.

Paul woke up a bit later than usual and answered a phone call to his mobile. "Yes, it's Paul speaking." As soon as Paul heard who it was, he listened intently then said, "Yes, I can speak." He listened again. "Yes, I have that and I am in total agreement."

"OK, I will meet you," he said after a moment and clicked off.

Emma's heart beat a little faster when she thought of Paul. Did she really want to get mixed up with someone who lived the sort of life he did? It was a question she answered herself very quickly, yes. She had never felt so alive. Yes, she was going to marry Paul and as soon as possible, she thought. She laughed to herself. God knows what her parents would say.

CHAPTER 7

Jeff and Karen were sitting in the office, going through the files on Jack Coombs and Richard Philips.

“Jesus! There's so much stuff, it’s incredible!" Said Karen.

Jeff had spent years reading and sifting through files and he hated that part of the job, in fact he hated all the paperwork he had to do. There had even been occasions when he should have arrested someone but didn’t, just because of the paperwork he would have had to write up. Jeff liked to be out on the manor visiting crime scenes, talking to people and getting evidence.

“Jeff, are you helping at all?” Asked Karen.

“No,” said Jeff, laughing.

“Well, I would appreciate if you did, please.” Karen knew exactly what Jeff was like and did not expect him to be reading through the huge pile of files on the two crooks.

“I know all I need to about those two bastards; I’ve arrested them at least, three times over the years and never got a conviction.”

“Why was that?” asked Karen, with interest.

Jeff thought for a moment. “Mostly witness intimidation, you think you’ve got a decent case and then suddenly all the witnesses get amnesia or just disappear.”

“Hmm, that doesn’t sound too good,” said Karen thoughtfully.

“It’s a fact of life, the whole world knows that those two bastards are into prostitution, drugs, gambling, robbery, you name it. They've done it or are doing it, but getting proof is another thing! Times have changed, Karen." Jeff was getting angry. "Money laundering is a fine art, off shore accounts, tax havens ... and the intimidation and violence is done carefully, with no lead back to the people that order the jobs done."

Karen was annoyed. "So what you're saying is, we are wasting our time before we even start."

"No, I am not saying that, what I'm saying is, it will be very difficult. The good thing is, if we have someone on the inside, then maybe, this time, we can get them, or at least, one of them."

"So, if you had to choose, which one would you take down?" asked Karen with interest.

"Easy question to answer," said Jeff. "Richard is the enforcer and has committed some horrendous crimes over the years. I'm not saying Jack is a saint but he is the brains, not the brawn, so yea, Richard would be the one, definitely."

Karen looked at her watch. "We better go and meet the whiz kids from the NCS then. You ready?"

"As soon as we get another coffee, I'll be ready," said Jeff as he stood up.

They made their way to Michael's office. They expected to see a couple of real whiz kid computer geeks, but what they saw was nothing like that. Andrew and Rob had worked for the NCS for about six years each and were both in their mid-forties, they had become a good team and their skills complimented each other. Andrew did most of the finance investigation while Rob concentrated on other intelligence material such as informers, phone tapping and the like. They loved their work and were known to go the extra mile to get evidence that could get a conviction. They were both married and had several children between them.

"OK, listen up," said Michael. "As you all know, we are going after Jack Coombs and Richard Philips. If I had to take one of them it would be Richard. He's a vicious bastard and needs to be taken out of circulation". Jeff laughed to himself; that was exactly what he had just said to Karen.

Michael looked at Jeff and Karen. "Andrew and Rob have been working on these two for the past three months. We even know what time of day they go for a crap!" everybody laughed and some of the tension left the room. "Jeff you and Karen will get a report from the guys which gives you a good breakdown of where we are at the moment. It's mostly finance but very thorough and incredibly eye opening, we estimate that their businesses are turning over about twenty million a year."

Jeff was shocked. He knew that prostitution, security and drugs were very profitable. But shit, that's a lot of money. Then he thought about his pathetic thirty five grand a year. He looked at Michael. "What do we reckon the net profit on that is then?"

Michael looked at Andrew and raised his eyebrows. Andrew cleared his throat and began to speak. "Well, we estimate about eight million," He looked at Jeff and Karen. "If you consider they've been at this for twenty five years, we reckon the total revenue could be about three hundred million, with one hundred million profits, you can imagine that both these gentlemen are worth millions."

"Andy, forget using the word gentlemen. As far as these two are concerned, they're scum, in fact, so you know what sort of people they are, I'm going to tell you a very quick true story." Jeff collected his thoughts for a moment.

"When these two 'gentlemen' started out, they muscled in on a pimping operation run by a guy called Monty. Monty was old school, loved girls and hated violence. Monty had a couple of brothels and made a good living. Well, to cut a long story very short, Monty ended up with no legs, and his meat and two veg down his throat. They found his legs standing upright on the eighteenth hole at his golf club, nice guys eh! Cause, we never proved it was them, but we all knew it was Richard!"

Karen had gone a bit pale after hearing this.

"Couple of right charmers then," said Rob. "It'll be good to get them inside."

"Listen, when we get them put away, the drinks will be on me for a week," said Jeff.

"OK, so we have established they need looking after and we are going to make sure it happens," said Michael. "Jeff, you and Karen read the reports and then we'll establish a plan of action. You will also be happy to hear we have a budget for surveillance on the ground and that a team will be in place in a couple of days' time. Good, let's get to it and good luck."

Jeff and Karen grabbed the reports and left.

"Hell, have you seen the size of this?" asked Jeff, holding up the report.

"Yea, I know, bedtime reading, I guess," said Karen.

"Well, I don't do much else in bed these days, "Jeff laughed.

"Speak for yourself," said Karen, with a twinkle in her eye.

Jeff had a mental image of Karen on all fours taking it from Michael from behind. Get a grip, he thought to himself, shaking his head.

"Are you alright Jeff?"

"Yes, fine thanks, just thinking." If only she knew, he thought! "Look, let's read the report and we can discuss the whole thing tomorrow."

"OK, it gets serious from tomorrow then. Good."

CHAPTER 8

Sunday 11th August

Emma Miller was twenty three. She lived in a beautiful five bedroom house with a swimming pool in leafy Kingswood Warren, in Surrey. She was the middle child of three. She had an older brother Ian who was twenty four and her sister Fifi was fifteen. I suppose most people would say she had been spoilt. She had Rufus, her horse, stabled up at Epsom Downs; she drove around in a brand new mini that her father had recently bought her; generally, she lived a great life. Peter Miller, her father, owned a chemical manufacturing company in Hatfield, Hertfordshire and made about two hundred and fifty thousand a year. Emma was currently between jobs; she had been working for an internet media company in London but had got pissed off making the tea all the time. Truth was, her father had gotten her the job through connections so he was not overjoyed when she came home one night and told him she had walked out. Emma had been fortunate to go to the City of London Freemen's School in Ashtead Park, an independent private school but had failed all her exams and left with no qualifications. She really didn't know what she wanted to do, but now she had met Paul Bolton, life had suddenly taken on new meaning. Emma had always been a bit of a wild child, and though she may not have done well academically, she was very street wise. Emma couldn't stop thinking about Paul, and the thought that he was somehow involved in some criminal activity excited her more than a little.

Paul had called Emma the next morning after the incident at the Tandoori Restaurant. He'd never been a great believer in love at first sight but he had now changed his mind. As soon as he saw her in the pub he knew he had to have her. She said she was fine and he said he would call her that night. She had said, "Make sure you do," which pleased him no end.

He also thought long and hard about all that had happened in the past couple of days. Dave, getting attacked in the Indian was incredible; that guy just did not know what he had done. The word was out and eventually, someone would see him, make a call and this time, he would really regret meeting the Bolton's.

There was also the meeting with Jack and Richard to think about and how best that relationship could be developed. Tony, was of course, dead against any involvement at all with them, other than putting them both in a helicopter and dropping them into the sea. Paul was worried about Tony; he hadn't moved with the times and could explode into violence at the drop of a hat. Paul smiled to himself. I just wish he would stop wearing those bloody awful clothes and spend some money on some good hand-made suits, he thought.

Letting Jack and Richard take over security in the pubs was not much of a loss, although with good steady money, Paul thought, the future was in the clubs. The profits in a well-run club could be huge and that was where he planned to focus.

He remembered he had to speak with Roddy about the deal with Jack and Richard that had to be tied up as quickly as possible, before they changed their minds.

In the early evening, Paul found a quiet spot in the club and made the call he had wanted to make all day. "Emma, its Paul. How are you?

At last, Emma said to herself. Mustn't appear too relieved or eager though.

"Oh, you found time to call then." Emma regretted saying that instantly.

"I wanted to call you hours ago," Paul said quickly. "In fact, I want to see you. Emma, the truth is, I haven't stopped thinking about you all day." Shit, he thought that was a bit over the top.

Emma was loving every minute of it; if Paul really liked her that much she wanted to hear it.

"Look Paul, I'm going to say some things a girl shouldn't say when she has just met someone."

"Really?" said Paul. "I'm all ears."

Emma was unsure how far to go. "I think we're going to get on really well. I woke up this morning and the first thing I thought of was you."

There was silence. Paul was taken aback.

"Are you still there?"

"Yes, sorry Emma, I'm still here." Paul made an instant decision. "I'm on my way now."

"You're coming to see me now?" asked Emma.

"Yes right now." Paul looked at his watch, it was 6pm. "I'll be there in just over an hour. Where do you want to meet?" Paul didn't really want to meet her parents quite yet, that would take some planning.

Emma quickly thought. "I tell you what, there's a Holiday Inn on Epsom Downs next to the race course. You can't miss it." Emma could feel her cheeks going red as she thought of the one night stand she had had with some bloke she met at the Derby last year. Christ, I can't even remember his name, she thought. The only thing she did remember was that he fucked her all night and she slept the whole of next day to get over that and the booze she'd drunk all day at the races.

"Yea, OK, that sounds good." Paul didn't have a clue where Epsom Downs was but he would switch on the Sat Nav and pray.

"Emma, I haven't got time to hang about, I'll see you soon."

"Yes Paul, don't get lost. See you soon." Jesus, Emma thought. What do I do first? Her mind was in turmoil. Shower, make up? What shall I wear? "Shit!" she said out loud and rushed to the bathroom.

Paul was in a similar state. Thank goodness, I had a shower and changed clothes at lunch time. I haven't got time to arse about, he thought. He shouted to Roddy who was sitting having a coffee.

"Rod, tell Tony I'm going to see Emma in Epsom!"

"Epsom! Where the fuck's that?" asked Roddy. Shit, yes, where is Epsom? Paul thought.

Paul rushed out to his car and pressed the key, the door opened and he went to get in. Hold on a minute, he thought. I don't need all this aggravation. He rushed back into the club, grabbed a phone and dialled the number he knew off the top of his head.

"I need a ride to Epsom Downs right now."

"Epsom Downs," repeated a voice at the other end of the phone.

"Yes, that's correct."

"I'm very sorry sir, but I don't think we can go that far."

"This is Paul at the Den. I have an account with you and spend a fortune every month."

"So sorry Mr Bolton, we'll have a cab for you in five minutes," said the taxi despatcher very quickly.

"That's better," said Paul and put the phone down.

Emma stripped off and jumped in the shower. She squirted some soap into her hand from the dispenser, it was the whitish clear colour and she thought of the joke she'd had with Mel when she stayed over about how it reminded them of semen. She lathered it over her firm breasts and imagined it was Paul with his hands; God she was getting wet already!

There was the sound of a car horn outside the club. Paul strode out to the cab and was about to get in the back but stopped and turned to the driver. "Don't ever press that horn if you come here again. Get off your fat arse, walk into the club and say you're here, is that alright?"

Max the driver was shocked, no one had ever spoken to him like that. "Alright guv, no harm meant."

"Good," said Paul as he opened the door but quickly shut it and said to the driver, "I'll be a second," and ran back into the club.

"Roddy, give me some cash quick," Paul held out his hand.

"How much do you want?" asked Roddy holding up a massive wedge of fifty quid notes.

"Thanks." Paul grabbed the whole lot and rushed back outside.

Emma was back in her bedroom, rummaging through her wardrobe. What the hell am I going to wear, she thought. Eventually she chose a classic black dress that showed her legs and breasts off perfectly. She suddenly remembered she'd been wearing black when they met in the pub. She didn't care, the black dress was tight and showed her slim body off really well. She put the dress on the bed and dropped her towel. She looked at her pussy and saw it was lovely and smooth, none of that au natural for me she thought. Emma had already chosen her underwear, she had picked out a matching set of black strapless corset, knickers, suspenders and stockings. Sophie wore stockings occasionally, but most of her friends didn't bother. Emma dabbed some perfume around her pussy, well you never know, could be a lucky night, she thought. She then moved over to stand in front of the full length mirror. She looked and liked what she saw, tall, sexy with waves of long blond hair falling down to her shoulders, and the stockings were sensational; she would do.

Paul jumped back into the cab beside the driver.

"Do you know where Epsom is?" he was looking at the driver.

"No idea," said the driver. "But the Sat Nav's working so we'll get there eventually," he added, smiling.

Paul turned away with a sinking feeling in his stomach, should have fucking driven myself, he thought.

Paul held up a fifty quid note "What's your name?"

"Max," the driver replied, eyeing the note.

"Keep your eyes on the road. Right, if you get me there sharpish, and I mean sharpish, you'll get one of these and when you take me back you'll get another, how does that sound?"

"Eh, what do you mean, when I take you back?"

"That's somewhat obvious, isn't it; I can't walk back to London"

"Nobody said I had to take you back. How long will you be?"

"Couple of hours; you can get a meal in the restaurant."

"I'll have to check with control," said Max in an appropriately serious voice.

"Yea, you do that Max, I can assure you, it won't be a problem."

Max was really quite chuffed for driving this geezer to and from Epsom. "Who's paying for dinner?" snapped Max.

Paul gave him a bit of a look and Max wondered if he had overstepped the mark. "I am of course." said Paul. "But don't go silly on the booze, eh?"

"Definitely not," said Max. Max was now thinking of a juicy filet steak with French fries. He gunned the engine and accelerated.

Emma was sitting in front of the dressing mirror, applying her war paint. She had decided to keep it simple and not slap on as much as usual. She wasn't sure why, but she thought Paul would like that. She finished her makeup, put on her five inch black heels and again looked in the mirror. Perfect, she thought. She looked at her gold Cartier watch, ten past seven. Wow, she had got ready in record time. I wonder what time Paul will get there, and he should arrive before me, she thought.

"How are we doing Max?"

"Good." He glanced at the Sat Nav. "We're only three miles from Epsom"

Paul looked at his watch, seven twenty. Not bad, he thought "We're going to the Holiday Inn next to the race course." He was a happy bunny; they'd be there in ten minutes. It was quicker than he would have done.

Soon the car pulled onto Epsom Downs. Paul looked around. "Bloody hell its dark up here, isn't it?" he was looking at Max.

"There's the hotel," said Max, Paul was admiring the vast white Grandstands that rose out of the darkness by the race course. They pulled into the Hotel. There was only about six cars in the car park and it all looked eerily quiet.

"This is the Holiday Inn, is it?" Paul was expecting a packed hotel with hundreds of guests; he kept looking around as though he was in the wrong place. This is strange he thought "Come on Max let's go." He made his way into the hotel and headed for reception. There was no staff, so he rang the bell. While waiting, he looked further into the reception area, not a soul; he was mystified how a hotel could survive with apparently no guests.

“Good evening Sir. How may I help you?” Paul turned to see a smartly dressed receptionist smiling at him.

“Paul was confused and looked at the woman. “Where is everybody?”

“Oh, It’s a very quiet night, you should be here when the racing is on,” she gushed.

Don’t think I’ll be rushing back here, Paul thought to himself as he again looked around. Then he thought of something and was really worried. "Is the restaurant open?"

“Yes, of course,” laughed the woman as though it was a stupid question. “Eh But it's a reduced menu tonight due to the number of guests.”

“Yes, but we can get a meal?”

“As I said, the restaurant is open, and I’m sure you will enjoy your meal.”

“I’m waiting for someone. Can we get some coffee while we wait please?”

“Of course,” replied the receptionist “What would you like?”

Paul turned to Max. “What do you want?”

“Latte for me," said Max.

“That’ll be two lattes please,” said Paul, turning back to the receptionist.

“That will be seven pounds please,” said the receptionist.

Paul fumbled in his pocket and wrapped his hand round the wedge of fifty’s. He tried to take one out but the elastic band was too tight. Shit, he thought. He pulled the whole bundle out and slipped one off the wedge. Max and the receptionist both noticed the wedge and couldn’t take their eyes off it.

Paul very quickly stuffed the money back in his pocket and handed the receptionist the fifty quid note.

“Do you have anything smaller? I can’t change that.” she said.

“Can’t change a fifty?” Paul was shocked. So now he knew what it was like to live in the sticks.

"I'll get these and handed the receptionist a ten pound note," offered Max.

"Thank you," said the receptionist and gave Max his three pounds change.

"We'll be sitting over there," said Paul as he turned to move away from the reception.

"Oh sorry, I better explain," said the woman. "You go in that small room over there." Paul and Max followed her pointing finger. "And help yourself to as much coffee as you like from the machines."

Paul and Max looked at each other with a look of disbelief. They were so shocked to be getting coffee from a machine in a Holiday Inn, they were speechless.

"Max, you get the coffees, I need to sit down," said Paul, shaking his head as he headed towards some reception chairs. He sat down and took out his Blackberry. He pressed the contact list icon and put in E. Emma Miller came up and he clicked the button and a second later, it started to ring.

"Hi Paul, how you getting on?" answered Emma immediately.

"I'm in the hotel."

"Oh great," says Emma... "I'm only five minutes away"

Paul was not sure whether to say anything or not but decided he would. "Emma, this hotel is very quiet, and I mean very quiet."

"Oh good, we can just concentrate on each other then."

"Sounds good to me, see you in a minute."

Emma was looking at her make up for the final time in the car mirror before she went in the hotel. She had seen Paul pull up in the cab and had decided to let him wait a few minutes before she went in.

"Now, listen Max, I'm meeting a young lady, so you better make yourself scarce. In the restaurant, sit at the other end to us, OK?"

"Of course, whatever you say," Max said as he sipped his coffee.

"Now, Max, she'll be here in a minute."

"Oh right, OK." Max was trying to finish his coffee quickly so he could get another free one as soon as possible. He moved away to a sofa, well away from Max.

Max now had a couple of minutes to think about Emma. He couldn't wait to see her, and for some reason felt like he did when he was fourteen on his first date. Bloody nerves, he thought. Suddenly, Emma appeared in the doorway. Paul was blown away. She looked fantastic! He stood up and moved towards her. They kissed cheeks and he led her to a comfy sofa.

"You look fantastic," Paul said as he took her hand. She laughed to herself. They were like two kids on a first date.

"Thanks Paul. How was the journey?"

"Yea, it was alright. It's very out in the sticks here, no street lights," he laughed. "And no people!"

Emma looked around and laughed. "I know. Where is everybody?"

"The receptionist said that they were busy during the horse racing," said Paul.

Emma gave her most brilliant smile to Paul. "So we have the whole hotel to ourselves, great."

They were still holding hands and Paul suddenly leaned towards Emma and gently kissed her on the lips. She closed her eyes and responded by pushing her tongue deep into his mouth. They kissed for a few seconds until Paul pulled away. "Wow you're a good kisser; I could do that for hours."

Emma just smiled at him as though to say yes, I don't mind, hours is fine by me.

"Emma, are you hungry?"

Emma loved it when Paul spoke her name, it was like she belonged to him.

"I'm bloody starving. I haven't eaten all day."

"Come on then, let's see what the restaurants like," Paul said as he stood up.

They were still holding hands as they entered the restaurant. They looked round, there were three tables with couples sitting at them. Max was stuffing his face at one end so Paul steered Emma to a table next to the window at the other end. Paul was trying to work out how the hotel could possibly survive with so few guests.

“Yes, I am here you know,” smiled Emma

“Sorry, I was trying to work out how this place survives.”

Emma looked around. “Yea, weird isn’t it?”

Paul was dying to hear all about Emma. “So Emma, I want to hear your whole life story, everything, don’t miss anything out.”

“Oh do I have to?” asked Emma. “I’d much rather hear about you.”

“I tell you what we’ll do then,” said Paul. “You go first and we’ll take it in turns.”

Emma laughed “Well, I was a beautiful baby."

“Is that it?” laughed Paul.

“’Fraid so. Your turn.”

They were both laughing and chatting away as though they had known each other for years.

“Well, I was born.”

“Yes,” interrupted Emma.

“I, eh, I’m not good at talking about myself,” Paul stuttered. “Well I was born in Bermondsey, I have a brother Tony and, and we’ve only just met but I have really fallen for you.

The romantic moment is broken by a waitress.

“Good evening. Would you like to order some drinks?”

Paul looked across at Emma. “What would you like, darling?” Darling. Where did that come from thought Emma, not that she didn’t like it.

“You order, Paul.”

“We’ll have a bottle of your best champagne, please,” Paul said, looking at the waitress.

Thank God for that, thought the waitress. Someone who's going to spend some money and possibly give me a good tip, something that is in very short supply working at this dead place.

The waitress handed Paul the menus. "That will be a bottle of Veuve Clicquot, I'll bring the champagne over in a minute."

Emma noticed that Paul didn't bother to ask the price of the champagne, she liked that.

"The menu's a bit limited but the steak looks good," said Paul loudly.

"Order me a good steak then as long as its medium rare, I'll be happy"

Paul smiled "Two filet steaks with all the trimmings sounds good to me."

They chatted away about anything and everything. The champagne arrived; the steaks were tender and succulent. It was a good meal.

"I had my doubts as to whether we would get a decent meal but it's been good," said Paul with a satisfied nod. He picked up his champagne and took a sip. He was thinking: should I hit on her and book a room? He looked at Emma. He imagined himself undressing her. He felt movement in his groin just thinking about it.

"I've really enjoyed it, thanks, Paul." Emma had drunk half the bottle and was becoming a bit giggly.

"What's next on the menu then, Paul?" she giggled.

"I hear they do a good ice cream," smiled Paul and winked.

Emma was desperate to give herself to Paul but she wanted him to make the move.

He leant across the table and whispered in her ear. "Let's get another bottle of champagne and get a room. If you didn't know it already, I'm madly in love with you."

Emma moved her hand up around Paul's neck, leaned over and kissed him slowly on the lips. "Sounds like a wonderful idea to me."

"Wait here, I'll see if they have a spare room," he whispered even though the hotel was practically empty.

"I'm not going anywhere," she said smiling at him.

Paul caught the waitress on the way out. “Another bottle of champagne and what’s the damage please.”

The waitress prepared the bill and handed it to Paul.

Paul looked at the bill, two hundred and sixty quid. He took the wad out of his pocket, peeled off six fifty quid notes and handed them to the waitress and asked her to keep the change. The waitress did the sum, forty quid tip! That’s more than she got paid by the hotel for a night's work!

"Thank you very much sir."

Paul told Emma he’d be back in a minute and headed for reception.

“Hi, I’ve decided to stay over," he said to the receptionist. "Your best double room please.”

The receptionist was pleasantly surprised.

"Of course sir, for one night?”

“Yes, thanks.”

“That will be eighty five pounds please.”

Once again, Paul took cash out and gave the receptionist two notes, she completed the paperwork and gave Paul the key.

“Room 34. I hope you enjoy your stay.”

“Thank you,” said Paul taking the key and he thought to himself yes I'm definitely going to enjoy the next hour or two.

Paul picked up the champagne and two clean glasses from the next table.

“Are you ready?” Paul asked.

“Very ready.” Emma got up and they strolled out of the restaurant towards the lifts.

Paul pressed floor three and turned to Emma. They smiled warmly and lovingly at each other. No words were necessary. Soon they got to the room, Paul opened the door and they walked in. Paul placed the champagne and glasses on the table and turned towards Emma.

"Paul, sit down please," Emma said as she took Paul by the shoulders and gently pushed him into the single chair. She then moved two feet away and stopped. Paul was wondering what Emma was going to do next. He didn't have long to wait.

Emma looked into Paul's eyes as she pulled the dress straps off her shoulders and then slowly undid the side zip. The dress fell to the floor and Emma pushed it to one side with her foot. Paul was transfixed; he was looking at the most gorgeous woman he had ever seen in his life. Emma turned a little to the side and gave a model like pose. For some reason, Paul remembered he didn't have any dessert with his meal. Well, he thought to himself, I'm going to have some now.

"Take the suspenders and knickers off," said Paul in a hoarse voice.

Emma did as she was told, pulling them down slowly and throwing them on the bed.

Paul noticed immediately Emma had a smooth pussy, thank goodness for that, he thought. Loads of pubic hair is old fashioned now; so this is what heaven is like. He licked his lips. He now had a massive hard on and had to use all his control and willpower to stop himself from just jumping on Emma. He wanted to take his time and make it special for her.

"Come here," he said holding out his hands. She sashayed over and stood directly in front of him.

"You are absolutely beautiful," he said, moving forward to the edge of the seat. He placed his hands on the cheeks of her arse and pulled her gently to him. He moved his mouth to cover her pussy and started to lick up and down. After a few seconds, he heard Emma groan and whisper to him.

"I'm in love with you, Paul." She groaned loudly again and started to move her hips back and forwards very slowly in time with Pauls tongue. Emma then grasped Pauls head with her hands and pulled it to her pussy in time with her movement. She was soon feeling weak at the knees and the sound of the licking was driving her crazy.

"Paul, move right back in the chair," she groaned. He pushed back and made himself comfortable. She climbed on the chair, spread her legs on either side of Paul and placed her hands against the wall, she then pushed her pussy back onto Paul's mouth, and she could now really enjoy it.

In the end, Emma could not stand up any longer; she moved back down and knelt on the floor in front of Paul. She undid the belt on his trousers, he lifted his arse and she pulled them and his pants down to his ankles and took them off. His huge cock leapt into the air and she took it in her hand and moved it up and down slowly, she then leant over and took his cock in her mouth. Paul loved it and kept looking down at Emma's face; she loved it too and was working really hard on it. Paul was getting too close to the end...

"Emma, let's go to the bed." She stopped and they moved onto the bed. He guided her to lie on her back and climbed on top. He kissed her passionately on the lips and then nuzzled her nipples. He could wait no longer and entered her hard. Emma gasped and adjusted her legs to curl round Paul's back. He stroked in and out, pumping faster and pushing harder. Emma was groaning and panting.

"Yes, Paul, you're so big I love it.

"Emma, you say all the right things," he panted.

Emma gasped again "Don't stop, harder!" she gasped, pushing herself harder against him. Paul pushed and pumped away even harder.

"Oh God, yes!" gasped Emma. They finally climaxed. Both screamed with ecstasy as they came together.

They were both exhausted and couldn't move.

"That was the best," said Emma after a while as she leaned over Paul and kissed him on his neck, then his nipple and then full on his lips. Paul began to feel his cock getting hard again. He took Emma and turned her over and entered her with a hard push from behind. Emma gasped and pushed her arse back to get the full pleasure. Paul ran his hand down Emma's arse and pressed his thumb into her arse hole; she pulled away, but Paul did the same again and this time, she moaned with pleasure. Paul came again and collapsed into a heap.

Emma reached over to the side and grabbed the champagne. She filled the glasses and handed one to Paul. They both drank greedily and emptied their glasses. Emma took Paul's glass and placed them both back on the side of the bed.

Emma nibbled Paul's ear and whispered.

"Paul, I want you to know you can do anything you want to me, anything that turns you on, anything at all, I want to make you happy, anything."

Paul was thinking to himself that not only was this woman beautiful, but she was the sexiest woman he had ever met.

"Emma, I want you now, I want you tomorrow and I want you for ever." he leaned over and kissed her on the lips again. "You get on top now," he whispered. Emma immediately sat astride him. She reached back with her hand and guided his cock into her wet pussy and started to move up and down. Paul grasped her breasts and fondled them, then pushed up and took each nipple in turn into his mouth. Emma was now groaning with every movement and Paul could feel himself coming again.

"Emma sixty nine!" Emma understood and turned round to face Paul's legs. She took his cock in her mouth again and sucked. Paul started licking Emma's pussy he couldn't stand it.

"I'm coming! Swallow it, swallow it!" he pushed his cock up into Emma's mouth and came. Emma took it and knew she had made Paul really happy. She kept her mouth round his cock until he was fully drained and the erection had gone soft.

"Was that good Paul?"

"Was that good!" he repeated. "That was sensational!"

Emma looked adoringly into Paul's eyes. "Have you had enough yet?"

Paul was exhausted. "Emma I am knackered, you are the best ever, and I'm going to have a job keeping up with you."

"That's funny," said Emma, laughing. "I was thinking exactly the same."

They fell into each other's arms.

CHAPTER 9

Jack and Richard had been expelled from school for beating a fellow pupil nearly to death. They had only escaped prison because Richard's father had threatened the boy's family and they dropped all the charges. Richard had been the leader in the beating and Jack had vowed afterword's he would always use his brains and leave the violence to Richard. The sight of the boy with his smashed face had given Jack nightmares, but he did recognise that violence would be needed at times to safeguard their interests and build a business.

Richard's father had set the pair of them up with a small business, running the doors at some local pubs. All pubs had to have security as there were constant fights, which someone had to sort out. In the early days, Richard was always out working somewhere, while Jack took care of all the admin, contacting bouncers and generally being the brains. Richard soon gained a reputation for sorting out trouble and this usually meant kicking the shit out of anyone who messed about in the pubs he was working at. The business, at first, was slow to take off; they were doing the doors on independent single pubs and Jack recognised the need to gain business with people who owned multiple outlets. He set up meetings with owners and offered good discounts on group business; slowly the business took off.

After about six months, they had forty odd pubs which was bringing in a tidy sum that enabled them to move out of their respective homes and rent a flat. They had upset a fair number of people on the way but Richard was gaining a reputation as someone not to mess with.

Jack's plan was to get to a hundred pubs and at the same time branch out into other areas like prostitution, clubs and drugs. Money was the sole motivator for Jack. He loved money so much, he would have sold his gran for a tenner, if he could have found someone to buy her!

The business reached about fifty pubs and then it stopped growing. Jack and Richard knew why; there were two guys who had control of the fifty other pubs they wanted, two separate businesses, one with twenty pubs and the other thirty.

They decided to start with the larger one, which was run by a man called Bruce Coyne. They contacted Bruce and asked him if he was interested in selling the pub doors. Bruce told them in no uncertain terms that they should fuck off and not bother him again.

They thought they might have luck with the smaller business run by a local nutcase with the nickname of Cruncher. Apparently, in his youth, he had been set upon by a gang in West Ham, he had gotten his mouth round one of the boy's arms and bitten him clean through to the bone.

Cruncher was a fair bit older than them, and in truth, he was getting fed up with the continual aggravation of running doors in pubs. Jack and Richard went to see him and put what they thought was a good proposal to him. A lump sum payment up front and a percentage of the take for a year, cash in an envelope every month. Cruncher drove a hard bargain and made them pay dearly for the business. In the end a deal was struck.

The fact was that, following the deal with Cruncher, Jack and Richard ran out of money. They certainly didn't have anywhere near enough to pay Bruce Coyne even if he had wanted to sell. They had to come up with a plan that would get rid of Coyne and leave them with the pubs.

They mulled over their plan while they were having a drink in the Ship, in Rotherhithe.

"Jack, leave it to me," said Richard. "We'll take Coyne out and muscle in on the pubs."

"Does that mean, kill him? Jesus, are you mad? We've never done anything like that before." Jack was worried that Richard was already out of control. "Look Richard, there must be another way. It's just finding the key, that's the issue."

"Well, you're the brains," said Richard, as he got up and went to the bar for another pint.

I might be the brains, thought Jack, but what to do, that was the question. Richard came back and sat down. Jack could see he was sulking.

"Richard, what's wrong?"

"I've told you, we get rid of that cunt Coyne, and move in. What could be simpler than that?" said Richard.

"Richard, you can't just get rid of people, you can't make people disappear."

Richard leaned forward with an intent expression. "Now, that is where you are wrong Jack, it can be done, believe me."

"Well, what did you have in mind then?" asked Jack, taking a large pull on his whiskey.

"Now, you're talking," said Richard rubbing his hands together as he started to talk in earnest.

"Coyne's got no family, he's a miserable fucker who lives to work and travel. His Achilles heel is his passion for jetting off to Spain and Portugal to top up his tan and that is where we can make him disappear."

Jack was knocking back his whiskey. "You make it all sound so easy."

"Jack, it is easy. You put a gun to someone's head and pull the trigger, boom! Problem solved."

"OK, I tell you what, work on a plan. Let me see it and we'll go from there. Remember we said at the start that we both have to agree to anything major happening in the business."

Richard picked up his pint and drained it. "Good, Jack, you're getting the hang of it now."

"Maybe," replied Jack. "Get me a large whiskey, I need one."

Richard needed some help to plan and carry out the disappearance of Bruce Coyne. He drafted in a couple of old mates who he knew he could trust, and who needed an envelope stuffed with loads of cash. Their names were Jim Telfer and Robin Scott. They were both hard nuts, not too many brains but good in a fight, loyal and would do as they were told, no questions asked.

Bruce Coyne holidayed in Torremolinos Costa del Sol in Spain every October for a month and on the Algarve in Portugal every April for two weeks. He was a confirmed bachelor and didn't particularly like women much. He always went on holiday alone and liked to stay in hotels where he was well known and had been to several times. He did have female company on his trips but only because he paid local prostitutes. As soon as Jack had agreed the hit, Richard found out exactly where Coyne was going on his next trip. It was good that it would be in October, as he would not be missed for a whole month. He then sent Jim, the slightly more intelligent of the two, out to Spain to recce the area where Coyne stayed.

Jim was out there for a week and most of that time was spent drinking in the bars and chatting up girls. Eventually, he returned to London and reported in to Richard.

"Jim, how was the trip?"

"Yea good, thanks Richard."

"So, give me the low down then." said Richard

"He stays in a big hotel on the seafront. It's a quiet place and the only people about are some tourists from here and Germany. I suggest we take him when he's walking somewhere, into a van and bob's your uncle."

Richard was looking at Jim thoughtfully. "What do we do with the body?"

"I went inland from the coast, there are miles of desolate shrub land that would be perfect for burying a body in."

"Sounds OK. Hmm, any problems you can foresee at all?" asked Richard.

"None, Richard, it's a piece of cake. From what you said, I'm assuming he'll be on his own?"

"Yea, but we are assuming straight away that he likes to take nice quiet walks in the pleasant evening coolness, but what if he doesn't?" Richard liked to cover all possibilities.

"Look, we can get him somewhere; he must go out for a meal sometime as long as we're on the case an opportunity will open for us"

"OK, we'll buy or hire a van once we get out there."

Richard had agreed to pay Jim and Robin ten grand each, plus he would pay all expenses.

Richard and Jack met the next night at the Frog.

"Get the drinks in Richard, before we start, I've a feeling I'm going to need a few tonight; make it a large one."

"Sure, Jack."

Richard gave Jack his large whiskey.

"So we're ready to go in October."

"Give me all the details, Richard."

"Jim's just come back from Spain," Jack interrupted.

"You sent Jim to Spain?"

"Yea, we now know the lay of the land and have a feel for the place; it will help when we go back."

Jack smiled at Richard. "I'm impressed, sending him out was a good idea. So, what's the plan?"

"We take him outside when he's not expecting it, into a van. Bullet in the head and bury him in the desert, easy peasy"

Jack looked concerned. "I don't ever want to hear the exact details, such as bullet in the head." "OK, sorry Jack," Richard said quickly.

"Anyway, it can be done without too many problems," added Richard confidently.

Jack was pleased to see Richard was confident but had his doubts that it would be as easy peasy as Richard put it.

“So, I’ll take care of Coyne," said Richard. "You need to make sure we get the business.”

Jack smiled confidently. “It’s all taken care of, so relax. You do your bit and I’ll do mine.”

Jack had already made contact with the pub owners in the guise quite truthfully of looking for new business. Once Richard was taken care of, it would be easy enough to muscle in and take over without too much aggro.

“Get the drinks in Richard,” said Jack, giving Richard his empty glass.

Richard started some serious planning. They needed a gun and that would have to be sourced in Spain. He didn’t fancy walking through Heathrow with a weapon in his pocket. There was always the option of going from a smaller airfield such as Luton or even taking a private jet, not sure what Jack would say about that though. It might sound like a small problem but Richard was worried. How do you go about getting a gun in Spain? Neither Jack nor Richard knew anybody over there. That problem was solved by Jack. He spoke to a mate in Manchester who knew someone, who knew someone who had gone to ground in Malaga following a Securicor armed robbery in Huddersfield. The gun problem was sorted and would be delivered to them in Spain; it would cost two grand in cash.

They needed to buy spades; you couldn't dig a hole big enough to put a body in without decent spades, especially in ground that was rock hard because of the heat. Richard felt confident it would go without a hitch, after all there would be three of them. It was two weeks till October first, so plenty of time as well.

CHAPTER 10

Jeff and Karen got into the nick early the next morning. Jeff hadn't been in early for about five years and all the coppers he met gave him strange looks and then asked him, either "Did you wet the bed?" or "Liz kicked you out of bed, then." Jeff didn't bother replying but just gave them a sort of knowing smile. Jeff had got home and was in good humour. Liz was surprised, very surprise. Jeff wasn't complaining, and hadn't told her Michael was a wanker, which he had told her every day for the last two years. Jeff was genuinely excited for the first time in ages; he had some of his mojo back and couldn't wait to get to work, which was really unheard of.

Jeff had nicked a fair few criminals over the years, especially in the old days when evidence and court proceedings were nothing like they are now. Things then were not so tight. Nowadays, things were crazy; one tiny mistake could blow years of work down the drain. He remembered well, Jordan Foster, a notorious east-end gangster getting let off because they hadn't had a search warrant when they found the weapon he had used to batter an elderly shopkeeper to death. Yes, times have changed, he thought.

Jeff was really waiting out his time before he could retire and get his pension. He'd done twenty three of the twenty five years and then he would be free. His mortgage was next to nothing and they could live on a grand a month, plus Steph's part time wage from her job at the Co-op. Jeff was feeling on top of the world and kept rubbing his hands together, a habit he had had for years.

Karen was very different to Jeff; she was very keen to prove herself and would happily work any hours required to get the job done. She was single at the moment, although Michael kept trying to get her into bed again. They had slept together once, when they were away at a conference. The sex hadn't been that memorable and she was concentrating on work at the moment. Karen was renting a one bedroom flat in Bermondsey, close to the nick, it was very handy when you finished work to be home in five minutes. Poor old Jeff spent an hour getting home and that was if he left on time at five pm. Karen liked Jeff, yes he was a bit staid and long in the tooth but after all his years of service, she wasn't surprised. Jeff knew and could handle people, especially the locals in Bermondsey. What Jeff had was likeability; everybody liked Jeff. Jeff was a bit slapdash and always looked at the big picture, Karen was clinical when it came to detail, as a copper nowadays needed to be, to make progress. She was a career cop, she wasn't pining for children and the thought of settling down with someone scared her to death. This new case could be a way to get her noticed, to make her mark. She was going to make sure she worked really hard on this case and also that Jeff did the same.

Neither Jeff nor Karen carried firearms in the course of their normal duties. Both had been trained in firearms and could, if necessary, carry them in an emergency, or on a planned basis. Jeff had fired a gun once in his career and had not hit who he was aiming at. But unfortunately, one of his colleagues, Toby Masters, had been shot in the head and killed. Jeff had never forgotten the funeral, where, it seemed, half the Met turned up. Toby's wife and children had cried from start to finish.

Karen had never fired a gun in anger and had always hoped she wouldn't have to. The fact they were now going after Richard Philips and Jack Coombs meant guns might well be needed. Karen knew that these two characters would, if necessary, definitely shoot to kill. Jeff and Karen were only recently discussing the difference between the UK and the US; eleven thousand gun deaths a year in the states, three hundred in the UK. That really said it all for the pair of them, never arm all UK coppers, it would be a big mistake.

Jeff got himself a coffee and breezed into the CID office.

"Karen, good morning how are you?"

"Fucking hell Jeff, what's happening?" Karen was concerned, Jeff must be in early for a reason.

"Don't you bloody start as well," said Jeff.

Karen gave Jeff a quizzical look. "What?"

"You know, wondering why I am in early for a change," grumbled Jeff.

"For a change, you've never been in early, as far as I know, EVER," laughed Karen loudly.

"Well, can I get you a coffee?" he suddenly winked at her.

"You don't do that very often either, have you won the lottery or something?" she asked, getting more amused.

Karen was mystified as to why Jeff was acting very strangely, albeit in a very positive way. She was looking at him and then she thought she knew why. Jeff was excited about getting back on the beat, after twenty odd years. He was going to make a difference once again, he was going to put the baddies in jail!

"Do you want a coffee or not?"

"Course I bloody do, you might not ask me for another hundred years." Karen was laughing again, she had never laughed so much. "It's good to see you happy for a change Jeff." She added.

He gave her a warm smile. "It's been known, you know. Now listen, let's have a chat before we see the rest of the team."

"OK, what's on your mind?" asked Karen.

"I just wanted to say that..." Jeff was looking seriously at Karen but couldn't get the words out.

"What is it Jeff? Please carry on."

"OK, look, I've not been the support to you that I should have been. There, I've said it. But, what I want you to know is that, while we are on this new case, I'll be there for you one hundred per cent; I really want to nail these bastards."

Karen stuck out her hand. "Partners."

Jeff gratefully took Karen's hand in his. "Yes, partners."

Jeff was very pleased he had got Karen back on his side and they could now concentrate on getting the evidence required to handcuff and read those glorious words to Richard Martin and Jack Coombs: "I am arresting you for...you have the right to remain silent but should you choose...."

“So, Karen, did you read the report?” asked Jeff

“Yes, it took me bloody ages and some of it was so complicated I could hardly understand it.”

“Yea I know what you mean," agreed Jeff. The financial trails take some understanding. But look, the key is this, they make a fortune through their brothels and as far as I’m concerned, that’s the easiest place to hit them and hurt them big time. Because not only are they illegal brothels but a lot of the girls working in them are trafficked over from Eastern Europe and then turned into drug addicts. It’s a very dirty business.”

Karen became very interested, she hated women traffickers. “But I couldn’t see how many brothels they have in the report.”

“They don’t know, except it must be quite a few to generate the cash that’s flying about,” said Jeff.

Jeff was chewing his nail. “Andrew and Rob will give us all the information we need. What time is the meeting?”

“Stop biting your nails. Six o clock,” said Karen

They talked through various aspects of the report and then arrived early to hear the full brief from Andrew and Rob, who were sitting at the conference table. Lisa, the receptionist came in with mugs of coffee on a tray, placed a mug in front of each person and left.

“OK, everybody, hush-up," said Michael. "Most of you know each other but I would like to introduce Kevin Ford. Kevin is in charge of the surveillance team out in the field and will be giving a briefing shortly. Andrew is in overall command of the office and field based intelligence, so over to you Andrew.”

“Thanks Michael," said Andrew, a big burly man with alert blue eyes. "The operational aim of this intelligence and surveillance operation is to provide CID based here, with enough evidence to produce a conviction for one or multiple crimes, by one, Richard Philips and one, Jack Coombs. The operation call sign is Raptor.” Andrew paused, to let that bit of information sink in.

“We are very fortunate to have a really crack team working on this operation,” he continued. At this point Jeff coughed. All heads turned towards him. Jeff raised his eyebrows and smiled.

“As you are probably aware," continued Andrew, "a large percentage of the Met’s NCS surveillance capability is spent in Counter Terrorism.” Andrew looked round the room. "This type of work is no different; it is based on building up an intelligence picture of suspects through continuous surveillance. Most of which, in this case will consist of following the two individuals by car and on foot. We will be picking up on behaviour patterns, who they speak to and where they go. We will document these with images and audio taping.” He looked at Jeff and Karen. “Teamwork is vital and an incredibly important part of surveillance. We will have a team of ten working on the two suspects, twenty four hours a day. Jeff, you and Karen may well be involved at some stage but your role is really to follow up every evidence and information that we gather for you, thereby building a case.

“From now on, each suspect will have a call sign. Philips is Falcon one and Coombs, Falcon two. This is purely so that if there is a slip of any sort and someone heard something, they will not know who we are talking about.

“Just so you know the procedure, authorisation has been granted by the Chief Constable to carry out a certain number of surveillance operations in the London and Essex areas. As we speak, surveillance is being set up at both home addresses, Falcon one in Billericay, Essex and Falcon two in Chelmsford, Essex. Permission has also been sought to intercept all phone conversations in and out. We will also “Hot Mike” the phones; in case you don’t know, this means that when the phone is not being used to make or receive a call, it is a microphone and will transmit audio to the surveillance team, this will be running from tomorrow. We are also looking at hacking into any available computers. We have also set up a static surveillance unit opposite a pub called The Frog, down the old Kent road. Interestingly enough, we already have some good quality images of meetings between both Falcons and unidentified individuals. We also think we have located one of the brothels in Peckham and we'll also be setting up a unit to monitor activity at that location. All this type of information will be fed to you and Karen, it will then be your responsibility to identify the individuals and then confirm whether you want them to be put on the surveillance list or not. Obviously, we can only take on so many individuals, so you have to be selective and prioritise." He paused and took a sip of his now lukewarm coffee.

"Now, lastly," he continued, "and maybe, most importantly, we have had some anonymous information, in fact two lots, that's all I'm going to say at the moment, but it is good material. Jeff, this will be made available to you after this meeting."

Kevin Ford then gave a presentation on how the surveillance team would work: there would always be one of the team in the newly set up ops room next to the CID office, his call sign would be Eagle. Eagle would be in touch with all operatives in the field and would co-ordinate activity within the team. Anything really important would be communicated to Jeff and Karen in live time.

Michael rose to close the meeting.

"As you heard, we have started some surveillance already and have some images for Jeff to look at. All the surveillance will be operating from 8 am tomorrow morning, so this is the start. Everybody's got to do their bit and with a good team effort, we can put Philips and Coombs behind bars for a very long time. So, Jeff you have a look at the Intel we already have and let's get going."

CHAPTER 11

“I’m telling you, Paul won’t like this one bit.” Roddy, Paul and Tony’s financial whiz kid was in the meeting with Richard Philips to sign the Club and Pub’s deal.

“Roddy it makes sense for everybody concerned," said Richard patiently. "Ryder knows the three clubs, he’s run them for years. He can help with the transition and then you’ll find he’s indispensable and be happy to let him keep running them.”

“Richard, I’ve looked at the books, Ryder has been running those clubs at a loss for years.”

“I know that, Roddy, but in truth he asked for investment a hundred times and we always said no. It’s not his fault. Once you invest in the clubs you will see what a shrewd and good businessman Ryder is.”

“I’ll run it by Paul and see what he says.”

“Look, Roddy, this is a deal breaker. If you don’t take Ryder, then the deal's off. I can’t be clearer than that.”

Roddy was well pissed off. Paul had said whatever happens, the future of their business was dependent on this deal. Fuck he thought, I’m going to have to go back and tell Paul he has a new employee.

“OK Richard,” Roddy stuck his hand out. Richard grabbed it as though his life depended on it and shook it vigorously.

“Good, now, how about a drink to celebrate,” said Richard, with a huge grin on his face.

“Large scotch please, Richard.” Roddy needed it after agreeing to Ryder coming on board.

The deal was done. Richard and Jack would add a further twenty pubs to their portfolio for the knock down price of fifty thousand. The three clubs would go to Paul and Tony for a nice round million quid. It was a good deal for everybody and the icing on the cake for Richard was getting rid of Ryder.

Roddy left the Frog and was dreading the next thing he had to do. He was under strict instructions to call Paul and confirm the deal was done with no hitches. Shit, that bastard Richard really stitched us up with that wanker Ryder, he thought to himself. He got back to his car and sat there for fully five minutes before he could dial the number.

“Give me the good news then, Roddy.” Paul sounded in a really good mood, probably been shagging that Emma again, that’s all he seemed to do these days, according to Tony anyway.

“It’s all good Paul, the deals done, the three clubs for a million and we get fifty thou for the pubs.”

“Great! When’s the completion?”

“As quickly as it can be done, probably eight weeks max.”

“Well done, Roddy. We need to have a drink on this, soon as poss.”

“That would be great, Paul.”

“OK look, I’ll catch up with you back at the den.”

Paul was about to click off but Roddy just managed to catch him in time.

“Paul, there’s just one small matter."

“What's that then?"

“Well, I had to agree that Ryder would come over for a few months to help with the transition.”

It went very quiet.

“It was a deal breaker Paul," continued Roddy quickly. "There was nothing I could do. He only has to stay six months and then we can just get rid of him, Paul. Hello, Paul are you there?” Shit! He's gone, thought Roddy.

In a way, Paul was not surprised with the Ryder situation because it's the sort of stunt Richard would pull, and although mightily hacked off with Roddy at first, he could see he had been in a corner with nowhere to turn. The only thing that interested him now was refurbishing the clubs, hiring new staff and getting them opened and seeing the tills fill up. Ryder could help out, it wasn't a huge problem but there was no way he was running those clubs once they were opened. Paul glanced at his watch, it was time to go and see Emma.

Paul had been dreading meeting the parents but he couldn't avoid it any longer. He hated going to Epsom or anywhere in the countryside. He was a real city boy who liked to be in the middle of millions of bricks and mortar. However hard he tried, he could not understand the attraction of being surrounded by grass, trees and fields. Paul knew where Kingswood was now and it was certainly an affluent area. Houses started at one million up to five or six for the really big mansions. Paul guessed Emma's house was probably worth about two mill. He was nearly there and he could feel the nerves setting in. Make it a quick dinner please, he prayed.

Emma was in her room, adjusting her makeup again. It was seven o clock, Paul should be here soon, as dinner had been agreed for eight pm. She was nervous for him; she knew how nervous of meeting her parents he was. Exactly why though, she couldn't understand. He was young, good looking, very successful and as Emma told her parents on numerous occasions, spoilt her rotten. The whole family were dying to see Paul, especially Fifi who, at fifteen was going on twenty. Ian had driven down and was chatting with dad in the lounge over a beer; mum was in the kitchen, panicking whether the coq au vin had enough red wine in it. Emma reflected on how well the relationship with Paul was going. The sex had been incredible, they couldn't keep their hands off each other. They must have tried every position possible but still kept finding new ones. There was no way to describe how she felt about

Paul; he was the love of her life. He was kind, considerate, thoughtful, generous, oh God, she better not tell him that or he won't get through the front door. Emma smiled to herself. She was sure Paul felt the same way about her. He did have difficulty with expressing his feelings but a couple of times under the covers, he had got serious and told her she meant the world to him. A tear came to her eye. She quickly wiped it away, pull yourself together, she said. Emma went downstairs to see if her mother wanted any help in the kitchen.

Paul pulled into the drive. The house was impressive close up. He had only ever seen it from a distance as he picked up or dropped Emma off. Well this is it, he thought. He reached over to the passenger seat and picked up the beautiful bouquet of flowers and the bag of presents, got out the car and walked up to the front door.

Emma had heard the car pull in and jumped with excitement, clapping her hands. "He's here, dad. Ian, Fifi, he's here."

"We know he's here," said Ian. "Shut up, for God's sake"

"Don't be so mean and horrible!" shouted Fifi.

The doorbell rang.

Emma yanked it open and threw herself at Paul. "Hello Handsome!" She had a huge grin on her face which cheered Paul up immediately. Emma hung onto Paul's arm.

"Come in! Come in!" said Emma excitedly. The family had all come into the Hall. Emma did the round of introductions. "Paul, this is my mum." Paul interrupted and held out a lovely bouquet to mum.

"Thank you so much for inviting me to dinner AND for having such a beautiful daughter." Everybody laughed.

Emma continued. "My dad, my brother, Ian and the little midget is Fifi, my sister." Paul shook hands all round and they all trooped into the lounge apart from mum, who went back to the kitchen.

Paul delved into his preze bag and took them out one at a time, he turned to dad. "Mr Miller, I hope you like Brandy," and handed it to him.

"Remy Martin VSOP, very nice. You better call me Peter."

"Thank you sir," said Paul. He delved into the bag again and brought out a bottle. "Ian, I hear you're a wine buff, I hope you enjoy that."

Ian opened the box and looked at the label: Chateau Petrus 2007, a very good red wine. "Thanks Paul, this is very nice and believe me, I will enjoy it."

"Fifi, I just didn't know what to get you, so I hope this is OK." Paul handed Fifi an envelope. Fifi quickly opened it and took out a card.

"Oh, great, it's a voucher for Topshop. One hundred pounds! Oh my God, I've got to tell my friends!" She rushed upstairs to her room. Everybody was laughing. The presents were going down well. Emma couldn't believe that Paul had the presents bang on for all the family. He really was a genius. But what about me?

"Oh, I forgot one," Paul said to the group. Taking a small box out of the bag, he handed it to Emma. Emma was apprehensive about opening it.

"Well, open it," said Ian.

"OK, OK," Emma said excitedly. She slowly opened the box and looked, then stared into the box without speaking and quickly shut it. Emma then burst into tears and ran out the lounge and up the stairs.

Peter and Ian looked at each other in shock.

"What was in the box?" asked Peter, looking even more concerned.

"An eternity ring."

Emma rushed into her room and slammed the door shut. She sat on the side of the bed and opened the box. She was still in shock. It was the most incredibly beautiful eternity ring she had ever seen. It must have cost a fortune, she thought. There were diamonds everywhere, sapphires, rubies and emeralds. It was just the best moment. Emma went and washed her face and headed back downstairs. The whole family asked if she was OK.

"I'm fine, don't worry."

When mum and dad saw the ring, they both looked at each other thoughtfully. This Paul is very serious about our Emma.

Paul had gone to Bond Street, looking for the ring. He had finally found the one he wanted. It cost seven thousand pounds. He had never bought anything so expensive for a girl before in his life.

The dinner was a great success and finally, Paul felt it was time to go. Emma walked him to his car.

“Paul, the ring is beautiful.” she showered him with kisses “Wait till I get you on your own and I’ll show you how pleased and happy I am.”

“I can’t wait,” said Paul.

Paul had one more surprise for Emma.

“Emma, I know it's quick, but I want you to move in with me, or if you like we can get our own place."

Emma was taken aback, things were moving so quickly. She didn’t care. “Yes, Yes I would love to. I love Chelsea Harbour and your flat is fabulous. When did you have in mind?”

“You think about it, for me, as soon as possible, I love you Emma Miller.” They kissed passionately.

“I’ll call you tomorrow,” said Paul as he reluctantly came up for air.

CHAPTER 12

Tony Bolton was a law unto himself and had been since he was five years old. He was a pain in the arse to his mum from an early age (His dad ran off when he was four) and never got any better. His teenage years were the worst. He hardly ever went to school and when he did, he was usually sent home for fighting or telling teachers to fuck off all the time. There was one occasion when he had chased a female teacher round the school shouting that he was going to kill her. She had finally locked herself in a toilet to escape him. The police were called and he was carted off. The local police were frequent visitors to see Tony, for crimes of shoplifting, public order offences, fighting in the street, threatening shopkeepers. You name it, Tony had done it all.

His nickname of 'Mad Tony' had come about because of a fight at a Millwall match. It was an away game at Birmingham and Tony and his mates had been looking for some trouble prior to kick off. They found it but were outnumbered by three to one. Instead of running, which may have been the sensible thing to do, Tony picked up a large piece of wood and charged at the Birmingham thugs single handed, screaming his head off. The boys with him all looked at each other and then did exactly the same thing, the Birmingham mob ran for their lives. When the boys caught up with Tony at least three of them called him fucking mad, and it stuck, "Mad Tony." Late teen years saw Tony progressing into more serious crime; car theft, burglary and robbery. Tony always had a big wedge of cash on him and started to act a bit like Al Capone; he didn't work and lived on his criminal proceeds. Tony was never scared to use violence from an early age. He and his brother Paul, were constantly in fights, although Paul leaned more towards using brains than brawn, and that was what happened. Paul learnt to make money in business and did not include violence, unless absolutely necessary.

Early in his twenties, Tony started to do things that he kept from his brother, and this had never changed. Tony had to have excitement and that meant criminal activity, usually with a smattering of violence. Little things like cigarettes; he would go into a local shop, walk round the back of the counter, take a packet of twenty and just walk out. If the shopkeeper said anything or made to stop him, he would get a severe beating. Once a shopkeeper called the police. Tony was taken to the local Nick, fingerprinted but then was soon released. Tony broke into that shop, stole all the booze and cigarettes and wrecked everything else, causing thousands of pounds worth of damage. He then went to see the shopkeeper the next morning, he just stood outside his shop and smiled at him through the window. He also silently mouthed the words "It was me," whilst pointing at himself. Afterwards, the shopkeeper dropped all the charges, saying he couldn't positively identify anybody. Tony liked to keep things from Paul because he knew he would disapprove and tell him to stop.

Tony eventually moved up to Jewellery shops and company payroll heists. He particularly liked the company payroll ones because someone told him they were insured and didn't really lose the money. He accepted that exactly at face value and thought nothing of it. All the money he earned from his personal side lines was put into an account at the Halifax Building Society, one of twelve bank and building society accounts he had.

Tony was planning his latest venture. He was in the globe, one of his favourite watering holes.

"Bout fucking time you two turned up." Bugsy and Tom were ten minutes late and Tony did not like to be kept waiting.

"Sorry Tony, had to clear up a bit of business."

"Oh yea, anything I should know about?" asked Tony.

"No, nothing at all, we got our money." Both of them were laughing.

"Get your drinks and sit down then."

"OK Tony, how are you?"

"Fuck off. Let's just get down to business," Tony looked around to see who was in and if anybody was close enough to hear their conversations. He saw an old boy sitting a bit too close for comfort.

Tony looked at him. "Oi, go and fucking sit somewhere else, this is private here." The old boy didn't look like he heard Tony.

"Go and sit somewhere else and your next pint is on me," he shouted to the old boy. You never saw anyone move so quickly.

"Very kind of you," said the old boy as he moved off to sit at the bar. The three of them laughed.

Tony went all serious. "So what have you got then?"

"Actually Tony we have heard about a nice little payroll that seems to be up for grabs," said tom.

"Sounds interesting," said Tony "Tell me more."

"Well, it's a company based in Plaistow, Arrow Logistics run by some Greeks. They pay the whole workforce in cash."

"How much?" asked Tony, with interest.

"One hundred employees' monthly wage at about fifteen hundred quid each, that's fifty thousand. A nice round number."

"Sounds good," said Tony thoughtfully. "Ok, tell me more.

"Monies delivered by Securicor at two fifty pm on the last Friday of the month. It goes into a downstairs secure office and is then given out through a hatch in a door. They start paying out at three pm and finish at five pm."

"So, how do we get in?"

"Well, we can either hit the boxes when they're being delivered or wait till the money is in the office and then grab it."

"And what do you think, Bugsy?"

"I think it's easier and a lot quicker to hit the Securicor guys when they carry the cash into the office," said Bugsy, matter of factly.

"How many guards, Tom?" asked Tony.

“Usually three, the driver and two carriers.”

“It won’t be that easy then.”

Tom looked surprised. “I never said it would be easy. Fifty thou’s a nice earner.”

“I agree. We need to plan this properly, but let’s go ahead; all those in favour.” Tony raised his glass and was quickly followed by Tom and Bugsy. All three drained their glasses.

Tony was in good humour now that a bit of business was in the pipeline.

“So, the last Friday is the twenty eighth, I’m looking forward to it already,” said Tony looking very pleased.

“Weapons?” He looked at the other two.

“We need pepper sprays and baseball bats minimum, could need a shooter to scare the shit out of them,” said Bugsy.

“As I see it,” said Tom. “One of us has to disable the van to stop the driver fucking off, the other two take the carriers and get the money.”

“Maybe we need a fourth person to drive, three of us will be outside the car, I don’t want any fuck ups when it’s time to leave.”

“I agree,” said Tom. “I’ll get someone in.”

“It’s an easy job, you should get someone for a couple of grand.” Tony was thinking hard. Look, we need a shooter, just in case. I’ll organise it. You two will get the money, I’ll take care of the van and driver.”

“OK, it should all take literally one minute from start to finish," said Tom. "Once we’re away, we head down to the lock up in Silverton, split the dough and disappear.”

“Good,” said Tony. “That’s the best bit, split the money and disappear. I like it.”

“Oh, Tom, who’s getting the car?” asked Tony.

“Yea, don’t worry, one of us will get it,” said Tom.

“Good. Is that everything?” Tony looked around. No one spoke. “I think it’s your round Bugsy.”

"Sure, Tony."

They had gone through the plan a hundred times. Tom had watched two Securicor deliveries and they were identical: two fifty pm delivery, driver and two guards on the last Friday of the month.

Phil would steal a car on the Friday morning and hide it in the lock up at Silvertown, prior to the heist. Tony, Tom and the driver called Phil, would join Bugsy at about two pm. The four of them would drive to Arrow Logistics and arrive at two forty pm. They would wait at the entrance to the industrial estate, as soon as the Securicor van passed them, they would put on balaclavas and follow at a safe distance until the last moment, when they would speed up and pull across the front of the van. Tony would shoot the tyres out, he would then threaten the driver by putting a shot through the side window, this would effectively stop the van from moving, and the shots would also scare the guards carrying the money boxes. At the same time, Tom and Bugsy would attack the two guards with pepper sprays and baseball bats and take the boxes. Everybody would get back in the car and they would travel at a sensible speed to Silvertown. Tony was happy that they had thought of all eventualities.

Phil stole a three year old silver Ford Mondeo in Canning Town on the Friday morning, at ten am; it was the sort of car that melted into the background. He filled the tank, checked the oil and then drove it to the lockup in Silvertown, arriving there at ten thirty five. He left the car and went to the Ace café round the corner and had a full English for a fiver, he liked to work on a full stomach.

Tony had had a lay in and told Paul he was having a lazy day doing nothing much, but that he would see him in the Den later that night. He also had a huge breakfast at the Bridge Café in Clements Road in

Bermondsey. He then met one of his contacts in Rotherhithe and picked up a Beretta M9 9mm pistol and fifteen rounds.

Tom took a call from Phil at ten fifteen am to say he had the car and all was well. Tom then met up with Bugsy and they had double Bacon and Egg McMuffins in McDonalds at East Ham with endless cups of coffee.

All four met at the lockup in Silvertown at around one thirty pm. Tony was the first to arrive and spent ten minutes looking over the car. He agreed it looked fine and told Phil he had done a good job. Tom and Bugsy arrived shortly afterwards. You could cut the atmosphere with a knife.

Tony had done this before and tried to reassure the boys. "Look everybody, chill out and relax, we'll go through the plan once more, and I don't want any mistakes."

"This is the last chance for questions." Tony was looking at the guys and felt confident they were up to it.

"OK, final words from me, if anybody gets caught now or later, mum is the word; families get looked after, is that clear?"

Tom, Bugsy and Phil all said "yes."

They all jumped in the car at two pm and Phil drove out the lock up at a slow steady speed. Phil had been the driver on a few jobs and he knew how difficult it was to drive slowly because the adrenalin is pumping so much. Tony was sat in the front with Tom and Bugsy in the back. There were pepper sprays and baseball bats in the back. Tony was carrying his favourite pistol, the Italian made 9mm Beretta, without question, one of the best pistols in the world.

They drove at twenty eight miles per hour to the Industrial Estate where Arrow logistics was situated and parked up near the entrance. This was the worst time, the waiting. Every second seemed like ten minutes.

Tony looked at his watch, it was two forty pm. "Ten minutes till the van arrives," he said to no one in particular. There was silence, all four were getting ready to hit hard and hit fast, the two ingredients for a successful job. Tony calmed himself; he could hear the steady breathing of Tom and Bugsy in the back.

Tony looked at his watch again, it was two forty five. "Five minutes to go." He took a deep breath and steeled his nerves, ready for action.

"Balaclavas ready," said Tony.

No one spoke, just complete silence.

"One minute," said Tony. He grasped his balaclava tight and felt his heart racing... He turned slightly and watched the entrance to the estate, time ticked on...

No van, Tony quickly looked at his watch again, it was two fifty two. "Two minutes late." More silence, more time ticked on...

Tony looked again: two fifty seven. "Seven minutes late, what the fuck's going on Tom?"

"I don't know," said Tom. "Keep calm, they could easily have been delayed by traffic, a hundred reasons," he added hopefully.

"Van's here!" Tony said suddenly, in a loud voice.

Phil pushed the accelerator slightly and pulled out a little behind the van.

"Not too close," said Tony. "Balaclavas on, weapons ready."

The Securicor van pulled up outside the Arrow offices, the back door opens and two guards jump out carrying money boxes.

"Go, Phil, quick!" said Tony urgently. Phil gunned the car, throwing gravel into the air as they screeched to a halt in front of the van. It all happened in a second. Tony jumped out and raised his gun. He fired a shot into each of the front tyres, while Tom and Bugsy charged out and attacked the two guards at the same time. They sprayed pepper at the guard's faces but they were wearing helmets with the visors down. They then started to hit the guards with baseball bats, but they would not let go of the boxes. The driver of the Securicor van had turned on the siren and it was making a hell of a noise. Tony was aiming the pistol at him through the window, shouting at him to get away from the horn. Tom and Bugsy were struggling with the two guards. People were now appearing from the offices.

Tom knew this had to end soon. He swung the baseball bat and nearly took the head off one of the guards, who dropped the box he was carrying and Tom quickly picked it up. He looked over to see Bugsy being held by two suited men, who must have come from the offices.

"Bugsy!" Tom shouted. He moved towards Bugsy but even more people were appearing from the offices.

"Shit!" shouted Tom. He stopped suddenly as he felt someone jump on him from behind. God, he thought, this is going to shit. He threw the box down and reached back and grabbed the man's balls and squeezed really hard. The man screamed and dropped down. Tony heard the scream and looked over. Jesus, he thought. This is bad, we've got to get out of here. He rushed over to help.

"Tom, we've got to get out of here!" Phil was sitting in the car trying hard to control himself. His first thought was to get out and go to help, but he knew he must stay where he was. The driver of the Securicor van could see Tom and Tony were in trouble. Even more people were piling out of the office. I could help, Phil thought. He jumped out of the van and attacked Tony from behind, getting him in a head lock and squeezing for all he's worth. Tony felt his air supply being cut off; he knew he did not have long. He made the decision and turned the gun, aiming it at the assailant's legs and fired. He heard a massive scream and felt the weight fall off him. He looked up. Tom and Bugsy were in big trouble. Tony had lost some control and there was only one thing he could do. He raised the gun and fired in the air.

"Everybody, get back!" Tony screamed. Tom broke free from his assailant.

"Tom, get in the car!" Tony raised the pistol again and fired. He felt his eyes being covered by sweat, he could hardly see. He rubbed his eyes and looked up. Some big cunt was charging towards him; he's so close now, I'm not going to prison, he thought. He raised the pistol and fired. The man fell like a stone and what was left of his face landed at Tony's feet. Tony looked over at Bugsy, he was lost. He turned and rushed for the car, grabbed the handle and jumped in. The car leapt forward before he could shut the door. Phil slammed his foot on the accelerator and pulled away at high speed. He swung the car round the corner towards the estate exit when a police car appeared, coming the other way, siren blasting.

Tony was in shock but still found the energy to shout, "Go left Phil!" Phil swerved left and hit the police car, bouncing off it and still speeding for the exit. Tony turned and saw that the police car had crashed into the side wall.

"Phil, slow down!"

Phil slowed down and pulled out of the exit onto the main road. He checked his speed meter and saw twenty eight miles per hour. He took a right turn on the way to Silvertown.

"Fucking hell! What a pile of shit! Fuck it! Couldn't have been much worse!" Tony was facing down and rubbing his face, neck and hair. "Shit, what a fuckup!"

Tom was leaning back, trying to catch his breath and thinking about poor, fucking Bugsy.

Tom started to cry. "We left Bugsy! Fuck! He's going to go down big time for this."

"Fuck! Fuck!" shouted Tony repeatedly

Phil was the only sane one in the car. "Both of you shut the fuck up till we get back to the lockup. You're drawing attention to us."

Tony could hear Tom whimpering in the back. Neither of them said another word till they pulled into the lockup and shut the gates.

There were four police cars and two ambulances outside Arrow Logistics. The entrance to the estate had been closed and most of the road and surrounding area were taped off.

Paramedics were desperately trying to stabilise the driver of the Securicor van. He had been shot in the thigh and had lost a lot of blood. He was strapped up and given pain killers. The ambulance driver turned on the blue lights and siren and headed towards Newham General Hospital.

The man who attacked Tony was dead. The bullet entered his left eye and exploded, taking off most of his face. He died instantly. The scene was still in chaos, about ten people from the company were milling about, too shocked to talk. They had all heard that Timius Papadakis had been shot and killed. Nobody could believe it.

Timius was Greek and brother of the owner of the company, Artan Papadakis. Artan was away on business in Albania and had all this to come back to.

The police officers turned to see who had arrived as a car pulled up near the offices. The car doors opened, Jeff Collins and Karen Foster got out.

Jeff and Karen strode over to the scene; a uniformed Sargent went towards them.

“Sounds like a bad one Simon,” said Jeff, surveying the scene. The Sargent responded “Shocker Jeff," said the Sargent. “Two shot, one dead civilian and the Securicor driver had a nasty bullet wound in his thigh. We also have the two guards and some members of the company with severe bruises. But the good news is we have one of the bastards in custody, he’s on his way to Rotherhithe now.”

“Do we know him?” asked Jeff quickly.

“Yea he’s a small time heavy in the local area.”

“Who’s the arresting officer?” asked Jeff.

“PC Cuthbert.”

“What were they after?” asked Karen.

“Payroll, about fifty grand. Why some companies still pay in cash, I don't know,” said Simon.

Jeff went into detective mode as he surveyed the scene more closely. “Make sure this whole area is sealed off, I don’t want any contamination of the scene. Are forensics on the way?”

“They should be here any minute, Chief Constable's on his way as well. Apparently, he needs to get out more and is gracing us with his presence.”

“In that case, Simon make sure everything is done by the book and most importantly, thoroughly. I don’t want any cock ups on this.”

Jeff turned to Karen. “Karen do what you're good at, we need all the witnesses' names, addresses, descriptions of the villains...”

“They were wearing balaclavas,” interrupted Simon.

“Check for CCTV," continued Jeff. "Nobody leaves here until we're happy we have everything we want.”

The forensics van trundled into view with a mini bus carrying a search team. The whole area would be locked down and gone over with a fine tooth comb. They all piled out and started to get to work.

"What about the vehicle?" asked Jeff, as he and Simon walked towards the offices.

"Ford Mondeo. It was reported stolen a few hours ago this morning."

Jeff was smiling as he turned towards Simon. "You know what, they've made a right fucking mess up of this, and we've got tons of evidence, lead witnesses and best of all, one of the little shits in the bag. I can't wait to have a chat with him."

Jeff was just a little concerned that his workload was getting out of control. Raptor and this investigation were just about all he could cope with. I must have a word with Michael, he thought.

Jeff and Simon disappeared into the offices.

Several things happened on the next Saturday and Sunday.

Artan Papadakis arrived back in the UK from Albania on Saturday. He went straight to the morgue where he identified his brother Timius as the person who had been shot by one of the robbers. The people at the morgue had done their best to patch up Timius's face but it had been difficult. He then had a meeting with senior managers at the company and told them to make sure employees who had been hurt were looked after. After sorting out everything he needed to, he went home to North London. Artan and Timius were very close and he was so upset he didn't know which way to turn. He drank far too much that night but had one thing to do before he tried to get some sleep.

Artan pressed the country number for Albania, followed by the area code and individual phone number. He steeled himself to make the call.

"Adnan, its Artan. How are you?"

"Long time, Artan. I hear you are making millions in the UK?"

"Just getting by Adnan, just getting by. I need your help"

"You know if I can help, I will."

"Timius my brother he has been murdered."

“What! Oh my God, Artan, I’m sorry. What the hell happened?”

“Robbery at the company. Timius was a hero and got shot in the head.”

Jesus, I don’t know what to say.”

“There is only one thing I want to hear. You will come over and help me find his killer and then we will make him pay, I will arrange everything.”

“Artan, I'll be on my way as soon as possible. I will bring Bashkim Amiti with me. He will be very useful.”

Artan was crying. “Yes, Adnan that is good. We will kill all these bastards who took my brother’s life.”

Adnan Ahmeti and Bashkim Amiti were both ex Albanian Army Special Forces. The very next day, they sourced some diplomatic passports and then boarded a British Airways flight to Heathrow, at Tirana Airport.

Nobody moved. Tony, Tom and Phil just sat in the car in silence for a full two minutes. Finally, Tony opened his car door and staggered out. Phil and Tom then slowly opened their doors and got out.

Tom was very upset. “Bugsy won’t talk, will he Tony?”

“No he won’t, if he does he’ll never see the courtroom.”

Tom was inconsolable. “He’ll get life, fucking life.”

“He knew what he was involved in, the rewards and the risks,” said Phil unhelpfully.

Tony and Tom sat down, Phil went into the office and came back out with three mugs and a bottle of scotch; it was meant to be drunk in celebration of a successful job but now it would blunt the pain, albeit only for a short time.

“What the fuck are we going to do now?” Tom mumbled grumpily.

“Nothing, until I’ve had a large fucking drink,” said Tony angrily as he held his glass out to Phil.

They all had a drink and tried to calm down.

Tony was feeling better as the whiskey hit the spot. "Right, there are several things to do.” He thought for a moment. “Phil get rid of the car, I don’t mean flog it for a grand and put it in your pocket, I mean get rid of it so it disappears. Either burn it or get it sorted at Mick's scrapyard. Tom, I want you to fuck off on holiday for a couple of weeks, go long distance. Caribbean's nice this time of year, I'll pay for everything, don't worry about money."

He thought again as he handed the gun to Phil. "Clean this and hide it here for a few days" He hesitated and added, "Listen both of you, I don't want to hear or see either of you for at least three months, is that clear?" He stared hard at both men. "If you get pulled, keep stum. Now, everyone, split and good luck." He walked out of the lockup and climbed into his car.

"Hi Paul, how are you?" said Tony as he walked into the den at nine pm.

"Yea, good thanks, how was your lazy day?"

"Oh, you know, boring really." If only you knew, thought Tony.

They got some drinks and sat down.

Paul took a sip of his beer.

"Hey, Tony, did you hear about the armed robbery in Plaistow?"

"No," said Tony. "What happened?"

"Right mess, by all accounts. One killed and the Securicor driver in intensive care, with gunshot wounds. Bloody amateurs, by the sound of it. Oh, and they caught one of the gang and they say there are so many leads they don't know where to start!" Paul laughed and looked over at Tony. Tony was deep in thought and looked really worried.

"You alright Tony?" asked Paul.

Tony lifted his glass and drained the large whiskey quickly. Paul noticed that his hand was shaking. I've never seen that before, he thought. Paul could sense something was not quite right, but what it was, he didn't know, yet.

The next morning, Tom headed to Heathrow. He wanted to be away as quickly as possible. He chose to go to Portugal. Nice bit of sunshine, some good food, good beer and if he's lucky, some nice female company.

The traffic was heavy as Tom drove through the tunnel into the airport. He was doing all of 5mph. He was casually looking across at the cars coming the other way to see if there was a nice girl he could smile at. He took no particular notice of the three Greek looking blokes in a big Blue Mercedes that passed him in the opposite direction.

CHAPTER 13

The plane circled Malaga airport. It had been a good flight; a few drinks and nibbles and before you knew it you were landing. Bruce Coyne was on his yearly trip to Torremolinos. October was cold and miserable in the UK and it was great to get away and have some decent weather.

Bruce smiled his way through Customs, if that's what you could really call it. Holiday makers were very welcome and he was out in to the sunshine in quick time.

He took a cab. It was eleven kilometres to Torremolinos, and within twenty minutes he was pulling into the front of the Marconfort Beach Club Hotel on the seafront. He got out the taxi and took a deep breath; at last he could start enjoying his holiday.

He booked into the hotel and soon found his air conditioned room on the fifth floor. He moved outside onto the balcony and looked out at the sea view, glorious. He had stayed at the hotel twice before and liked it very much. There was direct access to the sandy Playamar Beach, three swimming pools and hot tubs. He had booked fully inclusive so didn't even have to worry about carrying money. All in all, he was a happy bunny and his first night, he would make sure it was really memorable.

He changed into swimming trunks and made his way to the pool. He grabbed a sun lounger, stretched out and made himself comfortable. This is the life, he thought. He stayed on the sun lounger for a couple of hours, intermittently getting up to fetch another cold beer from the pool bar.

At six o clock, he went to see if the concierge was the same Pablo as the previous year. He was pleasantly surprised and Pablo seemed to remember him. He had given Pablo some really good tips and maybe, not too many of his guests asked him to supply girls.

"Pablo, I need a girl tonight."

"Don't worry Mr Bruce, I get you beautiful young girl." Pablo's English was not perfect but Bruce could understand him well enough.

"Not too young Pablo, over twenty, you understand. I do not want to end up in prison."

Pablo thought this was hilarious "You no end up in prison for loving girls."

"Pablo, girl must be pretty, not like one girl you sent me last year. You remember the girl that was looking straight at you but one of her eyes was looking the other way?"

Bruce doubted that Pablo understood that but tried with an easier approach. "Pablo, no fat ugly girls, you understand?"

"Sure, Mr Bruce, nice girl, no fat, no problem."

"Good. She can come and have dinner with me, say eight p.m. How much Pablo?

"Si, eh... very nice girl, for seventy euros."

"OK, thank you Pablo. You bring her to my room eight pm." No harm in repeating yourself with these wops, he thought.

Bruce thought that dinner would be good so he could suss the girl out and see if she was worth shagging for the cost. Bruce went back to his room and prepared for his guest.

A long lazy shower followed by a nice glass of chilled Cava and Bruce was sitting on the balcony waiting for his dinner date.

He checked his watch, eight fifteen and no sign of the very nice girl for seventy euros!

He took another long sip of the cava, shut his eyes and was soon nodding off. He woke with a start. Someone was banging loudly on his door. Shit, must be Pablo, he thought. He tried to rub the sleep from his face but probably made himself look worse and went over to open the door.

"Pablo, come in, come in." Pablo stood to one side and a Spanish girl entered the room. Bruce caught a glance and was not disappointed. Pablo followed her in and Bruce shut the door.

Bruce was surprised. In front of him was a really good looking slim Spanish woman in her early thirties.

"Mr Bruce, this is Maria." Bruce's first thought was, I bet that's not her real name, but who cares. The woman looked very middle class, certainly not like the scrubbers he turned up with last year. Maybe the recession has improved the class of tart, he thought.

"Hallo, Maria." Bruce held his hand out and Maria shook it gently.

There was a silence. "Eh, OK, Maria, do you speak English?"

"Yes, I learnt English at school." Bruce was happy. The strange English accent was so bloody sexy.

"Great, at least we can have a conversation over dinner. Pablo, I am very happy, so good bye and I will see you tomorrow, you understand?"

"Yes, Mr Bruce, I see you tomorrow, you have nice time, yes?"

"Yes, I have nice time," said Bruce as he almost shoved Pablo out the door.

"You are hungry, Maria?"

"I think the English expression is, I could eat a horse," said Maria

"Well, let's hope we're not having one of those. Shall we go to the restaurant?"

"Yes, let's go."

Maria seemed to be very happy, so Bruce was too. They made their way to the restaurant and sat in a window table with a lovely view of the pools and hot tubs.

"This hotel is very nice, is it not, Bruce?" Maria had the loveliest sexy voice when she spoke.

"Yes, it's very nice. Would you like some wine?" He poured some into a glass before Maria had the chance to say yes or no.

They chatted about nothing in particularly and ate their way through a mountain of food and several glasses of nice Cava. Bruce at one stage thought Maria could not have eaten for about a week; she ate so much.

Dinner had taken the best part of two hours and it was about ten thirty.

Bruce looked into Maria's eyes. "Shall we go up to my room for a nightcap?"

"What is this nightcap, Bruce?" Maria asked.

"A nice drink of whatever you like," said Bruce with a wink.

"I would love to, but it is getting very late and my friend is picking me up very soon." She looked at her watch. "But, it has been a very pleasant evening. I hope you have enjoyed it?"

"Yes, I suppose I have." Bruce was unsure what was going on but this woman was no prostitute and Pablo was going to get a good kicking.

Bruce walked Maria to the reception where she was picked up by another attractive younger girl.

"Thank you for a lovely evening. I enjoyed dinner very much," she said again, and disappeared.

Bruce strode over to the concierge's desk. Pablo was not there but he said to the man, "Tell Pablo to get his arse up to my room pronto, you understand?"

"Yes, of course," in perfect English, typical.

Bruce was well pissed off. Seventy euros for the privilege of taking someone to dinner.

There was a knock on the door. Bruce opened it to find a beaming Pablo.

"Pablo, you fucking numbskull, get in here." Pablo's smile disappeared as he could see Mr Bruce was not happy.

"Everything alright Mr Bruce?" Pablo asked.

"No, it fucking well isn't. Maria has gone!" He flicked his hand up to signify she had gone into the ether.

"Maria gone, si Mr Bruce, you have dinner, she go."

"No, Pablo I want girl, give dinner then up to room and jig jig." So Pablo understands exactly what he meant, he pushed his hips forward when he said jig.

"Jig jig Maria, no." Pablo was shaking his hand.

"I know that she has gone, you dimwit!" This is getting more like Faulty Towers every fucking minute, Bruce thought.

Pablo looked at Mr Bruce thoughtfully. "You say nice girl, Maria very nice girl no?"

"Yes she is a very nice girl, I want jig jig girl."

Pablo finally understood. "Yes, I see you want nice girl for jig jig." He does the hip pushing now.

"Yes ...!" Bruce couldn't say what he wanted to. "Pablo, can you get me jig jig girl, now?"

"Of course, is easy, one quick call girl here ten minutes for good jig jig."

Jesus! Why is life so complicated, thought Bruce. "Pablo, how much?"

"Eh, fifty euros one hour jig jig, very nice girl."

"Go and get the girl and bring her up to my room."

"Yes, I go now, come back ten minutes."

Bruce shut the door and went to his holdall and took out a duty free bottle of whiskey. He poured himself a good slug and knocked it back in one.

Fifteen minutes later, Pablo was back, this time, he was with a woman of about forty five, who had seen better days. The woman's name was Maria. What a fucking surprise, Bruce thought. He smiled at the woman. I need another whisky, he thought.

"You like jig jig," said Maria laughing mischievously.

Bruce smiled. At least she knew why she was here, he thought.

It was over pretty quickly and to be honest, not that satisfying. God forbid, he though, I might have to actually find myself a girlfriend while

I'm out here. It was too late to worry about anything else. Maria had gone and he was alone with his bottle of whiskey. He poured another large one and knew he would have a bad head in the morning.

CHAPTER 14

Police surveillance had commenced on all locations. Richard Philips, Falcon One in Billericay, Jack Coombs, Falcon Two in Chelmsford. The team at both locations consisted of two officers and one vehicle. When either Falcon left their location they were followed. A camera team had been set up in an office opposite the Frog pub in the Old Kent Road. Surveillance on the brothel in Peckham was again a camera team who were taking images of all individuals entering and leaving the premises. It had started pretty slowly as most surveillance operations do; the discipline required to stake out and stay concentrated for hours on end is quite remarkable.

Surveillance at the Frog had reaped literally hundreds of individuals captured on film. These were relayed to Eagle at Rotherhithe who then farmed them out to various resources, CID being the recipient of most of it. Jeff and Karen then spent time sifting through the images to pick out any known criminals or persons who could be of interest. They had spotted the usual local miscreants, such as Fred the Shed who made sheds for a living, but did car thefts to order as a side line; they saw Micky the Torch who liked setting fire to buildings and Tommy the Fence who took stolen property and sold it on for a vast profit. They had a small pile of images of people who they had an interest in. Amongst those images, there were several that Jeff had put there, purely because of his gut feeling or what was commonly referred to as copper's instinct. The images included both Falcons, who Jeff had recognised instantly and who were frequent visitors. There was an image of three men entering the pub that was of interest. Jeff thought he knew one of them. The three were Paul and Tony Bolton with Duke. There were also several images of nasty looking heavy types, who needed to be identified. Jeff had asked Karen to get a couple of local snitches in to help with that.

The surveillance operatives working on Falcon One had been running around all over London. The individual would always leave his home in Billericay at nine a.m. and return at four p.m.; he would then stay at home for a couple of hours and would usually go out again to clubs, pubs and restaurants all over the east end and further afield. He went to the Frog pub in the Old Kent Road regularly. He also visited a black woman in a flat in Canning Town. Further enquires revealed that the flat had been rented by Falcon One but that the resident was a Miss Julie Feather. It was believed that Falcon One and Miss Feather were in an extra marital relationship unknown to his wife. There were no visitors to the property.

Falcon Two, it seemed, on the surface, led a very disciplined and boring life. He left his mansion in Chelmsford on the dot at nine fifteen every day, he drove to the Frog pub in the Old Kent Road and stayed there until two pm. It was felt that he conducted all his business from the pub. He then returned home and did not leave the property again till next morning. There were no visitors to the property.

The phone taps on both residences were revealing nothing. Both Falcons had never used the house phones and were seen on various occasions with a selection of mobile phones. It was felt that multiple mobile phones were used for various different contacts; no mobile phones were registered personally to either Falcon. Neither of the Falcons used a computer.

What the police did not know was that both Falcons had a contract with a high tech company in West Ham that came on a monthly basis to sweep the properties and cars. No bugs were ever found but it was a necessary precaution that neither of them ever used the house phones as they thought they could well be hacked. Not only did both Falcons use multiple mobile phones but they were always pay as you go and untraceable. They were also changed frequently. Falcon Two also had a satellite phone which was housed in a briefcase which he used on occasions.

There was continuous camera footage of all persons entering and leaving the large house in Peckham that was thought to be a brothel. A group of young, and what could be described as attractive females, would arrive between ten and eleven o clock in the morning. The property would then have a succession of male visitors of all ages from twelve midday to three in the morning. An individual was identified by his car registration plates as Edward Frost, who was thought to be in charge of the premises. All vehicle plates of individuals who were seen entering the premises were read. A large number entered the property on foot, having probably parked some distance away. Falcon one had been identified entering the premises on one occasion and then leaving with a black girl who was later identified as a Miss Julie Feather. If it could be proven that the property was being run as a brothel, then the Met would consider contacting all known visitors with a view to prosecution.

Jeff and Karen were happy with the progress in what had been a few days. The image of Falcon One entering the property at Peckham showed a connection, but of course, there would be no connection in any ownership or rental agreements, which could tie Falcon One into running a brothel. To all intents and purposes, he could be a punter visiting for sex. The fact that Falcon One had seemed to have set up Miss Feather in the flat in Canning Town could possibly be useful in the future. Jeff was waiting desperately for identification of some of the people visiting the Frog that were of interest. Jeff and Karen had two massively important investigations going and they were as happy as pigs in shit.

CHAPTER 15

Jeff and Karen had put the word out on the street: they wanted information as to who was responsible for the armed robbery at Arrow Logistics. Securicor had offered a reward of fifty thousand pounds for information leading to a conviction. This was sure to bring information from all the local scum and it would then be a case of sifting through it all to see if any could be useful. The merest hint of a reward and some residents of Bermondsey would phone or send letters swearing it was their next door neighbour or even their parents or children.

"Sarg, take him in please; we'll let him sweat for ten minutes before we come in." Jeff and Karen went to get their fifth cup of coffee that morning.

Philip Mark Cooper, or better known locally, as Bugsy, was brought out of his cell and taken to a first floor interview room.

He had arrived at Rotherhithe nick direct from the armed robbery at Arrow Logistics. He was booked in, his full name and address were taken. He was fingerprinted, had his mouth swabbed for DNA and then photographed. He was then placed in a cell. The doctor arrived thirty minutes later to check him over and pronounced him fit, apart from a mass of bruises which would soon heal. His solicitor, who just happened to be passing nearby, was knocking on the reception counter demanding to see his client within an hour of Bugsy arriving. Terence Bradley, the solicitor, was an old school friend of Tony Bolton's. A couple of do gooders who visited cell prisoners to make sure they were being treated well, turned up. They only stayed two seconds as Bugsy told them to fuck off out of it.

Bugsy knew he was in deep shit; he had heard the gun shots and was praying that no one had been seriously injured or, God forbid, killed. He knew just for the armed robbery, he would get fifteen years, but if there were casualties, then he could get life. At least, his wife and kids would be taken care of. Tony would make sure they wanted for nothing. The thought of cutting a deal came to mind, but he knew that if he grassed the other guys up, he would end up dead in some prison washroom. The whole thing was just a complete fuck up.

It was a small interview room, four chairs and a small table with a tape recorder in the middle on one side. There was a copper standing near the side of the door. Bugsy was sitting in a chair on the other side of the table facing the door. He was tough but he was still shitting himself inside. He was not there for picking pockets. He looked around the room; if an opportunity arose for him to escape, maybe he would try it. Maybe Tony could spring him. It's too late to moan now so I've got to accept what comes and take it on the chin, he thought.

The door opened and the two detectives and what looked like a solicitor walked in and sat down on the free chairs.

"Hello Mr Cooper, I'm your solicitor." They shook hands and sat down.

Jeff looked at Bugsy, yes you should be sweating mate, he thought.

Jeff switched on the machine. "This is DC Jeffrey Collins CID, based at Rotherhithe Police Station. It is Friday the 9th of August 2013 at ten am. Those present are my colleague DC Karen Foster CID, and Solicitor, Mr Terence Bradley representing the accused. We are to question a suspect in connection with the armed robbery at Arrow Logistics on Thursday 8th August 2013."

Jeff turned to Bugsy. "Can you state your full name and address please."

"Philip Mark Cooper, Southwark Park Rd SE16"

"Thank you." said Jeff

"Mr Cooper, you were arrested at Arrow Logistics and were initially charged with armed robbery. I now have to tell you that charge has changed to the following." Jeff stopped to look at Bugsy. He could see he didn't want to hear, he wanted to wake up at home and think he'd had a bad dream. Jeff held his eye contact for a few more seconds then he delivered the words which would feel like a hammer blow to Bugsy.

“I am arresting you for the first degree murder of a Mr Timius Papadakis; the shooting and wounding of Securicor driver Mr Robert Jones; the armed robbery committed at the premises of Arrow Logistics and the possession and use of a firearm in the armed robbery.”

Jeff was staring at Bugsy to see his reaction. He had seen hardened criminals start to cry and beg for mercy but not this time. Bugsy just looked resigned to his fate. He glanced at the solicitor. He didn't look very happy. Caught at the scene, guns, people killed, this boy's in big trouble, thought Terence.

“Mr Cooper, can you explain to us what you were doing at Arrow Logistics on Thursday 8th August 2013 at two pm.”

Terence looked at Bugsy. “I recommend at this stage that you say nothing.”

“Detective Collins, I have not had time to talk to my client, so would request that you postpone this interview until I have had time to do so.” Terence looked Jeff in the eye knowing that he could do nothing but agree.

“This interview is terminated at ten eleven am so that the accused can deliberate with his solicitor.” Terence pushed his chair back to stand up but stopped as Jeff continued to speak, looking at Terence

“Because of the seriousness of the charges, it is my intention to re interview Mr Cooper at three pm later today.”

Bugsy and the solicitor headed off under escort to a room where they could speak in confidence.

“That solicitor’s more bent than a Yuri Geller spoon,” said Karen

Jeff looked at her as though he had never heard anything so strange in all his life.

“Yes, well everybody knows Terence hangs out with criminals, he seems to like that type of person. And of course, he’s a local lad you know, Bermondsey born and bred”

Bugsy and Terence sat down. Bugsy bowed his head and rubbed his face with his hands. “I guess I’m in deep shit.” He raised his head and looked at Terence wearily.

“I’m not going to sugar candy this, yes you’re in deep shit, and your friends send their regards.”

At that Bugsy looked up and slowly smiled. “Who exactly?”

“As I said, your friends are thinking of you," said the solicitor, keeping a straight face.

“As to what sort of deep shit you’re in I’m afraid it’s prison for a very long time”

Bugsy sighed in resignation. “Yes I know, life, I’m guessing.”

“Well, let’s see what we can do before thinking about that, so let’s get down to business”.

Bugsy and the solicitor spoke for an hour. Terence knew as soon as he heard the circumstances that there was nothing he could do, but he had to give Bugsy some hope.

“We’re going to play on the fact that you were brought up in the local area, that your family neglected you and that all your friends were criminals, so you had no chance of breaking out of that circle.”

“Before I go," said the solicitor in a serious tone. "Your friends will do everything they can to help you but you have to play ball. Jan, your wife and the rest of your family will be well cared for, they won’t have to worry about money.” The Solicitor took a deep breath and stared hard at a worried looking Bugsy. “The Police are going to put you under huge pressure to cut a deal and name the other gang members, they’ll promise you the earth, reduced sentence, protection, all sorts of things. Your friends say it would be very unwise for you to consider that course of action. You do understand that message?” He continued to stare hard at Bugsy.

“Yea, I understand. I keep stum and do my time or else.” Bugsy was not just worried that he could end up with a knife in his back; he was more concerned for his wife and kids.

The interview took place at 3pm and Bugsy answered every single question with the same answer, “No comment.”

Terence left the nick and had one thing to do before going home. “It’s me, he’s alright I don’t see any problems.” he heard the phone click.

He was taken back to his cell with the knowledge that very soon, he would be transferred, to be remanded at Her Majesty's Prison Belmarsh in Thamesmead.

Jeff and Karen were having a fag out the back.

"Jeff, you've got to squeeze him, he appears tough but you never know. Put him under pressure, promise him a new life, whatever it takes, he could give us those names." Jeff had said it was a waste of time. Bugsy had a wife and children and knew that they could be killed if he talked.

"OK, we'll give it a go. For a change, you be good cop and I'll be the bad arse."

The good cop, bad cop was so obvious but it still worked. Prisoners who had committed crimes were under immense pressure and felt the whole world was against them. A friendly word was like giving somebody dying of thirst in the Sahara desert a long glass of cold water.

"Let's get him in now while his head is in a real mess," said Jeff taking his last drag on his cigarette.

They came for Bugsy as he was trying to sleep.

"Can't a man get a bit of shut eye round here?" said Bugsy plaintively.

He was escorted back to the interview room. Karen walked in and sat opposite Bugsy and looked him square in the eyes.

"We want to have a chat with you Bugsy, but we're not going to tape it, OK?"

Bugsy was alert now. No tape, so it was all off the record; he could guess what was coming.

"Jeff will be along shortly." Karen was almost sneering at Bugsy.

"I hate people like you Bugsy, you think you're above the law. You're going to get life in prison. Do you know that life could be thirty years? Even if you only did twenty that will make you fifty when you come out. Your family won't even recognise you, not that they'll be around anyway. You don't think Jan's going to wait for you, do you?" That's a good start, Karen thought to herself. Let's see what this guy's made of.

“Do you, Bugsy? I’ll tell you how it works, shall I? She’ll come and see you for a few months and then it will dwindle to every few months until eventually, she won’t come, then you can be sure she’s got another man, another man in your house, in your bed, Bugsy, shagging your wife and bringing up your children.” Karen looked hard at Bugsy. “That’s what you deserve, Bugsy. You know the bloke shot at the scene? He was shot through the eye. Can you imagine that Bugsy? Do you think he fucking well deserved that? Well do you? DOA Bugsy. You know what that stands for, don’t you? Dead on arrival at Hospital."

Bugsy was feeling like shit.

“No, he didn’t deserve that.” Karen could see he was a bit tearful she pressed on relentlessly. “He had a wife and children, Bugsy, three kids, fatherless, and for what? Money, money, Bugsy. The Securicor guard that got shot: he’ll never walk without a limp; he may never work again. Was it all worth it, Bugsy?” Karen was nearly shouting at Bugsy and he was withering under the onslaught. “That’s why I don’t give a shit for scum like you, Bugsy.”

Bugsy jumped up from his chair. “Stop it for God’s sake! Stop!” The uniformed officer standing in the corner made towards Bugsy but Karen caught his sleeve and held him back.

“What's going on here?” demanded Jeff as he came through the door.

Silence.

Jeff looked at Karen. “I think you need to go and get yourself a coffee.” Karen got up and left the office.

Jeff looked at the uniformed officer and almost detected a smile.

“Bugsy, are you alright?”

Bugsy remained silent and sullen, still shaken from Karen's onslaught.

Jeff sat down and looked at Bugsy, who was now looking really ill...

“Bugsy, I expect you would like a cup of tea and a biscuit.” He smiled at Bugsy.

“Yea, one sugar.” Bugsy mumbled.

Jeff turned to the officer present and raises his eyebrows. The officer left the room to get Bugsy tea and saw Karen by the machine along the corridor.

“Bloody hell, Karen you deserve an Oscar for that performance.”

Karen chucked the empty paper coffee cup in the bin. “I actually believed a lot of what I said.” she strolled off towards her office.

“You know, Bugsy," Jeff was saying. "I’m from around here, same as you. I was lucky I could have easily ended up just like you. I could have been sitting in that chair.” Jeff was pleased with that. It sounded really good; that course on interviewing techniques wasn’t a complete waste of time then.

Bugsy looked up from his clammy hands. Jeff could feel he wanted to talk. “You’re local are you?”

“Born in Newham Hospital. Spent my whole life in Bermondsey and the surrounding areas,” said Jeff.

The door opened and the officer walked in, holding a mug of tea and a saucer, with digestive biscuits. He placed them in front of Bugsy, who took a good gulp of the steaming tea and coughed. He picked up a biscuit and nibbled at it. The hot tea seemed to put a bit of life in him. Jeff let him drink his tea and eat a biscuit for a minute.

“You know what, Bugsy, this is a fucking mess; dead bodies, people with gunshot wounds, and you didn’t even get away with any of the money.”

Bugsy was feeling a bit better. The sweet tea and biscuits were a godsend.

“Was it your idea to carry the shooter?”

“It wasn’t my fucking idea, are you mad? I’ve never carried a gun in my life, let alone used one.”

“That’s the trouble Bugsy, you weren’t carrying the gun but you’re taking the rap for it. If there hadn’t been a gun, nobody would have got killed. You might have only been looking at five years and been out in three.”

"You're right. If he hadn't been carrying, I wouldn't be in this mess," said Bugsy angrily.

Bugsy wanted to cry and scream and smash his fists on the table. He didn't do any of those things but he was thinking; forget Phil, he was only the driver, but Tony and Tom, he didn't even blame Tom much but that bastard Tony, why, why did he have to take that shooter and then start blazing away like a fucking madman?

Jeff needed to move it along.

"Yea, if that idiot hadn't taken the gun along then it would have all been different, especially for you now, Bugsy"

Bugsy had a picture of Tony in his head and he suddenly jumped. He could see Tony in his house with Jan and the kids, he had a gun, Jesus no, and Bugsy was now wide awake. Yea,

He hated Tony for shooting those people but did he really want to put his family at risk by snitching?

Bugsy finished his tea and looked up.

"Your name's Jeff, isn't it? I'm going to call you that, whether you like it or not. I know what you're up to. All this tea and fucking biscuits shit!"

"Let's cut to the chase then, Bugsy. You're going to rot in prison for twenty odd years while the people or more importantly, the shooter is out there enjoying life to the full. Are you happy with that?"

"Of course, I'm fucking not, but there's nothing I can do about it," said Bugsy

"That's where you're wrong Bugsy. I know the game. We can pick your family up in an hour's time and have them in a protected safe house.

You can spend your reduced sentence in Scotland in a section with other people just like you, it can be done."

Bugsy just sat there, thinking.

"What would my sentence be if I..." he was about to say snitched but stopped himself. "Cooperated?"

“I can’t promise anything but it could be reduced by half, you might only do ten years.”

Jeff was looking at Bugsy and couldn't believe he’d got this far.

“I could do my time in Scotland, are you serious?”

“Absolutely, Bugsy, you have my word on it.”

“I need to think about it.”

“OK,” said Jeff. “How long do you need?”

“An hour will be long enough, and I’ve suddenly become very hungry.”

“I’ll organise one of our delicious microwave meals for you. Look, make the right decision for you, Bugsy, not anyone else, you.”

Jeff got up and left the interview room and headed straight to the CID office.

“Karen, you won’t believe this but he’s thinking about it!”

“Yes, but you know what the answer will be. He’ll say get lost.”

Jeff thought back to what had happened. “You know what, I’m not so sure. I know it's unlikely but it’s possible. I told him he could serve his time in Scotland.”

“Are you serious? Can you fix that?” asked Karen.

“For a man who shot a defenceless civilian and wounded a Securicor driver, I think we would just about do anything.”

“Fingers crossed then,” said Karen dubiously.

Jeff spent an hour, looking through statements from witnesses at the scene. The hour went so slowly, it was mind numbing. It then went to an hour and a half, after one hour forty six minutes, he was informed that Bugsy would like to see him.

“Come on Karen, let’s go and see what Mr Cooper has to say.”

“Are you sure I should come?” asked Karen.

“Yes, it won’t make any difference; he’ll say what he wants to, whether you’re there or not.”

Jeff stopped outside the door to the interview room and turned to Karen. "Let's do it."

"Hello Bugsy." Jeff looked at Bugsy but could not detect any sign of a yes or no.

"So, here we are then," said Jeff briskly. "Are you going to help us Bugsy?"

Bugsy looked at Karen and then turned to Jeff; he looked at him for what seemed ages, but was probably only three or four seconds.

"The answer is," he hesitated, then said, "Yes I will cooperate with you, but I need to discuss the details with you."

Jeff and Karen looked at each other, trying not to appear shocked. Jeff turned back to Bugsy.

"That's really good news Bugsy and the right decision. Let's go through it all now shall we"

"I'm ready," said Bugsy, determinedly.

"So, who was the shooter?" said Jeff in a serious tone.

"Before I tell you that, I need to tell you my conditions."

"And what are they Bugsy?"

"First, I want my sentence reduced."

"That goes without saying," answered Jeff

"Next, I want to serve my sentence as far from London as possible."

"Agreed."

"Third I want my family moved somewhere a long way from London with new identities and protection."

"Agreed," said Jeff

"Last, once my family is safe I want to speak to my wife, and the second I hear my wife tell me she is happy and safe, I will give you one name, and that name will be the shooter."

Jeff was thoughtful for a couple of seconds, we can pick the family up first thing in the morning he thought, and there should be no hitches.

"OK, you have a deal." Jeff held out his hand, Bugsy took it and they shook hands looking into each other's eyes.

Jeff and Karen were ecstatic but Jeff was quick to point out nothing had been achieved until Bugsy's family were in a safe house.

Jeff and Karen rushed back to the CID office to put everything in motion.

Karen had never been so excited before. "Jeff, what time are we picking the family up?" She was almost overcome at the prospect of arresting the bastard shooter.

They were both so caught up in the moment that neither of them saw the smartly dressed man at the other end of the corridor stop and look at them, as he was about to leave the station.

They arrived at their office. "Karen, get the team organised for tomorrow morning's pick up. I'm just going to have a word with Andrew. I'll be back in a minute."

"OK," said Karen, as a million things she had to do started running through her mind.

"Andrew, I want a surveillance guy at an address in Tower Bridge Road like yesterday. We're going to pick up a family from that address tomorrow morning and I just want to make sure they're safe till then."

Andrew replied "Yea no problem Jeff. Can I send a squad car? We're short of unmarked at the moment."

Jeff thought for a moment "That's OK. Tell him not to fall asleep eh"

They both laughed.

Jeff gave Andrew the address and went back to his office.

"How you getting on, Karen?"

"Good, two unmarked cars, three coppers, one of them female to help with the kids, safe house is booked. We're ready, are you going?"

"No, I've got a copper outside the flat in..." He looked at his watch. "10 minutes, so we're covered but I want you to go. By the way, how old are the kids?"

"Two boys, sixteen and twelve, and a five year old girl. And it will be my pleasure to go."

"Karen, I want the wife to make the call once she is in the car."

"Sure," said Karen.

"I don't have to tell you this is a once in a lifetime opportunity, no hiccups OK?"

"Don't worry. I can see that promotion already," said Karen smiling.

Jeff was happy. They had a copper at the site and they could take their time in the morning and pick them up. There was no great rush. Jeff had had enough for one day and it was getting late.

"Karen, I'm off. See you at eight in the morning."

"Look forward to it. Goodnight."

Karen was smiling to herself. Jeff deserved a break and the arrest of the shooter would be an incredible coup for him. She sorted her files neatly into piles on her desk and then left for home.

Terence had left the police station a bit later than he had intended. He had had to see a new client and the interview had overrun. He was now at home in Hampstead, enjoying a glass of claret and looking at the tits on page three of The Sun newspaper. He couldn't put his finger on it, but something was nagging him and he didn't know what it was. His wife called him for dinner and he forgot about it.

Tony was at home in Billericay, doing nothing much, to the irritation of his wife who had asked him to fix a picture that had fallen off the wall in the dining room.

CHAPTER 16

Terence was up early the next morning. He had a coffee and some toast and was sitting in his office at home, opening the post from the day before. He paused for a moment, then picked up his phone and dialled Rotherhithe Police Station.

"Good Morning officer, this is Terence Bradley, Solicitor. I would like to book an appointment with my client, Mr Philip Cooper, for this morning, please."

"Hang on a moment please, sir," said the officer

The officer came back on the line. "I'm afraid, that won't be possible this morning as Mr Cooper is unwell."

"Oh, he was perfectly alright yesterday," said Terence with a frown.

"I'm only the duty receptionist," said the police officer

"OK, any chance of speaking with CID... Err... Jeff Collins or Karen Foster? I don't mind which."

"Hang on a moment, please, sir."

Terence was twiddling his thumbs as he was held waiting for some time.

"I'm sorry, both those officers are in conference at the moment and cannot be disturbed."

"Well, in that case I'll go and make myself another cup of coffee and try later," he said to the officer.

"Sounds like a very good idea to me, sir."

Terence clicked off the phone. He walked to the kitchen, filled the kettle and turned it on. Suddenly, a shiver ran down his spine. He was confused for a second while thoughts rushed at him. He glanced at the clock, it was nine forty am.

"Oh, Jesus!" he shouted at the top of his voice. He remembered at the Nick, the two happy CID officers, the words pick up, Bugsy supposedly being ill, no appointment this morning, no CID available. Shit!

Something's not right! Then suddenly, everything became clear and time froze. He knew what he had to do, but he couldn't move.

His wife walked into the kitchen. "What's wrong, darling? You're shouting." Terence just looked at her and then rushed past her into his office. He yanked the door open, grabbed his mobile and pressed contacts. Tony's name appeared and he pressed the button. He was shaking and was having difficulty breathing. Shit! Answer! It was ringing and ringing.

Tony heard his mobile ringing and picked it up. He saw the name and pushed the green answer button.

"Morning Terence, you're up bloody early this morning."

"Tony, listen, something's happening at Rotherhithe nick. I think Bugsy's done a deal."

As soon as Tony heard those words, his world suddenly changed. He felt sick and wanted to vomit. He couldn't breathe properly. He opened his mouth, but no words came out.

"Tony, can you hear me?" Terence was screaming down the phone. "Tony, you've got to get to his family. The police are picking them up this morning. Tony!"

Tony couldn't get his breathing under control, all he could see was a prison cell with a sign on the door: 'lifer, no remission.' "OK, OK, I'm here. Are you sure?"

"Cause, I'm fucking sure. Something's going on right now and I think they're going to pick his family up very soon, this morning, that's if we're not too late already."

Tony just clicked off the phone and stood still, in shock. How could I get Bugsy so wrong? He started thinking of options. It's either I do a runner or maybe if we can get Bugsy's family, then all can be saved. But why haven't the police turned up here, yet? Of course Bugsy will not give them any names until his wife and kids are safe, so they must still be at home. I've got to try.

Tony grabbed his mobile and made three quick calls in succession; the three men he called would be outside his house in ten minutes. He had to keep calm and think everything through. Shit, what a fucking mess. His last thought before dashing upstairs to get his Magnum was, I wish I could get Paul to help, but he couldn't; he would have to sort it out himself.

Tony pulled out of his driveway and picked up two of the men he called earlier, the third followed in another car; he didn't trust himself to drive, so told Ben, one of the boys, to get behind the wheel.

"Jesus! Ben! Put your fucking foot down, for Christ's sake!" Tony was still reeling from the news that Bugsy might well have done a deal. If they got to the flat and they had gone, Tony decided, he would go straight to Heathrow and get on the first flight to anywhere.

"Watch your speed Ben, we don't want to get stopped on the way." Tony could think of only one thing he would do to Bugsy, if it were possible for him to get hold of him.

Jeff and Karen had agreed to meet in the nick early; they were sitting in the CID office, on their second coffee.

"Don't worry Jeff, nothing can go wrong. Nobody knows anything about this, other than a couple of people here, so, don't get yourself all worked up."

"I know, but I want that bastard shooter so badly, I can taste it."

"I know what you mean, but keep cool, everything's in place." Karen couldn't believe how calm she was considering the seriousness of the morning.

"So, Karen, you get to the flat at ten thirty, pick up the family and take them to the safe house in Brighton, you then come back."

"Sounds good to me, Jeff." Both officers were a bit apprehensive but relaxed at the same time. They felt they were getting the upper hand at last. The time was now 10am. They would leave the nick at ten fifteen with an ETA at ten thirty.

Tony was sweating; he was sitting in the front passenger seat and was constantly fidgeting.

“Tony, try and sit fucking still for Christ’s sake!” said Ben irritably. Tony had a vision of walking into court with chains round his ankles and wrists, then realised they only do that in the States, not in the UK. He talked to Ben constantly. “Take the ring road south, we’re going to Tower Bridge road, remember."

“Jeff, this is going to be a big break for you,” said Karen thoughtfully while checking who was in the building for the pickup.

“Look Karen, let's get the job done, that’s all we focus on at the moment, the time for congratulations and all that is after the job’s done.” Jeff was feeling slightly tensed. He looked up at the clock high up on the wall. It was quarter past ten.

“You understand what to do," said Ben to the guy in the back of the car. "When we get to the address, Ben, you stay in the car while we go and get the family. It should be a doddle.”

Tony was near exhaustion and feeling a tightness in his chest. Jesus, I might die before we even get there, he thought. Suddenly he heard his mobile ringing. He pressed the red button. I can’t talk to Paul now, he mumbled to himself.

“Watch your speed, Ben. Keep in the left hand lane and watch that fucking bus!”

“Karen, are you all ready to go?” asked Jeff.

“Yea. Team are outside and ready to go.”

They looked at each other. “Go and do it then,” said Jeff. "And I'll see you soon."

The team piled into a car and a seven seater and pulled out of the nick into lower road.

Tony was entering onto Mansell Street. “Not far to go now.” His breathing was shallow and rasping.

It was now ten eighteen and Tony was five minutes from Tower Bridge road.

Karen and the police team were leaving Lower road and turning right into Prescott Street. She was ten minutes from Tower Bridge road.

Tony's car pulled into Tower Bridge road. He immediately noticed the police car outside the block of flats.

"Shit!" He pulled his pistol and shouted at Ben. "Park right behind the copper."

"What the fuck are you doing, Tony?" Ben screamed.

"I'm trying to stay out of fucking prison!" shouted Tony.

The surveillance police officer was Chris Morgan, a twenty eight year old married father of two girls. He glances in his mirror as the silver Astra pulled in behind him. Perhaps I'm being relieved, he thought. He pressed the window button and it came sliding down. A man got out of the Astra and walked to the passenger window. Chris leaned over and then a flash.

Tony leapt out of the car took four steps to the police car passenger window, raised his pistol and fired one shot into the officer's head.

Tony turned and shouted to his two accomplices. "Move it! Let's go!" They charged up two flights of steps and were at the front door to the flat.

Karen and her team were five minutes from Tower bridge road.

Tony knocked on the door. He could see a boy through the glass panel.

"Parcel delivery!" Tony shouted and rang the doorbell at the same time.

The boy opened the door three inches and peered out. Tony kicked the door and pushed the boy back in onto the floor. Tony rushed in, looking for Jan. She was in the kitchen.

"What do you want Tony? Get away from me," said Jan, backing away, with a sauce pan in her right hand.

"You're coming with me Jan, you need protection," said Tony hurriedly.

"We're alright here thanks, Tony." The boy entered the kitchen holding his head "What have you done to him Tony?" She rushed to the boy's side, putting an arm round him. "Are you alright?"

Karen and her team were three minutes from Tower Bridge road.

"I haven't got time to fuck about." said Tony impatiently. He turned to one of the heavies who had followed him into the flat. "Get the other kids, quickly!"

"No!" screamed Jan. Tony smashed her in the face with the back of his hand, grabbed her by the hair and started dragging her to the door. One of the heavies had the boy and the two of them moved out the door and down the stairs. Tony glanced back to see where the other guy was with the other children, but he could not see them. He couldn't wait. They were soon at the bottom of the stairs.

Karen and her team were one minute from Tower Bridge road.

Tony pushed Jan into the Astra and was quickly followed by the boy. Tony glanced up at the flat and saw the heavy coming down, no kids. He jumped into the car behind.

"Move Ben!" Ben pulled away, followed by the other car.

Karen and the team pulled into Tower Bridge road.

She could see the police car and for some reason, a crowd forming around it.

"Pull up behind the car, quick!" Karen had a sinking feeling that they were too late.

The car stopped. She jumped out and rushed to the police car.

"Police! Stand back everybody!" The crowd moved out of the way. Karen got to the passenger window and looked in.

"Oh God, no please!" she cried. The officer was slumped in the seat, blood and brains splattered everywhere. Karen turned to one of the officers with her. "Deal with this!" She turned and ran to the flat, taking the stairs two at a time. She was soon at the door of the flat, which was wide open. She knew, even before she went in, that they had already been taken. We've failed, she thought dismally. Jeff, where are you?

Help me! She ducked into the hall way and shouted: “Police! Is there anybody here?” Silence, just fucking silence. She turned to leave but heard a whimper. She followed the sound to the bedroom.

“This is the police. You're safe now, come out.” Karen scanned the room then suddenly, two children, a boy of about seven and a girl, five years old, appeared from a cupboard.

“Where’s my mummy?” asked the little girl.

Karen took the little girls hand, telling her not to worry, everything would be fine. Karen could feel tears trickling down her face as she walked out the flat with the two children.

A call came into Rotherhithe Nick at ten thirty five, reporting an officer shot at Tower Bridge road.

The CID office door opened and an officer walked in. “Jeff, an officer's just been killed at Tower Bridge road.”

“What?” Jeff couldn't take the news in. The operation was meant to be routine. “Do you know who it was?” Jeff asked

“Apparently a surveillance officer, Chris Morgan.”

Something has gone terribly wrong, thought Jeff. I’d better get down there. He jumped into a squad car and shot out of the nick towards Tower Bridge road. He was anxious and agitated. I’ve fucked up big time. But what exactly happened? His mobile rang shrilly. It was Karen.

“Karen! Are you alright?” he asked anxiously.

“Not too bad," said Karen wearily. "Two of the kids are here but Jan and the older boy have gone. I’m so sorry, Jeff.”

Jeff could hear and feel her tears. “Don’t worry. It’s not your fault. I’ll be there in five minutes.”

Jeff turned on the siren and blue light and watched as the traffic moved out of the way.

There was mayhem at Tower Bridge Road. The road had been closed off and Police cars were everywhere, ambulances and even a fire engine were in attendance. Police were everywhere. Jeff spotted Karen and headed towards her in the car. Karen saw Jeff and ran to him; she collapsed into his arms, crying.

“Jeff, I’m sorry, the officer in the car dead, shot in the head, is in pieces all over the car.” She was sobbing so much she could hardly get the words out.

“Don’t worry, it’s not your fault, we’re going to get this bastard, I promise you.”

The two cars headed straight out to Dagenham where Tony had a bolt hole. Tony was feeling better already. If that cunt Bugsy said one word to the filth, he would bury Jan and the boy alive. Thank God, I must have used up at least fifteen of my nine lives, he thought.

Tony left Jan and the boy at the Dagenham house with two of the heavies.

“So, what are we going to say to Bugsy? He’s already asked to see you once today.” Karen had recovered some of her composure.

“Karen, there’s one thing I want to know. How come they were there two minutes before us? Was it a coincidence? I don’t think so. Something is wrong and I can't put my finger on it.”

“You don’t think we have a mole here, do you?” Karen asked, looking very concerned.

“I can’t believe that, but then, not all coppers are straight, as we know.”

“Karen, I’ll be back in a minute," said Jeff suddenly and made his way to reception; Jim was at the desk. Good, he thought

“Jim, you know all about what happened this morning."

“Yea, nothing I hate more than a cop killer,” said Jim with feeling.

“You and me,” said Jeff.

“Jim, can we speak confidentially?”

“Course, what is it?”

“Well, I just cannot believe it was a coincidence that those fuckers turned up two minutes before us. What do you think?”

"I think it's very, very suspicious" said Jim. "Do you think there could be a leak here?"

"Possibly, I can't think of any other logical explanation," said Jeff thoughtfully.

The outer door suddenly opened and Terence Bradley entered reception.

"Good day to you, gentleman, how are you? Solved any major crimes recently?"

"What can we do for you, Mr Bradley?" Jim asked.

"Well, I want to see my client Mr Cooper, as soon as possible."

Something in Jeff stirred. No, surely, it's not possible, is it? But how?

"Perhaps, you would be good enough to take a seat in the waiting room while I see if that is possible," said Jim.

Jeff watched him walk into the waiting room and shut the door.

"I can't stand that bloke," said Jim, wrinkling his nose.

"Likewise," said Jeff, with a frown. "There's something about him; have you noticed anything strange about his behaviour in any way?"

"Not really. He rang in this morning asking to see Cooper. We told him he was sick and wasn't having visitors." Jim paused and frowned. "Oh, he also asked for you or Karen; we said you were in conference."

"Hmm," Jeff muttered, still frowning. "Well, he wasn't here yesterday when all this happened, so, I just don't know."

"All I know is, he left here at five p.m. yesterday," said Jim, helpfully.

"Five p.m. He left well before then, Jim," Jeff's frown deepened.

"Because I dislike him so much, I always remember when he comes and goes."

"He left at the same time we came out of the meeting with Cooper, that's it. He must have heard something. Christ, then this morning he got blanked on Cooper and me and Karen; he's put two and two together and got four. He's in league with the shooter."

“Sounds a bit farfetched, Jeff.”

“I’m telling you Jim, that bastard is in league with the devil!”

Jeff strode into the waiting room.

“Mr Bradley, I just want to let you know that you may see a few upset officers today. Did you hear that a police officer was murdered in Tower Bridge road this morning?” Jeff was watching him very closely.

Terrence went a little white but quickly regained his composure. “That is terrible news, I’m so sorry."

“He was a family man, married with two children,” added Jeff.

“Terrible, absolutely terrible,” said Terrence, shaking his head.

Jeff looked straight into his eyes.

“We will hunt the bastard that did this to the ends of the earth," he said. "Not only that, we will pursue with the same vigour anyone who has helped him, is hiding him, or knows him and does not come forward and inform the police. What do you think about that, Mr Bradley?”

“I am sure you will catch this individual very soon, officer.” He turned to study some papers on his lap.

Jeff walked out of the waiting room.

Terence Bradley was apoplectic. That Tony is a fucking maniac, and now I could be implicated in a cop murder, not forgetting the kidnapping. He thought quickly. There was only one thing; he would never ever see or speak to that lunatic again and he hoped the sooner Tony was off the streets, the better.

CHAPTER 17

Paul and Emma were still in love, were still making love ten times a week, were still buying each other silly presents and were still spending as much time together as they could. Paul had never realised what it was to find someone who you naturally thought you belonged with. They talked about everything and anything; they spoiled each other rotten and always thought of their partner rather than themselves. There had been a couple of moments when Paul hadn't really wanted to tell Emma about his past. He wasn't proud that he had been a football hooligan. But now, that was all in the past. Emma had changed his outlook on life. He wanted to settle down and have a family, and he wanted to have three kids with Emma. They had discussed it and Emma was excited to start a family, but first she wanted them to have some fun together. Emma had moved into the luxury apartment in Chelsea Harbour and took to domestic life like a duck to water. She also loved the cosmopolitan makeup of the Chelsea set. She loved the restaurant at the Wyndham Grand Hotel round the corner, loved walking in the Marina and wanted to see Chelsea play at Stamford Bridge, but Paul had said absolutely no chance. She loved cooking exotic meals and keeping the flat nice and tidy. She also enjoyed going out with Paul to the clubs where, of course, they were treated like royalty.

Paul had asked her how much housekeeping she needed, she had said she wasn't sure so Paul organised for a grand a week to be put in her Barclays account. Emma was very happy with that. She paid for the food and wine and had plenty left to get her favourite bits from Ann Summers. Emma liked to keep the sex spicy with dressing up and the purchase of toys. Neither of them could ever forget the evening Paul came home to find Emma dressed as a police woman with a huge strap-on.

They had even started having dinner parties. Paul would organise the wine and the music, which was always Madame Butterfly or La Boheme by Puccini. Emma had come home one day to find Paul crying his eyes out whilst listening to Madame Butterfly. It had moved him so much. Emma refused to let Tony come to another dinner after the fiasco of when he got drunk and abused some of her friends. In fact, she tried to keep well away from Tony as she considered him to be a total nutcase. His language was appalling and his temper could erupt at any time and for no reason whatsoever. Paul felt he was getting further and further away from Tony, who was still trapped in the good old days. Paul also had the feeling Tony wasn't telling him the truth about what he got up to. There were more and more phone calls where in the old days he would have answered them in front of Paul. He became secretive. He now preferred to go and talk privately on his mobile. He was also drinking far more than was sensible, and his temper was getting worse.

Business was booming. The empire was now ten clubs, money was rolling in. Turning the three clubs from Richard and Jack into lap dancing clubs was a masterstroke; tourists were packing in and spending big money. Paul had put Ryder in charge of the refurbishment and he had to give the guy his due: he had done a good job. Paul heard that Ryder personally interviewed all the girls. Boys will be boys. Paul had visited the clubs continually throughout the refurbishment and Ryder had said he could have whichever girls he wanted. Paul had declined, which had totally shocked Ryder. Paul had decided he was going to be a one woman man and that woman went by the name of Emma Miller.

Paul had decided to keep Ryder on; he had proven to be a hardworking and loyal worker, which was all Paul wanted. He was now the manager of the three lap dancing clubs, earning a very generous salary and profitability bonus, around a hundred grand a year.

Emma had found her sort of east end gangster. Whenever they went out as a couple or in a group, they always had protection with them. Duke was her favourite; he was as thick as a plank of wood but would do anything for her, and was very sweet. She loved the thrill of walking in a club and everybody looking at them. The truth was that, the clubs were legitimate businesses. The only dodgy bit was the fact that millions in cash was creamed off, so no tax was paid on it. The tax evasion was a major operation involving suitcases of cash going abroad, to several Swiss bank accounts. Paul had considered going totally legit in the future, but he needed to give that a lot of thought before even considering mentioning it to Tony. The truth was, did he really want his children to grow up in an environment that they would find it difficult, or impossible, to move away from?

Paul counted his blessings every day; a fantastic partner in Emma, a sound business that was making good profits, it couldn't get much better, could it? There was only one more personal landmark to achieve and that was to marry Emma, and Paul had plans to make that a very special event.

CHAPTER 18

Bruce Coyne woke up with a dreadful head and a mouth that was as dry as a vulture's crutch. He looked across at the table and saw the empty bottle of whiskey. No bloody wonder he had a bad head. He closed his eyes and lay back down. The room started spinning, so he sat up quickly and learned against the headboard. Never again, he thought. If he had a pound for every time he'd said that he'd be a rich man. He suddenly remembered the Maria fiasco. That bloody Pablo! Jesus! My head, he groaned.

Eventually, he made it to the mini bar where he drank six mini bottles of orange juice. This seemed to revive and perk him up, albeit not for long. He ended up back in bed, dozing fitfully.

Richard Philips had arranged to meet Jim Telfer and Robin Scott at the Mayflower pub in Rotherhithe Street near London Bridge. He'd gone a bit early, so he could have some lunch on his own, before meeting the guys at two pm. The food was excellent and Richard really enjoyed the house special of luxury Kobe steak burger topped with cheese and served with French fries.

Jim and Robin turned up at two fifteen and had obviously been drinking. Richard didn't mind people having a few but not when they were going to discuss business.

"Have you been in the pub all morning?" he asked the two boys.

"No, we had a couple in the Dog and Bell, that's all," said Jim.

Richard didn't look convinced. What are we? School kids and you, the fucking headmaster? Jim thought angrily to himself.

"Anyway, you're here now, so let's get down to business," said Richard briskly.

"Aren't we having a drink then?" Asked Robin, expectantly.

Richard hesitated for a second or two. "Well if you must, what do you want?"

"Two pints of Carling would be very nice, thank you, Richard," said a now cheerful Jim.

None of the three heard the click of the camera shutter as the surveillance operative took multiple images of the meeting.

Richard called over a waitress and ordered the drinks.

"So, can we get down to it now?" asked Richard impatiently.

"Yes of course, we're all ears, aren't we Robin?" said Jim.

Richard was getting just a touch pissed off. "OK, so are you two ready to leave tomorrow?"

"Yea, ready as we'll ever be. Flights are booked on Easy jet from Luton. We'll find a hotel when we arrive."

"Good, get something not too close to where the bastard is staying," said Richard thoughtfully. "I'm booked into the Sol Principe Hotel. It's just down the coast from the Marconfort Beach Club. I don't want the three of us to be seen together. Did you get new mobiles?"

"Yea, got them both from Sol, pay as you go, never been used," said Jim.

Richard was mentally going through his checklist. "Give me the numbers before you go, they need to be dumped in Spain when we leave, OK?"

"Sure," said Jim

"What about the van?"

"We'll hire one with fake IDs and pay cash the morning of the gig," said Robin.

"Good." Richard was feeling a bit better as the two of them seemed to be on the case.

"Have you booked return tickets?"

"No, we plan to take an internal flight to Madrid or Barcelona, stay there a couple of days and then fly back."

Richard thought that was a really good idea but didn't bother telling them.

The images of Falcon One and two unknown males were transmitted to Eagle two minutes after the meeting split up. They were on Jeff Collins' desk, five minutes later.

"Karen, any idea who these two are with Martin?"

Karen leaned over Jeff's shoulder. "Don't know them."

"Could be interesting. Ask Jim, he knows every villain within ten miles of here."

"Will do, Jeff."

The next morning, Falcon One left his house at ten am, which was an hour later than usual. It was noted by his surveillance that he appeared to be placing a large suitcase in his car boot which obviously meant he was going on a trip. This information was relayed to Eagle and then quickly to CID in Rotherhithe.

Andrew had popped in to see Jeff. "Falcon One has left his house an hour later than usual and has a very large suitcase in the boot of his car."

Jeff wasn't sure what to make of that.

"So, he's going on a trip." Jeff thought for a second then asked. "Which direction is he headed?"

"Well, let's find out." Andrew and Jeff headed quickly towards the Raptor operations room.

Terry was on duty. Andrew and Jeff entered the room. Jeff nodded at Terry.

"Falcon One, what direction is he headed in?" asked Andrew.

Terry pressed a button on a phone consul. "Eagle calling Falcon One."

The three of them were standing over the consul, nothing.

Terry repeated, "Eagle calling Falcon One, come in."

The speaker burst into life. "Falcon one, hear you loud and clear."

"Current location and direction of Falcon One."

"Currently, he is on the M25 heading South towards the Dartford Bridge."

"Where the fuck is he going then," asked Jeff, surprised.

"We won't know till he gets there," said Andrew thoughtfully.

"What happens if he pulls into Heathrow?" asked Jeff, looking concerned.

"That's a good question, what do you want to do if that happens? "Asked Andrew.

"Me?" said Jeff.

"Well, you're in overall charge of the operation."

"Well, in that case, we follow him," said Jeff.

"Hmm, well, if he heads into Heathrow, we need to find out what flight he's on. Hold on, let me make a call."

Andrew found a seat in a corner, picked up the phone and pressed some numbers.

"I need the number for head of intelligence security at Heathrow."

The call was put through to Heathrow, via a secure link from New Scotland Yard.

"I'm putting you through now,"

"Heathrow security," said another voice.

"Is Bob Grey there?" asked Andrew.

"Who's speaking please?"

"Andrew Homer..."

"Give me a call sign and I will check the list"

"Raptor."

"Hold please."

Bob came onto the phone. "Andrew what can I do for you?"

"I need some info. Male passenger, Richard Philips, booked on any flights today?"

"It will take two minutes."

Andrew was holding the phone, praying for some good luck.

"Yes, we have a Richard Philips booked on flight BA162 departing Terminal 1 at one pm, destination Malaga, ETA three twenty."

Andrew was over the moon. He turned to Jeff and Terry and almost screamed. "Going to Malaga at one pm bingo!"

"Find out if there are any spare seats on the flight," said Jeff quickly.

"Are you able to tell me if there are any spare seats on the flight?" asked Andrew into the phone.

"Please hold."

The tension in the operations room was palpable.

"There are four seats available as we speak."

Andrew held up four fingers and smiled at Jeff. "How many do you want" he asked Jeff quietly.

The truth was, Jeff was not sure what to do but told himself to be positive. "Two seats," he mouthed to Andrew.

Andrew was back to Heathrow Security. "Can we have two of those seats please, officers will be at Heathrow as soon as possible."

"OK, if you need further help do not hesitate to ask."

Andrew was very appreciative of the assistance. "You've been very helpful, thank you."

Andrew turned to Jeff. "So, who's going and what's the plan?"

"I want Karen to go and can your surveillance guy accompany her? They can act like a couple going on holiday; it's perfect."

"Yea," said Andrew. "Although Max Foot is one hell of a lot younger than Karen."

"Well, let's hope Karen likes them young." Jeff and Andrew laughed.

Jeff walked quickly back to CID. “Karen, is your passport up to date?”

“Eh, yes. Where are we going?”

“Not 'we' Karen, you. You’re off to sunny Malaga with Max Foot.”

“Malaga? And who the hell’s Max Foot and what sort of name is that?”

“Listen, we haven’t got time to discuss this now. Get a squad car and driver, get the siren on, go to your place, and pick up everything you need for a couple of days away and get to Heathrow, pronto.”

"Now?" asked Karen with a mixture of delight and anxiety.

“Yes, now. You’re on the one pm BA flight landing at three twenty, I’ll go through channels to get some Spanish police assistance.”

Karen was still standing, staring at Jeff.

Jeff held out his hands out and looked at her with raised eye brows. “Well, are you going to stand there all day?”

“Err, no, I’m on my way.” She grabbed her bag and jacket

“Well, get going then; I’ll speak to you en route.”

Karen was soon on the way to her flat. She was slightly worried. Foreign country with a stranger, nowhere to stay. The most worrying thing though is that she didn't want to let Jeff down. She thought this was almost certainly a waste of time. Richard was probably going for a few days R and R. Oh well, I might as well pack my bikini.

Jeff went back to the ops room. “Andrew, how far is Falcon One from Heathrow?”

“He’s just come over the Dartford Bridge. So as long as there are no holdups, probably about an hour.”

Jeff looked at his watch. “Well, in that case, he’ll get there about eleven forty five, that is of course as long as there are no accidents or holdups; we are talking about the M25 after all.”

Jeff was talking loudly. “Karen will be in a squad car with a siren on, so I estimate she should get there about twelve thirty. It will still be tight; let’s hope there’s no cock ups.”

Jeff phoned Karen. “Karen, where are you now?”

Karen was slightly annoyed. “I’m packing my case.”

“OK, keep your hair on, I’m only asking. You must be at Heathrow at twelve thirty.”

“You better tell the driver then.”

“OK, I’ll speak to you soon.” I'll let her get on with it, he thought.

He picked up the internal phone. “Andrew, you’d better organise flying documents for Max to pick up with his ticket; I don’t suppose he’ll have his passport with him.”

Andrew was feeling good now. “Already done, Jeff. Karen on her way?”

“Ha! She’s still packing her case, she’s probably packing enough stuff for a two week holiday in the Seychelles. Women!”

Jeff felt hungry. He had skipped breakfast and his stomach was now telling him it needed something. He headed for the canteen. Toasted bacon sandwich with brown sauce and a latte will sort that out. He tried to forget about Falcon, Karen, Malaga and everything else to do with Raptor for just five minutes; he gave up after ten seconds and headed back down to his office to start all over again. He was also aware that he had a huge amount of work to do on the Arrow Logistics robbery. I’ll devote some time to that tomorrow, he promised himself.

“Falcon one is at Junction 7, he’s on time,” said Andrew as he came into Andrew's office. OK, anything we haven’t done?”

“As long as Karen gets to Heathrow on time, then we’re on course.”

“Unfortunately, I need to set something up with our Spanish friends. Remember we have no jurisdiction at all in Malaga, maybe a liaison officer and preferably one who speaks a little English."

Jeff got on to Scotland Yard to sort the Spanish connection and requested for the Spanish liaison and this was agreed. Karen and Max would be met by a plain clothes police officer at Malaga airport.

Jeff was thinking this was a lot of work for what probably was Philips going on a short bloody holiday. He wished for a second he was going with Karen, a few drinks one night, you never know what could have happened. He put that out of his head very quickly and went back to the job in hand.

Jeff looked up as Andrew stuck his head round the door.

"Falcon is still on schedule, he's past the A3 turnoff and heading towards Heathrow. How's Karen doing?" Jeff didn't answer and gave 'a don't ask' look. Andrew shut the door quickly.

I suppose I'll have to call Karen, Jeff thought. She must be on her way to Heathrow by now. He looked up at the clock. It was eleven fifteen.

"Hi Karen." He could hear the siren blaring. "We're making good progress, a plain clothes Spanish liaison officer will meet you at Malaga airport. Falcon one is on schedule and should be at the rendezvous at twelve. How are you getting on?" He hated asking but he wanted to know.

"Well, I got out to the car and the driver had disappeared."

"What?" Jeff was incredulous.

"Yes, he wasn't in the effing car, gone to get himself a coffee down the road, can you believe it?"

Jeff was feeling physically sick. "So exactly where are you now?"

"Err we're ..." Karen was looking out the window of the car and he heard her ask the driver, "Where are we?"

"We are heading into central London."

"Did you hear that, Jeff?"

"Yes, central London."

"No," said Karen "we are heading towards central London."

"OK, Karen great I've got to go, speak to you soon."

"Shit, we haven't even started and I'm pulling my hair out." Jeff was dismayed at the way things were turning out and went to get another coffee and took it back to his office.

His phone rang. "It's Andrew. Falcon one has decided to stop at Cobham Services; apparently, he had a pee, bought a coffee and was now heading back onto the M25."

"OK, so he'll soon be turning off at junction 15 for the M4, and he's nearly there"

"Yea, we'll keep you updated."

"Thanks Andrew."

Richard was happily driving towards Heathrow, totally oblivious of all the activity that was surrounding him. He took the M4 turn off then left the M4 at junction 4 and was soon through the Tunnel into Heathrow itself. He headed straight to Terminal 1 and used the Valet Meet and Greet Parking service. How the other half live. Richard walked into the

Terminal while a driver took his car for secure parking. The car would be delivered back to Terminal 1 when he returned.

Richard headed straight to check in and went through passport control airside. He checked the flight number and then strolled off to gate 6. It was twelve ten, and boarding was in ten minutes.

"Den, how much longer do you think we'll be?" Karen was worried and thought they might not make the flight. She looked at her watch again, twelve thirty. She was also worried that Den would crash and kill the pair of them or even worse, some eighty six year old granny out buying her groceries.

"Traffic's bloody awful even with the siren on, Jesus, some people are so stupid!" he shouted as someone else blocked his path. "You better tell Jeff we're at the Chiswick Roundabout just coming onto the M4, if we get a good run we'll be there at one o clock."

Jeff looked at his ringing mobile. "Hi Karen, what's new?"

"Den says we're on the M4 half way between junctions two and three. ETA is one o' clock."

"OK, I'll see if we can delay the plane; speak to you in a minute"

"Andrew, I know this is asking a lot but can they hold the plane for us? ETA for Karen is one o' clock."

"Jesus, they don't like holding flights up you know, but leave it with me."

"Bob, Its Andrew again. Can we hold that plane for ten minutes? The second officer will be in the terminal at one o 'clock?"

"Bloody hell, Andrew we don't like holding up flights, you know." Andrew smiled wearily.

"OK, we'll sit at the gate longer than usual but tell them to get a bloody shift on!"

Jeff's straight on the phone "Karen they're holding the plane, tell Den to floor it."

"It's already on the floor, I'll be lucky to get there alive."

The tannoy system burst into life. "BA162 Flight to Malaga at Gate 6 is now boarding, business class first, please."

Richard looked smug as he stood up. He was second onto the plane and had booked a seat right at the front with extra leg room. He sat down and immediately checked out the stewardesses. He sat back with a sigh and stretched. Why was it that BA now always had such old frumpy stewardesses?

The plane filled up and everybody was expecting to take off on time.

"Den, how much further?"

"We're as good as there."

Den was happy he was finally approaching Heathrow.

"What's the time?"

Karen checked her watch. "Twelve fifty five. Don't slowdown."

Finally, the police car screeched to a halt outside the entrance to terminal one. Karen thanked Den and ran for the door. She charged over to book in; the staff had been expecting her. She heard someone on a walkie talkie. "Parcel has arrived." Her luggage was tagged, passport checked and ticket issued.

"Come with me please." A lady in BA uniform took Karen's arm. It's ten past one.

Falcon one was looking at his watch. He put his hand up to attract the attention of the nearest stewardess. "Is there some delay?" he asked.

"A late passenger is just coming on board," smiled the stewardess reassuringly.

"OK."

Karen was rushed through security and was soon striding down the tunnel connection to the plane. She showed her ticket for the last time and was accompanied to her seat by one of the stewardesses.

Falcon one looked up to see who was keeping the entire plane waiting. He caught a quick side view as the lady almost ran down the gangway to her seat.

"This is your seat madam, enjoy the flight."

Karen looked to the side of the empty seat and saw a ruggedly handsome young man. God, is this Max Foot? She wondered.

The young man turned to Karen and smiled. "Hi, I'm Max, you must be Karen."

Karen smiled and thought that the trip could be even more interesting than she had anticipated.

A member of Heathrow security rang Rotherhithe to inform them that BA162 had left Heathrow at one fifteen, with both parcels on board.

CHAPTER 19

Artan Papadakis was born in Athens, Greece but spent most of his life in Albania and the last ten years in the UK. Artan lived with his wife and two children in a beautiful five bedroom house in Totteridge, North London. The family were popular and mixed in well with the local community and joined in with all the communal activities undertaken by the Residents Association of which they were keen members. Artan had spent the last ten years building up his business, Arrow Logistics, into a profitable multimillion pound turnover company. Arrow Logistics specialised in transporting containers of Food Products all over the world.

The shock of the robbery and the killing of Timius hit Artan like a sledge hammer; he could still not believe it had happened. Artan's wife, Eleni, had had to visit her doctor and was prescribed valium. The two children were traumatised and had hardly left the house.

But that had all changed for Artan the minute he picked up Adnan and Bashkim from Heathrow. Now he was focused, he wanted action and he wanted it as soon as possible. They were on their way back to Totteridge, in Artan's Mercedes.

"Adnan, first of all, you must not tell Eleni why you are really here; I have told her you and Bashkim have come early for the funeral and to offer your support to the family."

"No problem." Adnan is a man of few words, striking in appearance due to a scar that ran from his left eye down to his chin. During his military service, he had served in the Balkans as an advisor and had been injured in a firefight when he shouldn't have even been there. Where Adnan was broad shouldered and tall, Bashkim was the opposite, small, slim and wiry with the courage of a lion.

"It is good that you spent long hours learning English," said Artan. "I knew it would come in useful one day."

"It doesn't matter that Bashkim does not speak English, he is not here to chat up girls or attend English Ladies' tea parties," chuckled Adnan. Artan smiled thinly. The mood was of solemnity and a fierce feeling of wanting revenge for the death of Timious.

"It will be difficult; we are not in our homeland," said Adnan.

"You are right Adnan, but the same rules apply, if you want information you pay for it, money talks, money can do anything, and believe me I will spend every penny I have to get those bastards who killed an unarmed man defending his colleagues. Timius will be avenged or I will die in the attempt."

They arrived home to be welcomed by Eleni and a well laid table. *Tave kosi* (baked lamb with yogurt), *gjelle me arra* (veal with walnuts), *byrek shqiptar me Perime* (meat pies) and *spec ate mbushura* (stuffed peppers) followed by *bakllava* and *hallve*. Artan, Eleni and the children didn't eat much but Adnan and Bashkim were in heaven and ate every plate clean.

The three men then went to the study. Eleni brought in a decanter of brandy with glasses and left them to talk.

Artan poured three large brandies and they all drank a good measure with loud smacking of lips, a tribute to the quantity and quality of the food and brandy.

"So, to business," said Artan, settling back in his seat. "The Security Van Company Securicor have posted a fifty thousand pound reward for information leading to the arrest and conviction of any of the men involved in the robbery."

"That is a huge amount of money," said Adnan, looking suitably impressed.

"It is not that much money here, Adnan, but it may bring one or two worms out of the woodwork." said Artan, taking a log pull on his brandy. "The very good news is that I have paid someone in the Securicor Company to let me have this information the minute it arrives, that way we can get to the person or persons before the police"

“What about the police, Artan?” said Adnan.

“I am only going to say this once," said Artan looking at both men. "No one must be killed or even injured, other than the perpetrators of the crime, especially no one from the Metropolitan Police.”

“So, we wait. We have the funeral next Friday to organise and when we get the lead we want we will act very quickly.” He topped up all the glasses and raised his in the air. *“Se Hetan*” (success) they emptied their glasses and Artan suddenly began to cry, raising his hands to the heavens.

There was no immediate news. The funeral was held and it was a very good send off for Timius. Artan shut the factory and bussed all the workers up to Totteridge. There was much crying and wailing and afterwards copious quantities of whisky and brandy were drunk. Artan got home afterwards and was happy it was over. Now he could concentrate on finding the scum that did it.

It was Saturday morning. Artan’s mobile rang suddenly. He listened to a voice at the other end.

“A name has been mentioned twice, Philip Evans, apparently he drinks in a pub called the Adam and Eve in Rotherhithe, have you got that?”

“Oh yes, I have that.” Artan clicked off and a chilly smile came to his lips.

“Adnan, tonight we get the first one. Get prepared.”

Adnan told Bashkim that they were going out to get the first name. Bashkim was over the moon; just to get out the house for a few hours would be wonderful.

“Bashkim, check the weapons again.” For Adnan and Bashkim, the night could not come soon enough.

Adnan had recently gone to the Albanian Embassy and picked up a case containing two Uzi sub machine guns and ammunition. The Albanian Special Forces had tried hundreds of guns but nothing compared to the Israeli produced Uzi.

Artan got home and found that Adnan and Bashkim had gone out for a run. A good idea, he thought, get the blood flowing to wake them up.

Artan switched on his computer and googled the Adam and Eve Pub, Rotherhithe. 47 Swan street, Rotherhithe, London SE16 4JN. That was it really, a non-descript pub in a non-descript place.

Artan was thinking ahead: we drive up park outside, go in ask for him, drag him out into the car and we're gone. Hold on, he might be built like a tank and have several similar friends. Hmm, well an Uzi soon separates the men from the boys. He turned to look at Adnan and Bashkim who had just came into the room slightly breathless from their run.

"Ah, Adnan I was just thinking of you. How do you think we should play it tonight?"

"Simple, one of us goes in, identifies the mark then leaves. When the mark comes out we take him. It will be dark and with luck, he would be on his own."

"Just what I was thinking," lied Artan.

Adnan looked worried. "Sometimes, it is easy to forget the simplest elements. Where are we taking the man? Surely, not back here."

"Good God, no, I have already taken care of that. There's an old iron works five miles from here, it has back access and there'll be no one for miles."

"Excellent," said Adnan, rubbing his hands enthusiastically

"Rotherhithe is a long way from here so we need to get going about five pm, dark clothes." "Yes," said Adnan and Bashkim.

At five p.m., the three Albanians set off for Rotherhithe and drove at a leisurely pace until they arrived in Rotherhithe. They continued to Swan Street and drove past the pub, noting the location of the doors and layout of the surrounding streets. It was a smallish pub, so there certainly would not be hundreds of people, which could sometimes be an advantage, sometimes not. It was now eight pm and they found a quiet side street to park, with a view of the pub. It was decided that Artan would go into the pub and see if he could find out if Philip Evans was in and if possible, identify him.

Artan opened the door and walked in. He quickly looked around and noted there were about fifteen people in the bar, mostly men and a couple of woman.

He approached the bar. “A pint of your best bitter, please.”

The landlord silently picked up a glass and filled it with beer. Artan paid three pounds and sat down. He looked round the pub again and it struck him that this was a pub where asking questions could be dangerous. It looked like a pub where villains might hang out. He was sure they were in the right place. He sipped his pint and pretended to read a paper, but he was listening to as many conversations as he could. He began to think he was wasting his time and then he heard someone say loudly, "Your round, Phil." He didn’t look up immediately. He didn't want to attract attention. He then casually looked over to see a medium sized man get up from a table and make his way to the bar. He noted his medium height, his short brown hair, brown shoes, cream trousers and brown jumper. No doubt, he'd have a coat which would probably be hanging up somewhere, thus making it difficult for Artan to identify. Artan glanced over to the table he was sitting at. Three other men who all looked capable of handling themselves. Hmm, could be tricky, he thought. He left the pub and went back to the car.

“He's in the pub.”

Adnan and Bashkim smiled. Adnan rubbed his hands vigorously. “Good, we look forward to making his acquaintance.”

“Now, we wait.” said Artan, making himself comfortable in the back seat.

It was ten to eleven.

Artan rubbed his eyes. “It’s ten to eleven, we must be alert, and the pub will close soon.”

Adnan and Baskim shook themselves and looked out the window at the pub doors. It came to eleven, eleven fifteen, eleven thirty, eleven forty five.

“Jesus, what are they doing in there?” said Artan plaintively.

"I'm not sure what the English expression is, but in Albania, we call it after hours drinking," said Bashkim.

Adnan looked at Artan anxiously. "They could leave by the back; we will not see them."

"I'm the only one who can identify him. We stay here," said Artan thoughtfully. Twenty minutes later, all the lights but one went off in the pub. Doors opened and people spilled out onto the street. Artan was searching the group anxiously.

"There he is, in the long brown coat."

"Yes, I see him," whispered Adnan.

They watched as the four men shook hands and disappeared in different directions. The mark was on his own, heading towards the car.

"Shit! He's going to walk past the car." Artan thought quickly: "You two get out and get behind the car. When he walks past, take him."

Adnan and Bashkim jumped out and hid behind the car.

Phil was strolling towards the car with his hands in his pockets. He'd had a good few pints and was in good humour. He was whistling tunelessly.

He stopped whistling as he came level with the blue Mercedes and glanced in. Nice car, he thought. Artan turned towards him at exactly the same second and their eyes met. Danger! Phil's hesitation for one second decided his fate. He turned to run back to the pub. He took one step and felt a blow on the head and then nothing.

Adnan and Bashkim grabbed Phil and piled him into the back of the Mercedes. They tied his hands and legs, taped his mouth and pushed him onto the floor. Artan pulled away and headed for the iron works in North London.

"Well done, boys." Artan passed back two miniature bottles of whiskey. Adnan and Bashkim looked at them and laughed.

"What are these?" Adnan asked.

“It is to warm you up for the work ahead, but you cannot have much, we need to keep clear heads.”

Adnan and Bashkim look at each other and both laughed loudly. “Gezuar, Cheers, Salut, Skol, Sante, Prost."

It was very late as the Mercedes pulled into the entrance of the works, the back of the car stank of urine; Phil had pissed himself twice on the journey.

“Get that piece of shit inside!” said Artan angrily.

Adnan first laid a carpet of plastic sheeting to cover the office floor before he and Bashkim dragged Phil inside and tied him to a chair.

The three Albanians stood looking at him.

“Remember, boys, we want the man who shot Timius," said Artan, looking down at him. "If he is that man good, if not, he must tell us who he is, that means we need him alive to tell us, so remember that, ok?”

Phil opened his eyes and lift his head slowly and painfully, to see three very frightening Greek looking blokes standing over him. He knew he was in deep shit. He felt the plastic covering underneath his feet and that really worried him. He shook his head and looked up clearly at the three men. “Who are you and what do you want with me?”

“Hello Philip, or, can I call you Phil?” asked Artan, coldly.

“I don’t know you, any of you. What do you want? I think you have the wrong person.”

“Phil, that is why you are here so we can establish whether you are the right person or not.”

Who the fuck are these guys? Phil wondered. He was scared they were speaking quietly but the menace in their faces was disturbing, particularly the one with the huge scar on his face.

“Have you heard of Arrow Logistics?” continued Artan in his quiet but cold voice.

Phil tried to give nothing away. “Never heard of it.”Adnan was watching him very closely and as soon as Artan said Arrow Logistics Phil showed a tiny flicker of identification in his eyes.

Adnan raised his voice. “You are lying! Do not think you can fool us?! We have conducted hundreds of interrogations. We are professionals, it is in your interest to tell us the truth.”

“I can’t tell you the truth if I have no idea what you are talking about. Ask my friends, they’ll vouch for me. I’m an unemployed plasterer. You have the wrong person.”

For a second Artan, thought maybe it was possible. Idiots phone up and blame people for things out of revenge or spite, or a million other reasons.

“Phil, where do you live?”

“Local.”

“Where, exactly?”

“I know where you live, Phil, I have been there,” added Artan.

Phil jumped up as if to attack Artan, shouting at him. “You bastards, you touch my family, I swear I’ll come for you!”

Bashkim smashed his fist into Phil’s chest. Phil reeled back, fell back into the chair, gasping for breath. He stopped moving the chair and tried to control his breathing and anger, eventually he was taking slow deep breaths. He was now really terrified, thinking he could be killed or even worse, tortured, slowly.

“So, Phil, you were there?”

Phil looked up at Artan, still grimacing from the blow to his chest. I was only the fucking driver after all he thought. “Yes, I was the driver,” he mumbled.

“Good, now we are getting somewhere. I want you to understand that you are in serious trouble. I am going to ask you a series of questions and I want the truth. If I feel you are lying, then my two friends will...” he made a slight gesture with his hands which said more than words ever could.

“Are you sure you were the driver? Was it not you who used the gun?”

“I’ve never used a gun in my life. I am a professional driver for hire to anybody who will pay me.”

"I believe you, Phil. Tell me about your part in the job."

Phil took a deep breath, and tried to look and sound convincing. These three are no fools, he thought. "Well I don't know why but I was called in at the last minute. I stole a car on that morning and was told to pick up three men at the Angel pub in Bermondsey Wall East, at four o' clock that afternoon. It was purely a driving job; I had no idea there were guns involved or I wouldn't have taken the job. I'm small time, ask my mates, they'll vouch for me."

"What car did you steal?"

"Ford Mondeo."

"During the heist, did you get out of the car?"

"No, I sat in the car throughout."

"What is the name of the person the police have in custody?"

"I don't know. I was not allowed to know the names of the three other guys; they do that for security."

Artan looked at Bashkim and nodded. Bashkim took one step towards Phil and smashed his right fist into Phil's stomach and then followed that with a left hook to the jaw. Phil couldn't breathe and thought that his jaw was broken. The pain was agonising.

"I'm telling the truth, for God's sake!" he said desperately.

"God is not going to help you, Phil." Artan nodded again at Bashkim.

Bashkim took a pair of pliers out of his pocket. Adnan went behind Phil whose eyes widened in terror. Adnan got his head in a vice-like grip. Bashkim then held Phil by the hair at the front of his head; he pushed the pliers into Phil's month and clamped them onto one of his top front teeth, he turned his wrist and felt the tooth break. Phil gave a blood curdling scream.

"Now, Philip, you must see that we are serious. What is the name of the man who shot and killed my brother?"

The pain was excruciating, Phil felt as if he was going to pass out any minute. And he knew it would be hopeless and worse for him if he kept lying. But as soon as he told them what they wanted to know, what was going to happen to him? He know they would not let him go because he could identify them plus he would go straight to Tony. No, they were going to kill him anyway. I'll just give them a false name; that might delay them but they would still come back and finish me off. Why did I ever do that job? Smack! Phil suddenly felt a blow to the side of his face.

Bashkim was good at his job. They didn't want to kill him. They wanted information, then of course, they would kill him.

"The name, Phil," persisted Artan, patiently.

Bashkim took a long bladed razor sharp knife and sliced at Phil's ear. It was like a knife through butter. The ear fell to the floor, a fountain of blood shot into the air. Phil let out another blood curdling high pitched scream. A moment later, anger galvanise Phil into action. He lifted the chair and charged at Bashkim knocking him back against the wall while he fell to the floor at the same time. Adnan was seriously annoyed. He grabbed Phil and the chair and threw them back upright. Adnan then took the knife and cut all Phil's clothes off. Phil felt even more defenceless now as he looked down at his blood soaked body.

"The name, Phil," repeated Artan in a cold deadly voice.

Phil was in shock; his body had taken a real hammering, he was in agony from several wounds. He then felt one of the men grab his hand and place it on a table, he heard one of the men say 'two,' this was followed by screaming pain in his right hand. They had cut two of his fingers off. This was the first moment he wished for death.

"The name, Phil."

They worked on Phil for the next thirty minutes. They crushed the toes on his right foot, broke his left arm, smashed his ribs and cursed him endlessly. Phil was in so much pain, new pain didn't make much difference. He wished for death several times. They then cut off his penis and testicles and the amount of blood loss was incredible. It gushed out of the wound. Finally, a metal pole was inserted into his anus and hammered up into his body, causing massive internal damage. His final words were 'Fuck you, Greek cunts'.It had been a messy affair and Artan was shocked that the man had not given them the name.

They must learn lessons from it for the next time. They dug a deep hole well away from the office and piled all the bloody plastic sheets and the remains of Phil into it. They drove home, all had showers followed by a good meal, plenty of whiskey and then sleep.

CHAPTER 20

"Let him sit in the fucking waiting room all day for all I care!" Jeff was in a really foul mood; he was convinced Terence Bradley had told the shooter about Bugsy doing a deal, which had resulted in the shooting of the police officer and Jan and the eldest boy being taken. Now, he had to see Bugsy before that Bradley bastard.

Jeff was sitting in the interview room facing the door. He was not looking forward to the imminent arrival of Bugsy. He decided it would be pointless sugar coating it or trying to hide anything, he would tell it exactly as it was.

He stood up as Bugsy entered the room. "Hello Bugsy."

"So, what the hell has happened to my phone call?" Bugsy asked plaintively, eye balling Jeff. Bugsy knew that something was wrong.

"What the fuck has happened, Jeff?"

Jeff rubbed his face wearily. "Bugsy, last night I ordered a policeman to stay outside your flat, he did that and we turned up at ten thirty this morning to pick up Jan and the kids. The police officer was killed, shot in the head. Jan and your eldest have gone, the other two are being cared for by social services. They were two minutes ahead of us, I have my suspicions as to how they got the information that we had agreed a deal.

"Was it a copper?" Bugsy managed to get the words out.

"No, but I suspect you will know who it was very shortly."

"You're talking in riddles Jeff, I don't understand."

"As I said, you will know shortly."

"Jesus! The madman has Jan and Chris, I'm in a canoe with no fucking paddle!" Bugsy had tears in his eyes.

"We have to get this guy off the streets. Bugsy, you can still help us."

"Are you fucking mad Jeff? He's a killer! He'll kill them both, like that!" Bugsy snapped his fingers.

"Look, we all need time to reflect." Jeff got up, followed by Bugsy. "Stay here Bugsy. Your solicitor is here to see you." Jeff added meaningfully, staring hard at Bugsy.

Bugsy sat back down with a worried frown.

The door opened. "Mr Cooper, good morning, how are you?" Bugsy looked at him and remembered the other day how he'd said "Your friends send their regards." He was in touch with Tony and had told him a deal had been done.

"You want to be very careful, Mr Bradley or I could tell Jeff in CID that you are a known associate and friend of Tony Bolton."

"I am no friend of that lunatic and you should watch what you say if you know what is good for you. Remember, I am the one walking out of here."

"You do realise that if I wanted, you could actually be joining me in here. I think you can help me a lot more than you are at the moment, Mr Bradley."

"I think I might have to become ill and pass your case onto a colleague." Bradley was getting worried. He could see his whole career was now in jeopardy.

Bugsy drew close to Bradley and snarled, "That psychopath has my wife and eldest son; I will do anything to keep them safe."

"You better do your time then," said Bradley.

Bugsy leaned back in his chair and studied Bradley pensively.

"I want you to find out where they're being kept."

"I have to be honest with you Mr Cooper, I no longer have a relationship with the gentleman that we are talking about."

“And why might that be?” Bugsy hadn’t anticipated this.

“He has recently killed two people, one of whom was a policemen. They'll never rest until he's caught and when he is, there’ll be a lot of falling out; I don’t intend to have my career, family and my life taken away because of that madman.”

“I want you to find out where they are being held and let me know as soon as possible.” Bugsy persisted.

“Even if I wanted to, he’s not going to tell me. There's not one good reason I could give for him to tell me that; his brother doesn’t even know anything about any of this.”

“Perhaps, he ought to know then.” Bugsy was looking for the key that could unlock the mess that Jan and Chris were in, and added hopefully, “You must have done work on all the properties he owns.”

“Yes, I have, and the portfolio is extensive. Of course, nothing’s in his name other than where he lives.”

“So, it’s almost certain he's using one of those properties as a safe house to hold Jan and Chris.”

“Maybe, but he usually spreads any risk, so for all I know, he might have five solicitors doing work for him.”

Bugsy leaned forward, resting both hands, tightly clasped, on the table and stared earnestly at Bradley. “Bradley, you and I can help each other here. Have a sniff round, see what is happening with his properties at the moment, and look for any that are empty and not making him money." He paused and frowned. "The other thing I need you to do, is, keep me out of Belmarsh for as long as you can, because once I’m in that shithole, anything can happen.”

“I’ve got to go. I’ll see what I can do.” Bradley stood up to leave.

“You do that. I look forward to hearing from you soon.”

CHAPTER 21

Life was good for Paul Bolton, the clubs were doing really well. The three clubs from Jack and Richard were going from strength to strength, sales were improving every month and the contribution to group profits was significant. They were grossing more than the other established clubs, which were more drinking clubs with striptease and girls working the tables. Lap dancing was a real money spinner; not only were the clubs making a fortune, the girls who worked in them were, as well. It was not uncommon for a girl to go home with a grand in her pocket for a night's work. Paul also knew some of the girls attended private parties for clients, paying thousands of pounds; tits and bums can be very lucrative.

Emma had pestered Paul to take her to one of the lap dancing clubs to see how it all worked. Paul had kept putting her off but eventually admitted defeat, as he knew she would continue till she got her own way.

It was a Saturday night, ten p.m. They arrived at the Spotlight club in Kingly Street near Oxford Circus. Paul and Emma went in through the door marked Staff Only. The doorman immediately phoned through to Ryder and informed him that Paul and Emma had arrived.

"Paul, how are you?"

"Fine, thanks Ryder. This is Emma."

"Emma, very pleased to meet you."

"Let's have a drink and then I'll give you a guided tour."

"Let's do the tour, then we can relax." Paul wanted the tour before it got crazily busy.

"Yea, great let's go. We've done something upstairs you are going to love."

Ryder did the ground floor first, then the bar area with pole dancing, girls' changing rooms, coffee and rest room, offices and the rooms used for private shows. Paul had seen it all before but Emma was totally transfixed by it all. Several things surprised her; one was how stunningly attractive most of the girls were, and she was also shocked by how much money they could earn. Ryder then took them upstairs.

"Paul, you are going to love this." Rider was excited.

Paul laughed. "This better be good, Ryder."

"Don't worry, its sensational. We call it the wet experience."

Ryder took them into a room and flicked the light. Paul and Emma laughed at the same time. They were in a room that, for all intents and purposes, had transported them to the Caribbean: palm trees and beautiful beaches. Ryder pressed another switch and the sound of waves crashing against the shore, and Honolulu music, filled the room. There were nice bench seats on the two sides with a sort of stage at the end which could take about eight punters at a time. Paul looked closely at the end of the small room, he took in the discreetly hidden shower heads and the bathroom style floor.

"Ryder, this is great! Is it popular?" Paul looked around admiringly.

"The punters love it, the girls took some convincing though, what with all the water and having to dry off all the time. But the take is good, so that cheers them up."

Paul looked thoughtful. "I wish we could see it in action."

"Well, that's possible. We have five wet rooms and one of them has a secret viewing room."

"You pervert, Ryder," said Emma, smiling, as she walked towards the palm trees and beautiful beaches.

"No, no; we use it to see new girls and also to check periodically on girls who have been here for some time, to make sure they're not getting rusty."

“Great, so we’ll have a look soon. Now, how about that drink?”

“Yea, let’s go down to the bar.”

The club was filling up. Japanese and Chinese tourists seemed to outnumber everybody else put together.

They got a bottle of champagne and took a booth in the corner. The pole dancer was twisting and turning on the pole and removing items of clothing until she was fully naked. Emma was watching Paul out of the corner of her eye and could see that he couldn't take his eyes off the naked girl. She was not surprised. The girl was gorgeous, with a fabulous body. Maybe I could take pole dancing lessons to excite Paul at home, she thought. Ryder was also enjoying the show. Women had always been his weakness and he made full use of the girls at the clubs. They finished the champagne and made their way up to the wet rooms. Ryder opened a door and they entered a very small room with two chairs facing a curtained wall. He pulled the curtain to reveal a one way mirror.

“I’m going to leave you to it, come down when you’ve seen enough.”

Paul and Emma looked at each other and then looked at the wet room. It was empty and not very inspiring.

“Paul, I love this place. Maybe I should learn the business and run a club.” Paul couldn't believe she said that and just gave her one of his ‘Are you mad?’ looks.

Suddenly, they heard the music come on and six tipsy oriental punters came into the room and sat down. There was now a bit of electricity in the room. A tall beautiful girl with long natural blond hair wearing a bikini, came on to the stage and started to dance. The punters couldn’t take their eyes off the girl, following her every move. Then the showers came on. The girl was quickly soaking wet and she pushed her hair back with her hands and thrust her large firm breasts out; the punters were drooling. Emma was getting excited and looked at Paul, he was loving it just as much. The dancing girl then removed her bikini top and her large firm breasts were now on show. The punters were leaning forward, desperate to touch but knowing they could not. The dancer then slipped her bikini bottoms off. You could cut the atmosphere with a knife. The music increased in volume and tempo, the girl was dancing faster and sexily. Emma couldn't take her eyes off the girl, she was stunning; she would love to have been in the room, closer to the girl. She reached over and grasped Paul's hand. They both leaned closer to the one way mirror. The girl was good. She was running her hands all over her body, exciting the punters to boiling point. Emma could stand it no longer. To Paul's amazement, she stood up, pulled her short dress up and took her knickers off. She then pushed her arse in front of Paul. He realised what she was getting up to and quickly undid his trousers and released his huge erection. He leant Emma over so she had her hands on the mirror, watching the girl dancing. He then entered her with a hard thrust. Emma gasped as she felt him inside her. She wished the dancing girl could have joined them. It was all over very quickly and Paul groaned loudly as he came inside her. The music stopped. The punters were clapping and taking notes out of their wallets. The girl took the money, saying thank you many times; she must have received at least a hundred quid tip.

“That was most interesting, Ryder," said Paul, as they ordered some drinks at the bar. "I expect to see good profits at the end of the month.”

“Yes, thank you for tonight. It's been a real eye opener,” added Emma with a grin.

Paul later found out from Ryder that the dancer's name was Lexi.

Paul and Emma skipped out the Club and went round the corner into Beak Street. They entered an Irish Bar called Waxy's Little Sister where they could have a quiet drink in private. They sank into the comfortable armchairs and Paul ordered a Brandy and Emma had a large dry white wine.

“Well, what did you think of that?” asked Paul.

Emma laughed. “Well if you want the truth it turned me on so much I could scream, the girl's dancing was just electric.”

“Yes, I could see it turned you on, especially when you took your knickers off. I wasn't really expecting that at all. So now, you're interested in women as well?”

"Paul, we always said we would be truthful with each other. I'll try anything once but I would never do anything that you felt uncomfortable with."

"Glad to hear it. That girl was gorgeous, wasn't she?"

"Her bloody legs went on forever and that smooth pussy looked divine," Emma laughed.

"Stop it, Emma! You're getting excited and so am I!" Paul slipped his hand under the table and moved it up her thigh. "You're not wearing knickers!"

"No, I put them in my pocket." She groaned as he rubbed her pussy.

"Let's drink up and go home so you can finish what you have started." They almost fell over each other as they moved towards the door.

CHAPTER 22

"Yes, I'm Karen, good to meet you."

Karen gave Max one of her best smiles. He was young and good looking and they're going to Malaga. What could be more romantic than that? Max was also looking at Karen; he guessed early thirties, quite fit, but not really his type.

"So Karen, you just made it."

"Just being the operative word. The drive from Rotherhithe to Heathrow was hairy, to say the least. I'm thankful to be alive."

"Were you driving?"

"Good God, no, the driver was doing a hundred miles per hour the whole way, I had my eyes shut half the time."

"So, this is all very last minute, Falcon one could easily be going for a couple of days break."

"Well, if that's the case, I shall unpack my bikini and enjoy the beach, plus this is all on expenses, so good food and loads of booze is the order of the day."

Max laughed. "I'm with you on that Karen, we may as well start now. What do you want to drink?"

"We are on duty, Max, but OK, a nice glass of chilled, dry white wine, sounds good to me."

"Coming up." Max looked at one of the stewardesses who came over and took his order.

"Did you see where Falcon sat?" asked Karen in a serious, low tone.

"Yes, he's right at the front, on the right hand side."

"I hope to God he didn't get a good view of me when I came on board." Karen was worried she could be compromised and they hadn't even got to Malaga yet.

"I don't think he would have seen you, it's possible he may have got a bit of a side view but you were moving very quickly, so, it would only have been a fleeting glance."

"I bloody well hope so, otherwise, we really are wasting our time."

Karen and Max both ordered the Mediterranean chicken and spent five minutes discussing what exactly, if anything, was Mediterranean about it. Karen glanced through the inflight magazine and told Max some interesting facts about Malaga airport.

"Last year, there were one hundred and two thousand flights into Malaga airport carrying twelve million passengers, that's a lot of holiday makers, and a large percentage were from the UK."

Max was nodding off. "Fascinating, Karen." And just to emphasise how boring that piece of information was, he snored loudly.

"Please yourself." Karen said with a huff and put the magazine back in the seat holder, and then leant back and shut her eyes.

The captain was explaining that they were going to land in approximately ten minutes. Karen leaned over and gently shook Max.

"Max, we're landing shortly."

"Oh, OK." Max rubbed his eyes. "That was quick." He suppressed a yawn and squinted at his watch.

"Time does go quickly when you sleep for most of the journey," said Karen.

Max was now wide awake. "Right, I gather we're meeting a Spanish copper at the airport. I hope he knows what he's doing."

"So do I."

Max laughed and said in a serious tone, "Falcon has a large suitcase, so he will have to collect that."

“One of us can follow him and the other can go and find the Spanish copper. Anyway, let’s see how we get on.

The plane landed and Max and Karen moved up the aisle quickly to get reasonably close to Falcon. They followed him off the plane and headed to passport control. Falcon was having a problem and had been taken out of the line.

“I wonder what’s going on,” said Karen to Max.

“We’ll wait at the exit into the airport, he can’t go any other way.”

Max and Karen continued to the exit into the airport. They then stop and waited for the Spanish police.

“Let’s hope they come before Falcon turns up.” Karen is glancing around, trying to identify anyone who looked like a copper.

A man was making his way towards them but he didn’t look too much like a copper. He was now smiling at Max and Karen.

“Mr Foot and Miss Foster?”

“Yes,” Karen smiled and shook hands, followed by Max.

“Soy el Detective Miguel a su servicio,” said the man in rapid Spanish.

“We’re hoping you speak English Miguel?” asked Karen.

“Yes of course, I speak the English. How are you today?”

“Very well, thank you. The man we are following is still in customs. Do you have a car?” asked Max.

“The man will remain in customs until we are ready to meet him.” Miguel said holding up his phone. “As soon as we're ready we will send him along.”

“Very good, Miguel; we follow him to his hotel, one of us will stay there while we organise somewhere for us to stay.”

“That is all taken care of, your rooms are booked.”

“OK, well, in that case do you want to release Falcon?”

“Si, we can do that now.” Miguel got on the phone and spoke rapidly in Spanish.

"He is on his way now, about five minutes."

"Where are we staying? I hope it's a nice 5 star hotel?" Karen could guess at the small budget that would be available.

"Well, we were asked to put you in value accommodation but I have, how would you say, um, flashed my badge and got you upgraded to four star." Miguel knew this would get the glamorous Scotland Yard detectives on his side straight away.

"I'm impressed Miguel," said Karen, pleased. "Thank you. I hope you'll have dinner with us tonight, circumstances allowing."

"I would be delighted, circumstances allowing," smiled Miguel.

Miguel's phone rang; he answered, "Si," and slipped the phone into his pocket. He is here, he will be a few seconds." Thirty seconds later Falcon walked into the airport. He then collected his suitcase and headed to the exit and the taxi rank.

"Follow me," said Miguel. They walked to the end of the taxi rank and waited. Falcon got into a cab and they pulled away. Karen was about to say something to Miguel when a car pulled up in front of them. Miguel turned to Max and Karen. "Let's go."

Falcon was taking the Torremolinos route and after twenty odd minutes was dropped off at the Sol Principe Hotel.

"I suggest Max stays here and keeps watch on Falcon, yes I shall call him that as well. Karen you will please come with me to your hotel, it is not far away."

"Sounds good to me. Max, behave and I'll be back shortly. I'm in your hands Miguel."

Miguel smiled but was confused. I had heard that English girls were easy, he thought, but surely this woman was not offering herself to me? I have only just met her. Miguel and Karen jumped in the car and were racing south down the coast. Karen was loving it, beautiful weather, and a handsome Spanish liaison officer; perhaps there could be a bit more liaising than there was meant to be. They soon pulled up outside the Sol Don Pedro Hotel.

"This looks very beautiful, Miguel," said Karen, admiring the tall white building, the deep orange blooms of the climbing Begonias and pink Bougainvillias adding glorious shimmers of colour with the shimmering deep blue swimming pool at the front of the hotel.

"Yes, I chose it for you myself. They have very good rooms and the food is more Spanish than most round here. Let me take your bag."

They entered the hotel reception.

"Hello, Maria," said Miguel to the receptionist. "This is Miss Karen Foster, a very important person from London in the United Kingdom. Her colleague, Mr Max Foot, will be arriving later. I would like you to make sure that Miss Foster and Mr Foot have everything they need to make their stay enjoyable and unforgettable."

"Do not worry, we will look after them very well, Miguel." The receptionist smiled and Karen noticed she winked at him and wondered if she was one of Miguel's girlfriends. He was wearing a wedding ring; but nowadays, that meant nothing. The booking and formalities done, Miguel handed Karen her bag back.

"Karen, go and settle in your room, I will have a coffee and wait for you. Please, do not rush, take your time."

Karen took the lift to the fourth floor and found room 401. She loved the room. It had a balcony overlooking the pool and the sea. I know where I'm having my coffee in the morning, she thought, with a satisfied grin.

She went back downstairs but there was no sign of Miguel. He suddenly appeared from the back of reception, looking rather dishevelled. A moment later, Maria came out from the same place, looking much the same. I don't believe this, they've just had a bloody bunk up, no wonder he wanted me to take my time.

Karen thought she would have some fun. "Are you alright Miguel? You look so tired."

Miguel looked sheepish and muttered, not meeting her gaze. "I am fine, thank you for asking, Miss Foster."

"I think we need to get back to see Max, if you don't mind, Miguel."

"Yes, let us go immediately." He was still trying to avoid Karen's eyes.

They got in the car. Karen was trying to think of when she last had sex. God, it was over six months ago; some nookie in the afternoon with a sexy man would be most welcome, but highly unlikely. They were back at the Sol Principe Hotel very quickly and found Max in the restaurant having a coffee.

"Wow! Max, I love this restaurant, the tiled floor and the tables with their white tablecloths... it all looks so Spanish."

Max was condescending. "We are in Spain, darling."

"So, how is the surveillance going?" Karen is back being in charge.

"Nothing. He's been in his room and hasn't come out at all."

"Hmm, I'm sure he'll come out for dinner later; I wonder if he'll eat in the restaurant or go out."

Miguel was looking thoughtful. "I think it is a good time to remind you that if this Falcon commits a crime of any sort, then the Spanish police will have to arrest him; you cannot be involved."

"Yes, we know that Miguel, it may well be that he is just here for a break. We will see."

"So, where's my coffee Max?"

Miguel quickly spoke to one of the waitresses. "Un café de la dame veiled."

"Shit, he's in reception," whispered Max.

"Karen and Max sat down and acted as though they were holiday makers, chatting and laughing.

"Jesus, he's coming into the restaurant."

Falcon was dressed in cream chinos with a crisp white shirt and a big gold watch on his wrist. He was looking very much like the well to do Brit on holiday. He's walked towards Max and Karen. "Good evening," he smiled at them.

Karen's heartbeat was going through the roof. She looked up and smiled' "Good evening." He walked over to a table for two by the window and sat down. People were starting to fill the tables, which gave Max and Karen some comfort.

Miguel looked at Max and Karen. "Why don't we have dinner here, it's perfect. We can eat and watch him at the same time."

"Yea, why not?" Agreed Karen.

"OK. I could eat a camel!" said Max, rubbing his stomach.

Karen looked at Max and shook her head.

"Good, I will order all the food and wine, wonderful," smiled Miguel happily. "Let's have a drink before we eat. What would you like?"

"Wine for me, beer for Max."

"Good, now let me look at the menu," says Miguel, opening the large menu.

They didn't have to wait long, the food arrived by the bucket load. *Garbanzos con espinacas* (Chickpeas and Spinach), *Chorizo en Sidra* (Chorizo in Cider), *almejas a la marinera* (Clams in white wine), *coctel de gambas y aguacate* (spiced prawns and avocado), *txangurro* (spider crab), and *langostinos al fino* (Jumbo shrimp in sherry sauce).

Main course was a huge dish of fish Paella, placed in the middle of the table. It looked and tasted delicious, the yellow of the rice, the multitude of fish and jumbo prawns.

Karen was trying not to drink too much wine but she was finding it very difficult. "Max you're on duty tonight. I leave it up to you when you feel safe enough to leave and come back to the hotel. I'll take the early morning shift, starting at six thirty a.m." She turned to Miguel with a satisfied smile. "That was a lovely meal, Miguel. I'd like to go back to my hotel now, please."

"Of course Karen, let's go."

At the hotel, Karen went straight to bed. She'd had too much to eat and drink, and felt slightly guilty. She was worried that they were treating the trip like a holiday and was determined to get back on track the next morning.

Max had been left at the hotel on surveillance. Falcon finished his dinner at ten thirty and went back up to his room. He did not come out of his room again and Max returned to the hotel at midnight.

The next morning Karen, was up at five a.m. She had a slightly bad head but nothing to worry about. She was determined to make sure the surveillance was a professional operation and that started from when she got to the Sol Principe Hotel. She made herself a coffee, opened the balcony door and took in the view. She then thought of dirty grubby Bermondsey and Rotherhithe; it may be home but I could get used to this, she thought.

She took a taxi to the Sol Principe. She enjoyed the short journey. The sun was coming out and in the distance, she could see mountain tops; it really was very beautiful. At the hotel, she paid the driver and made her way into reception. It was now six thirty and the hotel reception was very quiet. She made her way to the coffee bar and decided to try some Spanish.

"Buenos Dias, Como Estas?"

"Good Morning, I am fine thank you. That was very good Spanish," said a smiling Spanish Barrista.

"Well, I'm not sure about that but I am trying," laughed Karen.

"I want to learn about Spanish coffee, can you teach me?"

"Well I could do but first, we must introduce ourselves. I am Placido Sanchez."

"Well, hello Placido. I am Karen Foster and your English is so good."

"I worked in London hotels for five years, so I learnt a bit. Now, about the coffee."

"Placido, Spanish people drink loads of different coffee. What should I have and when?"

"OK, your first cup of the day should be a Café con Leche, which is half a café solo and half hot milk. In the evening you should have a Café Solo, which is a strong Espresso with lots of sugar. Have you got that?"

"I think so. In that case, I would like a café con Leche, por favour."

"That's a good start. You can have this on the house."

"Thank you, Placido."

While Placido turned to make the coffee, Karen admired his stocky frame and typical Spanish good looks. He must be about forty, she thought.

"How long are you here for, Karen?" he asked as he gave her cafe con leche in a tall thin glass.

"A few days," not really sure myself, she pondered.

Karen took a sip "Delicious, thank you Placido"

"It is my pleasure, Miss Foster"

Karen suddenly remembered the reason she was here. "Placido, I must go, but I'm sure I will be back for more of your fabulous coffee." She took a step away from the counter then turned. "Yes, I'm a Miss. See you later."

"I will be here, Miss Karen Foster."

Karen strolled into the reception area and sank into a sofa in the corner, well away from the entrance and reception desk. She could see everywhere whilst being tucked away out of site. It was now seven a.m.

One or two Spanish people came in with papers but it was very quiet. She phoned Max and delighted in waking him up.

"Max, sorry, we didn't agree a time. Can you be here at, say, ten?"

"Yea, cool. See you then."

Karen was scanning the reception area, people were beginning to wander down for breakfast. There seemed to be a real mixture of nationalities. Lots of Germans, which was typical, some local Spanish, quite a few Brits and a few odds and sods. Karen took out her mobile.

"Jeff, its Karen. How are you coping without me?"

Jeff was laughing and seemed wide awake. "We're managing, don't worry. I'm on my way into the office."

"I thought I heard cars. Bloody hell, you'll be in the office early again!"

“I’m in early every day now. What’s happening out there?

“Nothing much at the moment. Falcon's relaxing and not doing much at all. Maybe he’s just here for a break.”

“Maybe,” said Jeff

“What’s happening with the Arrow Logistics case?”

“Well, we haven’t had any new names in that area of interest but we are making progress.”

“And what about Bugsy?”

“I don’t want to say too much on the phone but that’s gone very quiet. And the other connection was the solicitor, if that makes sense?”

“My God, if I’m getting that right that is incredible.”

“Yea, well it’s something else for us to look at as soon as you’re back. So, how is the Sangria?”

“I don’t know, I haven’t had any yet.”

“How’s the liaison officer?”

“Yea, he’s OK and seems to be very on the ball.” Karen was trying to be matter of fact and professional.

“Karen, we think Falcon is out there for a reason and it’s not to have a break.”

“OK.” Karen was not going to push for more information whilst on the phone, maybe that came from the anonymous source, she thought.

“Keep alert and safe.” said Jeff

“Speak to you soon, Jeff, take care.”

She looked around. Nothing happening of any interest, the breakfast buffet could be worth a visit though, she thought.

Karen headed into the restaurant and took a seat, allowing her to see the reception and hotel entrance. She then helped herself to some fresh fruit compote and more coffee.

After breakfast, she took up her old seat in the reception area.

Jim Telfer and Robin Scott were sitting in the bar of the Los Jazmines Hotel, a two star establishment just down the coast from the Sol Principe, where Falcon was staying. They got drunk on the Easyjet flight over from Luton and got even more drunk on their first night in Torremolinos. They were suffering from hangovers but were still managing to knock back a few Tequilas whilst eyeing up the Bikini clad girls in the pool.

Jim was speaking to Robin. "I guess we better watch the drinking. Remember, we get the other five grand only on completion of the job, and we've got to see that smarmy bastard Philips, tonight."

"Yea, I guess. Where are we meeting?"

"La Luna Blanca, some shit hotel miles away from here. We better hire a car this afternoon so we can get about easier."

"Good idea to have our own wheels," agreed Robin.

Falcon came down for breakfast at eight thirty and ate his way through the entire buffet. He then returned to his room. Max and Miguel turned up at ten past nine and a progress meeting was held outside on the sun terrace in view of the hotel entrance.

"Max spoke first. "So nothing to report then, Karen?"

"No, he's been a good boy, but I have spoken to London and they seem pretty sure he's over here for a reason, other than to top up his tan."

"So, we need to be alert and ready for anything."

"Yes, that's right Max, on our toes, as it were."

"On our toes, what on earth does that mean?" asked Miguel, twisting his face into a grimace.

"Don't worry Miguel, it's a crazy English expression." laughed Max.

At eleven on the dot, Falcon appeared and headed to the pool. He grabbed a sunbed and made himself comfortable, and then rubbed suntan lotion over himself. He was constantly scanning the pool, eyeing up the gorgeous young women in their Bikinis and thongs. He stayed at the pool till two o clock and then returned to his room. Miguel told

Karen and Max that Falcon was very sensible for probably taking an afternoon siesta. Karen also decided to have some time off in her room and Miguel disappeared to see someone for coffee. Karen wondered if he was going to see Maria the receptionist for a good shag; she was slightly jealous. The team reconvened at the Sol Principe at five o clock. Nothing had changed; Falcon was still in his room.

"I hope something of interest is going to happen soon," said Miguel.

"Miguel, I have done surveillance for weeks on end when nothing happens, but things do happen and when they do, it can be very quick; that is why we need to always be alert."

Miguel felt like he'd just been told off and decided to go for a wander.

"Keep Miguel on side, for God's sake, Max."

"I'm only telling him how it is," Max said defensively.

Nothing had happened and time marched on. It was now 8.00 pm and the three of them decided to eat. They all ordered different meals and were picking at some olives when Karen suddenly tensed.

"Falcon is in reception. Miguel go and see what he's up to." Miguel meandered over to the reception desk and pretended to look at the postcards. Two minutes later he returned to the table.

"He's booked a taxi; he's going out for dinner."

Max was well pissed off. "Shit! I was looking forward to my dinner."

"Let's go outside to the car so we are ready to follow him," advised Miguel.

Five minutes later, a taxi pulled up and the driver went into the hotel. He came back out, closely followed by Falcon. Just as Falcon was about to get in he stopped and took a good look round the drive, satisfied everything was OK he got in and the taxi pulled away and headed towards the coast road.

"Our man is up to something", said Karen.

"Yes, I agree," said Miguel.The taxi driver made his way onto the coast road and headed south. He passed numerous hotels and eventually pulled into a hotel called Los Jazmines.

Max and Karen were looking at the hotel. “This is not really Falcons style,” observed Max.

“Two star, at a push,” said Miguel.

“Hmm, Miguel, go in and see what’s going on, be careful.”

Miguel got out the car and disappeared into the hotel, he was in there at least twenty minutes and then reappeared, coming out of the hotel, heading towards the car. Karen and Max watched him anxiously as he headed back towards them and got back into the car.

He smiled at Max and Karen. “Something is happening, or do you say, something is going down.”

“Well?” said Karen impatiently.

“He’s met two very shady looking men, they're having a drink.”

Karen turned to Max. “We need a picture of the two men, even better, of the three together.”

Miguel was smiling as he took two pieces of paper out of his jacket pocket and handed them to Karen.

Karen looked at them and grinned. “Well done Miguel, excuse my language, this is fucking fantastic!”

“What is it?” Max asked.

“It is a copy of the passports of our two friends," said Miguel. "I got the manager to make copies for me, remember, all foreigners deposit their passports with hotel management."

Karen was still looking at the two passport copies. “This is good news and you may be surprised to hear that I saw a picture of these two only a couple of days ago, they were in a pub in Rotherhithe with Falcon." She handed Max the copies. "Max, get copies of these over to London as soon as we get back to the hotel. It’s a pity we can’t hear what they’re talking about!” She added, looking up at the hotel entrance. She was looking pleased; at least things were getting more interesting, she thought.

CHAPTER 23

Jeff was sitting in the CID office at Rotherhithe Nick drinking one of the endless coffees that he had every day. It was a time to take stock and look at everything and see where they were. The surveillance on Falcon Two was getting nowhere at all, Jack Coombs lived the most boring life anyone could ever imagine. He left home every morning, went to the Frog pub down the Old Kent Road, worked there till 2.00 p.m. and then went home. He never used the home phone and surveillance could not hack into any of his numerous mobiles. He never did anything or went anywhere, for a man with millions, he led a very quiet life. Jeff thought for a second how he would live if he was a multimillionaire. He soon snapped out of it; it's never going to happen, he thought.

Falcon one was in Spain and things were just getting interesting. The news that Jim Telfer and Robin Scott had had a meeting with him was a step forward and who knew where it might lead. Jeff missed Karen and hoped she would be OK. Falcon One was an animal, and now he had two local thugs with him, things could possibly get nasty.

Surveillance on the address in Peckham had proved, without doubt, that it was being run as a Brothel. There were now hundreds of images of visitors to the establishment, including, among others, an MP and a police officer. The police officer would get a big surprise when shown the image.

The Arrow Logistics case was just coming together. All the physical evidence had been gathered and were now ready to be considered. Masses of spent shell cases had shown the weapon to be a 9mm Beretta pistol. The burnt out shell of a Ford Mondeo, which almost certainly had been used in the raid, had been found down a side street in Bermondsey. The fifty thousand Securicor reward, had brought in loads of names, but the only one of interest was Philip Evans, but they had been unable to locate him. The Met were going to post their own reward of twenty five thousand, alongside the Securicor money, so, hopefully, that would bring in some more leads. The local snitches had all gone to ground and the one they did speak to was so terrified, he almost crapped himself. The man who shot Timius Papadikis and the Securicor driver had no compunction in using extreme violence and obviously, anyone who knew him was very wary.

The Met had now received three anonymous letters with reference to Falcon One. The first two had been to establish some sort of relationship. The third had given concise information that Falcon One was going to Malaga in Spain to commit a serious crime. Again, Jeff thought of Karen and that he could have placed her in harm's way by sending her to Malaga. He really wished he could have been there with her. Karen was a good cop, but was she ready to go toe to toe with an armed nutter? Jeff also wished they could open up some sort of discussion with the informer, but there was no information gleaned from the letters, to point to his or her identity.

CHAPTER 24

Paul and Tony were having a quiet drink at the Den Club in Soho. Paul was getting more and more worried about Tony's state of mind. It was difficult to mention anything to Tony without him flying off the handle. He seemed constantly agitated and was drinking far too much. Something was going on in Tony's life that Paul did not know about and he was really concerned.

"Tony, you're drinking far too much these days. What's going on?"

"Nothing! I'm allowed to relax, aren't I?" Tony was on his fifth large whiskey and it's only 7.00 pm.

Paul tried to lighten the atmosphere. "How's the best team in the world doing then?"

"Go and see them and then you'll find out." Tony snapped and took another slug of his whiskey.

Tony's a hard case but having wounded one and killed two people in the past few days had gotten to him, especially killing the copper. Tony knew the Met would move heaven and earth to find the man responsible. Maybe it was time to join the other ex-pat villains on the Costa del Sol, he thought. His mobile rang, he didn't know the number but he pressed the green button.

"Yea."

"Hi, look you don't know me. My name's Daniel. I've got some information for you." The voice sounded anxious.

"Yea, what's that then?" Tony couldn't get to excited.

"I understand your looking for a big geezer called Steve; you had some trouble with him in an Indian, recently."

Tony came to life. This was just what he needed to cheer himself up.

"Well, Daniel, it's your lucky day. Where is he?"

"Is there a drink in it for me?" asked Daniel.

"Daniel, do you know the Den club in Kingsley Street, Soho?"

"Yea, I'm very close by and so is your boy, Steve."

"Once you've told me where he is, come round to the club and have a drink with me and we'll look after you."

"OK, he's in Madame Jojos club, in Brewer Street."

"Jesus, he's five minutes away from us. Thanks, see you shortly."

"Paul, that wanker who did Dave with the bottle is at Madame Jojos."

Tony was going to continue talking but Paul held his hand up to stop him. He took his phone out and looked at his contact list. He found what he was after and pressed the green button.

"Arnie, its Paul at the Den Club. I need a favour."

"No problem. What can we do for you?"

"There's a punter in your club, he's about six five, big build, dark hair, if I remember correctly. I don't want him leaving before I get there."

"He shouldn't be too difficult to spot. Don't worry, he won't be going anywhere."

"Great. See you shortly."

Tony was looking at Paul approvingly. "Good idea, let's get going."

"One more call, Tony." Paul looked through his contacts again.

"Dave, its Paul. Get over here as soon as you can; your friend from the Indian restaurant has shown up."

"I'm on my way," said Dave at the other end of the phone.

Paul looked at Tony. "Tony, get Duke and two other boys, we don't know how many of the bastards there are."

Tony rushed off to gather the crew and soon they were on their way to Madame Jojos.

“What are we going to do with him then, Paul?”

“Well, I think we’ll leave it to Dave to have a chat with this piece of shit first, if there’s anything left, then you can reintroduce yourself.”

Steve was at Madame Jojos with a girlfriend called Trixie. He had completely forgotten about the trouble in the Old Kent Road and at the Indian restaurant.

Tony and the crew arrived at the Club and piled out of the car.

Paul looked at the crew. “OK Tony, you, me and Duke will go in and suss out what’s happening. If we can’t handle it, we’ll come back for the rest of you.”

They got to the door and were stopped by security.

“We’re here to see Arnie. My name is Paul Bolton.”

The security guard spoke into his wrist and turned back to Paul.

“Terry here will take you to another more discreet entrance round the back. Arnie will be waiting for you.”

They walked round to the back entrance and Arnie was there to greet them.

“Paul, Tony, how are you? Long time.” He nodded at Duke.

“Come in, Come in, your friend is here with a girl. No one else.”

“Good that makes life easier,” said Tony, looking please

“Come up to the office.” Arnie led the way upstairs into an office overlooking the bar and dance floor. “He’s..., well, I hope it’s him. He’s in the bar there at the end with the redhead.”

“Paul and Tony looked where Arnie was pointing. “Yup, it’s him, the little fucker!” said Tony loudly.

Arnie looked serious. “Obviously, we don’t want any trouble in the club, so you need to get him outside.”

“Yea. Can you put the fire alarm on?” Tony's face was grim.

“No, I can’t. Once they go out, they’ll all fuck off home.”

Paul was looking thoughtful. “He could be in here for hours.”

“Punch in the guts and just frog march him out; it’s easy,” said Arnie.

“I don’t want to cause any trouble. Can we put something in his drink?” asked Paul.

“Brilliant idea Paul, and we have just the thing. We’ll give him half a tablet of Lunch Money, better known to you guys as Rohypnol. It takes effect within thirty minutes and he’ll be totally zoncked out.”

“Agreed. Sounds good to me,” said Paul. Tony nodded.

“I’ll go and get it done.”

Paul, Tony and Duke went to the window and watched the bar. Arnie appeared and called the hostess over to him. He whispered in her ear and she nodded and then went back to serving. Ten minutes later they all watched as Steve the Mark called the hostess over and ordered drinks. The hostess turned to the back of the bar and they saw her slide back a very small hatch door built into the wooden backdrop. She then poured a pint of beer and put it down in the hatch and closed it. She poured a white wine and reopened the hatch and took the pint of beer.

She returned to the mark and gave them the drinks, took the money and moved away.

“Fucking hell! That was smooth, wasn’t it?” exclaimed Tony.

Paul couldn't take his eyes off the bar. “You learn something every day eh.”

Arnie returned with a girl who took the drinks order and prepared them in the corner bar. “What did you think then?” he was looking at Paul and Tony, smiling.

“Genius. I love the idea of the hatch, as long as the punter is not directly in front of it, no one would ever see it.”

“Yes Paul, that’s why we have two hatches,” laughed Arnie.

They sipped there drinks and continued to watch Steve at the bar.

It took about twenty minutes before they saw a reaction. Steve rubbed his head and spoke to the girl. She took his arm and looked at him sympathetically. He steadied himself for a minute but then stumbled and had to reach out to hold the bar to stop himself from falling over. The girl was getting more concerned and motioned the hostess over. They spoke and the girl nodded a few times, then went back to speaking to Steve.

The hostess suggested the woman should take Steve home to sleep it off. Arnie turned to Paul. “They’ll be leaving in a minute, over to you.”

“Thanks Arnie, if you ever ...”

Arnie didn’t give him time to finish. “No prob.”

Tony, Paul and Duke left through the back door. They strolled round to the main club entrance and waited for Steve. One of the cars was placed just to the side of the entrance with the back door open. Steve and the redhead appeared. Steve was clearly disorientated and kept looking from side to side. It all happened very quickly. One of the crew took the redhead's arm and started to march her down the street while Tony and Duke each took Steve’s arms and pushed him into the back of the car and drove off. The men dropped the redhead's arms, turned and walked off in the opposite direction. She started looking round for Steve and headed back to the club.

“Hello Mate, what’s your name by the way?” asked Tony.

“Steve. Is this a taxi? Where’s Annie?” He was confused and not really sure what was going on. They had given him a very small dose and it would clear up in an hour or two.

“When we get back, stick him in the back office and give him tons of coffee," said Paul. "I want him awake and compos mentis as soon as possible.”

Steve had the constitution of a horse and was wide awake and alert within an hour. He was sat on a chair in the office, hands cuffed and looking up at a guy who was bigger than him. “Where am I, mate?”

“I’m not your mate and you’ll find out in a minute”

Steve tried to act tough. “I’ll remember your face.” Duke just smiled evilly at him.

“Dave, it’s your call with this guy, a hard lesson, yes, but I don’t want a dead body in the club, understood? Plus, he doesn’t know where he is. I want it to stay that way and no names.”

"Understood, Paul."

"Well, let's go and say hello, shall we?"

Paul, Tony and Dave headed to the back office.

"Hello Steve," said Paul, standing directly in front of Steve. "You may remember us; this gentleman here slapped you in the pub when you were chatting up three girls down the Old Kent Road and this is the guy you smashed with a wine bottle in the tandoori, do you remember?"

Steve could not believe this, he was in big trouble. "Listen, I didn't mean nothing by it. Let's all have a drink and make up, eh?"

Tony grabbed Steve's collar. "Have a drink and make up, you cunt!" he drew back his hand and smashed Steve hard in the chest forcing him to gasp for breath.

Tony looked at Dave. "He's all yours."

Dave hadn't forgotten the bottle over the head and still had stiches in one of the wounds. He took a fearsome set of knuckle dusters out of his pocket, put them on his hands and went to work. Punch after punch slammed into Steve; this lasted till Dave could hardly lift his hands. He stood back and looked at his handiwork. There wasn't an inch of Steve that did not have cuts and bruises, both his eyes were closed and swollen; he would take a long time to recover. Dave turned to Tony. "That's me done." He took off the knuckle dusters, put them in his pocket and sat down.

Tony took a long, hard look at Steve "I don't think he's had enough yet. Have you had enough Steve?" Steve was out for the count.

Tony went to a cupboard and took out a large screw driver and approached Steve. He lifted his right hand and placed it on one of the other chairs. He lifted the screw driver and slammed it down onto and through Steve's hand. He did the same with the left hand. Even though Steve was out of it, he still felt the pain and emitted a loud scream and passed out again.

"Duke, take this bastard and drop him outside University College Hospital A and E."

Tony and Dave went into the bar. “Two large whiskeys, Carrie.” the drinks turned up and they both took a good slug. “That’s better,” said Tony appreciatively.

One of the doormen approached Tony with a man. “Tony, you asked to see Daniel as soon as he came in.”

Tony looked at the man. “Hi Daniel.” He turned back to the doorman. “See to it Daniel has drinks and a meal on the house, then take him to see Roddy." He turned back to Daniel. “Stay as long as you like; free drinks all night, plus you’ll leave with a monkey, how’s that?”

“I’m very happy with that, thank you.” The doorman took him to the bar.

Paul walked in. “So, it’s finished.”

“Yea, he won’t be worrying anybody for a good long time,” said Tony, lifting his glass.

CHAPTER 25

"Paul, what time are you coming home?"

"About midnight. Why? You alright?"

"Yes, I'm fine. I just, you know, wanted to see you."

"If something's wrong, I'll come home now."

"No, nothing's wrong. I'm just being silly."

Paul was not sure what was wrong with Emma but he was going to go home early to find out. He left the club at 9.00 pm and was home at 10.00 pm. He opened the front door and announced his arrival loudly. "There's a very handsome horny man inside the apartment, is there anybody home?"

Emma rushed out the kitchen and threw herself into Paul's arms. "You're home so early." She smothered him with kisses.

"What have I done to deserve this?" Paul was looking and feeling very pleased.

"Well, you know ..., I can't wait for you to stick that big thing of yours into me and you know what happens when you do that."

Paul tried to look confused. "You mean, apart from you enjoying it; hmm keep going."

"I'm pregnant, we're going to have a baby."

Paul could not speak and stared at her. He was close to tears. "Paul, you're going to be a dad," she repeated happily. That was it for Paul. The tears started to flow, he couldn't stop them. Emma started as well and they held each other tightly.

She pulled herself away, looking worried. “Tell me you’re happy, please, Paul.”

Paul held Emma’s shoulders and held her gaze. “It’s the most wonderful news I’ve ever had in my lifetime; I am overjoyed, so happy.” Paul was sobbing, smiling and laughing. “Get the Champagne out! Who can I call? Have you told your mum and dad? How far gone are you?”

“How could I tell anyone before you, Paul? This is our baby, a little Paul and Emma.”

“I’m sorry Emma, you must think me hopeless.” There were more tears in his eyes.

“No Paul, I see your very hard side, and it is wonderful to see your soft side as well. You know, you are my hero and I just know you will be a fantastic father.”

“Thanks Emma.” he took her in his arms and kissed her passionately on the lips. “I suppose, this means, no more nookie?”

“No, it bloody well doesn’t. We just need to be more inventive.”

“Well, we’ve never had a problem with that before,” he said and they both burst out laughing.

Phone calls were made. Mum and Dad were ecstatic; Tony was drunk and happy; all Emma’s friends were overjoyed; it was a time of great celebration. They talked about whether they wanted to know the gender of the baby and decided against it. Whatever turned up was fine by them as long as the baby was healthy. Paul secretly wanted a boy and Emma really didn’t mind as she planned on having a few. The one thing Emma really wanted was for Paul to ask her to marry him before she got too big. Emma thought the baby was conceived at the Spotlight club whilst watching the gorgeous lap dancing girl in the wet room. They agreed that’s something that they wouldn’t be telling the child when he or she was older.

Paul had been thinking about marriage as well. He never thought he would find a woman who would fulfil his every dream. That isn’t to say they never argued, but it was very rare and arguments never lasted very long. They were just very compatible, especially sexually, as they still jumped into bed, got on the sofa, rolled on the floor, did it in the train, the car. It was a bit like the song, "Any time, any place anywhere, there's a wonderful world we can share" and Paul and Emma liked to share.

Paul was going to propose to Emma and he wanted to make it very special, but the first thing he had to do was to go and see Peter Miller and ask for his daughter's hand. Bit old fashioned but Paul thought Emma would like it, so he did it. Her father was delighted and opened a very nice bottle of Champagne in honour of the occasion. The next thing was to plan something really special for when he officially asked for her hand in marriage.

Paul came up with a special lunch trip to Paris. He told Emma to dress smart casual and they left the apartment and went by taxi to London City Airport. They were waved in through customs and boarded a Lear jet 45, a really superb private jet. They had Champagne and canapés on the very fast forty five minute journey to Charles de Gaulle airport where they were greeted by a chauffeur-driven Mercedes. They were then whisked into central Paris to the Hotel Meurice. Once inside the hotel, they were escorted to the three Michelin-starred Restaurant. They sat down and took in the sumptuous décor, the beautiful mosaic floor and the fabulous crystal chandeliers. There were quite a few diners at the other tables.

"Paul, you are spoiling me rotten and I love it. Spending some time on our own is just wonderful; I wish we could do it more often."

"You are just so worth spoiling; I wish I could do it more often but the clubs don't run themselves. So this is a very special occasion; and Miss Miller I have brought you here for a reason."

"I know that, you want to have your evil way with me on the way back in the plane."

Paul laughed and then got down on one knee. "Oh my God," said Emma loudly and excitedly.

"Miss Karen Miller, would you do me the honour of becoming my wife?" Paul's voice was solemn. It seemed the whole restaurant had gone quiet.

"Yes!" screamed Emma. "Yes, I'd love to become Mrs Paul Bolton!" all the other diners suddenly burst into spontaneous applause. Emma and

Paul smiled at the other diners and then grabbed the large menus to hide behind. The meal was superb. They had the tasting menu which included crispy green ravioli with a fricassee of snails and wild garlic, spit roasted pigeon with red cabbage and apple juice and the best crème brulee and raspberries ever. The journey back was spent phoning relations and friends, telling everyone they were getting married. They wanted the wedding to be as quick as possible as Emma didn't want to walk down the aisle with a huge tummy. The honeymoon was booked in the Seychelles; massive shopping expeditions were undertaken to bridal shops and then life went pretty much back to normal.

The only bad news was that Tony had already said he was going to be the best man, that's if he stayed sober long enough, Paul thought. Paul also had to do something for Emma's birthday; and with everything else going on he was having trouble thinking of something suitable. Then he had a brainwave.

"Ryder, its Paul, I'll be popping into the club about 10' o clock. Make sure Lexi is OK."

"Sure Paul, special night?"

"See you later." That Ryder is a nosy git, thought Paul. He always wants to know what's going on.

It had all been arranged they would go out for dinner to Le Gavroche in Upper Brook Street, Mayfair. They had the tasting menu at £190 each, plus £200 on drinks. The only reason they went there was because Emma had happened to watch a television program called Master Chef; she had seen Michael Roux Junior and wanted to eat at his restaurant. Paul didn't mind, it was a two-starred Michelin restaurant.

After dinner, they made their way to the spotlight club for a nightcap. Paul and Emma entered the club and made for the bar. Ryder joined them and ordered champagne.

"Are you paying for that Ryder, or am I?"

"That's a good question. I'll pay for this out of my own pocket," said Ryder.

Paul didn't think for one minute that Ryder would pay for it out of his own pocket; he treated the clubs like his own personal property.

"Thank you for that Ryder."

Emma was not drinking much because she was pregnant, so Paul drank most of the champagne; one of his pet hates was wasting good food or drink.

Paul took Emma's hand. "Happy birthday darling." He leaned and whispered in her ear, "I've got a nice surprise for you."

"Oh good, you know I love surprises."

"Let's go then." Paul pulled her up and headed towards the stairs.

Paul had already sorted out with Ryder that Lexi should put on a private dance for them in one of the wet rooms.

Paul and Emma entered one of the wet rooms and Paul immediately checked to make sure there was no one way mirror.

"Oh my God! This is a real surprise Paul, I can't wait!" They sat together on one side and suddenly, the music started.

The music was on for a few seconds and then a girl appeared on the stage.

Emma noticed straight away it was the same girl they saw last time. She turned and smiled at Paul. "It's the girl we saw last time."

"Is it really?" said Paul with a knowing look.

Emma turned to watch the girl and Paul whispered in her ear. "Her name is Lexi."

The music got louder. Lexi was gyrating and the atmosphere was becoming electric. The showers came on, water cascaded onto Lexi.

She ran her hands over her body. Emma couldn't take her eyes of the girl; she was just so sexy. Lexi was wearing a black bikini which barely covered anything. Emma was wishing her to take of the bikini top so she could see her gorgeous firm breasts.

"Lexi, take the bikini off!" Emma shouted excitedly. Lexi looked surprised. Paul was even more surprised.

Lexi looked at Emma and motioned her to join her on the stage. Emma held back for a second and then stood up and took a step towards Lexi.

She stopped and looked at Paul as if to ask his permission. Paul smiled and nodded. Emma joined Lexi who started rubbing her wet body against Emma. Emma wrapped her arms round Lexi's back and undid her bikini top, releasing her voluptuous breasts. Emma watched Lexis' breasts swing from side to side. She then bent down and took hold of Lexis bikini bottoms and slid them down her legs and took them off. Emma was almost out of control; she started to remove her own clothes, helped by Lexi who couldn't get them off quick enough. Both girls were now naked.

Paul was dribbling and had a massive hard-on; he couldn't take his eyes off the women. Emma moved behind the dancing Lexi and started to fondle her breasts from behind. She then moved one hand down to massage Lexi's smooth pussy. Lexi could only stand so much of it and had to break away. She turned and bent down and grabbed Emma's arse cheeks with her hands and pulled her towards her mouth. Lexi licked and nibbled at Emma's pussy, enjoying the musky taste. Emma glanced over at Paul to see him wide eyed. She whispered to Lexi and they both moved towards Paul. They undressed him to expose what they thought was the biggest erection they had ever seen. Emma took his huge cock as far down her throat as she could; at the same time Lexi had one of Paul's balls in her mouth and was sucking and pulling at it. Paul lasted only a minute and sprayed semen over Emma and Lexis' faces.

All three of them went into the shower and lathered soap over each other, enjoying the pleasure of sticking soapy fingers up each other's arses and pussies. Emma and Lexi jerked Paul off once more and then he dried himself off and got dressed. Emma and Lexi brought each other to organism and then collapse onto the seat. In a few minutes, they were fully dressed.

Emma was looking very pleased and satiated. "Lexi, I want you to come and visit me very soon. Will you come?"

"You bet I will. You are one sexy woman and the boss is not bad either."

"Here's my number, call me and let's set something up, yea?"

"Happy birthday Emma, and I'll see you soon."

Paul and Emma went back to the bar and had another drink.

“Wow! That was sensational wasn’t it?” said Paul.

“I’ve invited Emma to visit, you OK with that Paul?”

“Yes, I’m OK with that. Shall we get going?”

“Yea, let’s get home; I need some more attention.” said Emma, hooking her arm into Tony's.

What Ryder hadn’t told them was that, as well as the room with the one way mirror, there was a room that had a number of secret video cameras that recorded the action from all angles.

Ryder gave Lexi a bundle of notes for a job well done and made his way to the wet room Paul and Emma had just vacated. He entered the room and opened secret panels and took film cartridges out of three cameras. He then went back to his office and locked the door. He inserted the first cartridge into his player and saw Paul and Emma enter the room. He fast forwarded to when Lexi came on stage, adjusted to play, sat down and had a swig of a bottle of beer. He then watched as Emma and

Lexi got naked and started to caress each other. He took another swig of beer and a triumphant smile spread across his face.

CHAPTER 26

Karen said that she wanted Telfer and Scott followed but they only had one car. Miguel quickly organised an extra car and driver who turned up at the hotel in twenty minutes. Max would follow the two men to find out where they were staying and then report back to Karen. Karen and Miguel would stay with Falcon and see what he was up to. The meeting in the hotel broke up at 10.30. The three men shook hands and got in their cars and drove out of the hotel. Max followed Telfer and Scott back to the Los Jazmines hotel where he saw them go straight into the bar. He settled down to wait for them to go up to their room and when that happened, he would go back and see Karen. Karen and Miguel followed Falcon back to his hotel where he immediately went up to his room.

Karen, Max and Miguel met up back at the Sol Don Pedro hotel.

"OK, we now have two marks to follow," said Karen. "Max, you and your driver Alfonse, will take Telfer and Scott. It's going to be tricky and exhausting for you but it has to be done. Miguel and I will continue with Falcon. I honestly think that something is going down and it's going to happen in the very near future. We need to be on the ball." She turned to Miguel. "Miguel, do you usually carry a firearm?"

"No I don't, but I am licenced to, if I want to. Do you think it is necessary?"

"Definitely, and also Alfonse, if possible."

"Is there any way we can be issued with a firearm?"

"I will speak with my superiors. I honestly do not know what the protocol for this is."

"Miguel, we know in the past, Falcon had used firearms. It may well be necessary to combat that threat with our own; I don't really want to face a gun with no means of defence."

She turned to Max. "So Max, you're back on station at 6.00 am, same for us Miguel. Everybody get a good night's sleep."

Jim and Scott went straight into the bar when they got back to their hotel. They hit the tequilas and finished the night with a couple of large brandies. Jim was pissed off with Philips; he was such a slimy toe rag, giving out orders like he was some sort of Mafia Don. They had agreed to get the Spades and look at vans for hire the next day, Wednesday. They also had to recce the Marconfort Beach Club and make visual contact with Bruce Coyne. Falcon had said he wanted to get the job done as quickly as possible and be back in the UK in a couple of days' time. The day of the hit was scheduled for Thursday.

Max and Alfonse were outside the Los Jazmines Hotel at just after six am the next morning. Alfonse was armed and carried a Glock 17 9mm pistol, a first class weapon in any one's book. Telfer and Scott as usual had bloody awful hangovers the next morning, they got up late and headed down for breakfast at ten o clock, they didn't eat much but drank copious cups of coffee. They then went back up to their room and emerged thirty minutes later carrying bags and looking as though they were going somewhere a bit of a way off. Max contacted Karen and informed her Telfer and Scott were on the move. Telfer and Scott drove out of the hotel and headed towards the town centre, on the main road into town they pulled into a Garden Centre parked up and started wandering around. They picked up a barrow and were then seen to be looking at Garden Tools. They placed in the barrow two large good quality garden spades and two very sharp looking machetes. As soon as they saw this, Max and Alfonse looked at each other. Max phoned this through to Karen who thought this was a major development; she also told them Falcon had eaten breakfast but had stayed in his room all morning since. Telfer and Scott left the garden centre and headed north up the coast road towards the Marconfort Beach Club Hotel.

Bruce Coyne had now settled in and was really enjoying his break. Pablo had found him a very sexy nice Amiga (lady) called Consuela, who took care of all his physical needs. He spent most of the day sunbathing and drinking cold beers at the pool, in the evening he would have dinner in the hotel, followed by an hour's shagging. It was a great itinery.

Telfer and Scott then pulled into a car and van hire centre. They looked at various vans, filled out some paperwork in the office, got back in their car and headed north.

Alfonse phoned the van hire centre and spoke at length in Spanish. He clicked the phone off and turned to Max. "They've hired a van to pick up on Friday morning," he said.

Twenty minutes later, Telfer and Scott pulled into the Marconfort Beach Club Hotel car park. They got out the car and strolled round to the pool. They scanned the area and then seemed to recognise someone and moved back round to the car park. They spoke for a few minutes, got in the car. Max quickly made for the pool to see if he could recognise anyone that Telfer and Scott had seen. He took a good look round but could not see anyone. He went back to the car and rang Karen to report.

"Ask Alfonse to get copies of all the UK guest passports staying at the Hotel. Have a look yourself and then get them over to me. One of them must be the mark. Also, send copies to London, Jeff may know someone."

"I'll get on it straight away," said Max

Max and Alfonse eventually drove back to the Los Jazmines hotel. They spent hours in the bar, drinking tequila and both left sozzled, at midnight.

Falcon stayed at the hotel all day, eating, drinking and relaxing. He then spent an hour with Consuela and didn't emerge from his room again that night.

CHAPTER 27

Bugsy was well fucked off; he was pulled at nine forty five in the morning and told he was going to be remanded at Her Majesty's Prison Belmarsh, awaiting trial. Belmarsh was a category A men's prison and therefore very secure. That bastard solicitor, Bradley, hadn't been back to see him and now he was off to fucking Belmarsh. Bugsy had spent a year in Belmarsh in 2002 for stealing cars and knew what a dump it was. Actually, that wasn't strictly true; it had only been opened in 1991, so compared to somewhere like Wormwood Scrubs, it was ultra-modern. You could wear your own clothes, had power in your cell and could have TV for a pound a week. Bugsy knew where he was heading, House Block 3 which was for prisoners on remand. If he was lucky, he could get a single cell, but more than likely, he would find himself in a double, or worse, a multi-occupancy cell. He thought back to the time he was in Belmarsh, he'd spent a fair time in the gym trying to get some muscles but usually ended up playing basketball or volleyball. One good thing about Belmarsh was that, they helped him with his reading and writing and he also tried his hand at learning plumbing.

What to do about that shit Bradley, was the focal point of Bugsy's thoughts as he travelled to Belmarsh in the prison van. It was a short journey and before long, they were driving down western way in Thamesmead and into the prison premises. Bugsy could look forward to hours of mind boggling boredom, only slightly off set by the fact that he could get his teeth done and have his eyes checked by the optician, all for free. He thought about what else he could sign up for; Art, Cookery, Maths, Music, but the one he fancied this time was Computer Studies. If nothing else, he could learn how to access porn. He remembered someone telling him that it cost just under seventy thousand pounds to keep a prisoner in jail for a year. It seemed a huge amount of money to

Bugsy. There were about nine hundred prisoners in Belmarsh, so that makes sense, yea, he thought. Well, it makes a lot of money to keep this prison open. He found out later it was about forty million quid a year to run Belmarsh. He couldn't believe it.

Bugsy went through induction: the rub down search, the metal detectors and drugs; dogs giving him a good sniff. He was then moved to House Block 3 which was where he thought he would end up. It wasn't too bad. He got a double cell and was sharing with a fence called Toby who was a local from Woolwich. Toby had been in and out of prison more times than he could remember and knew the ropes. Bugsy still couldn't get that bastard Bradley out of his mind; he had to do something. If he did nothing, then Jan and Chris would be OK. So maybe, he should just do his time. But I'll probably get twenty five years minimum, he thought.

He was in a group that were welcomed to Belmarsh by Dick Thomas, the Governor. "Do your time, learn as much as you can while you're here to prepare yourself for when you leave; we don't want to see you again."

Bugsy knew that at the first association time, he would no doubt see people he knew and some who were in Belmarsh during his last visit.

He immediately put in a request to see his solicitor and phoned his office to tell him to get his finger out, but he was not available, what a surprise. He was also told to expect a visit from CID at Rotherhithe. That Jeff's not going to give up easily, he thought.

Bugsy sat in his cell, trying to weigh up the options. He was tempted to call Tony's bluff and give the cops his name. He would just love to see Tony go down for life, but he knew that Tony would kill Jan and Chris. He also undoubtedly had friends in Belmarsh who would quite happily stick a knife in his throat. In the end, Bugsy finally knew what he was going to do. He was now looking forward to that bastard, Bradley, coming in.

Bugsy was in interview room 1 on the first floor where legal meetings took place. He had a plan and if Tony didn't agree then he would fuck him big time.

Terence wanted to get rid of Bugsy's case but Tony wouldn't let him as he wanted to know what Bugsy was up to. Terence hated going to Belmarsh; all the clanging of doors and the turning of keys made him jittery, even more so now that he was implicated in the killing of a police officer. He had some messages for Bugsy from Jan and Tony. He strode into the Interview room, intent on being in charge.

"Morning Mr Cooper, and how are you?"

"Don't good morning me, you wanker. Where have you been?"

"I've been very busy. I have other cases, you know."

"Listen, you jumped up piece of shit. Get this straight, you start taking an interest in my welfare or I'll fuck you, don't underestimate me, I mean it." Bugsy was up for this meeting and was not going to take any shit from this smooth talking wanker.

"Mr Cooper, I have a couple of messages for you."

"Oh yea? What are they?"

"Firstly, from your wife. She says she's fine and everything is good."

Bugsy said nothing. That's what Tony told Bradley to tell me, he thought.

"Secondly, Tony has friends in here who can make your stay more comfortable as long as you play ball."

Yeah, thought Bugsy. And if I don't play ball, there are people in here who will take care of me.

He looked at Terrence and smiled. "Well, I'm mightily comforted by those words. Thanks, Bradley."

He leaned forward and snarled at Bradley. "Now, this is what I want you to tell that fucking cunt, Tony Bolton. Are you listening?"

Terrence had a feeling he was not going to like this. "Yes I'm listening."

"Good, now you tell Tony this: whatever happens, I'm looking at twenty, twenty-five years, so when I next travel to court, Tony is going to spring me and then he's going to set me and my family up in Spain." he looked at Bradley to see his reaction. Bradley said nothing.

"Well?"

“You’re off your fucking trolley! Why on earth would he do that?”

“Because if he doesn’t, the following is going to happen. One, I will give his and your name to the authorities. CID from Rotherhithe are coming to see me tomorrow, so that would be a good opportunity. Secondly, once I have spilled the beans, as they say, I will go to Block 4 where it will be much harder for Tony to get to me and then I’ll be moved a very long way from here."

Terrence looked thoughtful. “You seem to have forgotten one major item, and that is Jan and your son. He will kill them, you know.”

Bugsy took a few seconds to reply. “I have no wife and no children until I get out of this place for good.”

Terence always said nothing surprised him, but Bugsy possibly sacrificing his family, came as a bit of a shock. He looked at Bugsy's calm demeanour and knew he was serious.

“Well, the sooner I leave, the sooner he’ll get the message,” said Terence as he got up and made for the door. Bugsy stopped him in his tracks. “Bradley, I’ll call your office at four pm this afternoon. I want a yes or no, is that clear?”

“Perfectly clear Mr Cooper.” Terrence strode out into the corridor and disappeared from view.

Bugsy had played his cards and now had to wait.

Terence was shitting himself again. He could see his whole life going up in flames. He got in his car and dialled Tony's number.

“Terence, how are you? What happened at the meet?

There was silence, as Terence took a deep breath.

“It’s looking bad Tony. Bugsy wants you to spring him on his next trip to court or he’s going to talk, we will both be in the shit then."

“Whatever happens at some time, he is going to die, nobody fucks with me!"

“I suggest you keep calm and think this through, I don’t think he’s kidding. He says he’ll do his time in Block 4 until he gets moved, also he doesn’t give a shit about Jan and the boy.”

"Call me back in an hour." Tony clicked the phone off. He sat down and looked out the window. Fuck! This is not looking good at all, he thought angrily. Spring Bugsy from a prison van? Shit! That will be a tough one. People will get hurt, possibly killed. Well, I've killed one copper, so if a prison guard has to kop it as well, so what, I'll get life anyway if they catch me.

Tony decided not to wait for the call from Bradley. "Terence, tell that toe rag Bugsy it's a deal. Listen, I need to know when they're going to move him."

"I don't want to get involved any more Tony. My career is at stake here."

"Terence, it's a lot more than your career that is at stake here, you do understand?"

Jesus! Thought Terence, now the bastard's threatening me, and what about my family.

"I'll do this for you Tony but then that is it, we're finished."

"Hey, we're friends, aren't we? I'll get it all organised but the date and time is what I need. Speak to you soon, Terence."

Terence was glad he was off the phone from that madman. Well, if you sit with the devil long enough, eventually you get burnt, he thought. Now I'll try and find out when Bugsy might be back in court.

Bugsy had been worrying all day; would Tony go for it or not? You could never really tell with a lunatic like him. It eventually came to 3.55 pm and Bugsy made for the phones.

He dialled the number and it was answered immediately. "Good Afternoon, Malone and Bradley. How may I help you?"

Bugsy licked his lips and cleared his throat. "Mr Bradley, please."

"Who may I say is calling please?"

"It's Mr Cooper."

"Hang on a moment please, sir."

“Ah, Mr Cooper good afternoon. The answer to your question is yes, I’ll be in to see you shortly, so please be as prepared as you can, is that clear?”

“Loud and clear. Thank you Mr Bradley; see you soon.” Everybody knew the phone calls were listened to, so you had to be careful what you said.

Bugsy put the phone down and walked away. He was so fucking happy he could have shouted from the rooftops. What he did do was walk back to his cell as though absolutely everything was perfectly normal. He entered his cell, sat on his bunk bed and allowed himself a huge smile. He should be getting out of this mess pretty soon.

Bradley put the phone down and prayed that he would soon be out of this mess for ever.

Tony had started putting a crew together to attack the prison van and spring Bugsy. The first person he rang was Tom.

CHAPTER 28

“Artan, we cannot go on like this," said Adnan. "Nothing is happening, we are going crazy here.” Artan, Adnan and Bashkim were having a progress meeting at Artan’s house.

“I understand it is very difficult, but what can we do?" Said Artan lifting his hands to the heavens.

Adnan and Bashkim spent nearly all their time at the house in Totteridge. It’s a very comfortable house and Eleni was cooking all their favourite Albanian and Greek dishes, but they were going mad with boredom.

“We need to be more pro-active,” said Adnan.

“Tell me Adnan, what can we do? Tell me, please. I want results the same as you. The police have put a new twenty five thousand Pound reward, that’s seventy five grand in total. Someone must come forward soon.”

“Maybe people will not come forward because they are too scared of this killer,” offered Bashkin.

“I agree,” said Adnan. “The man called Cooper, in Prison, is a local man; from that we can assume that the other members of the gang are also local.”

Artan looked thoughtful. “So, come on, we’ve been in difficult situations before; how do we flush these bastards out?”

“Artan, you said money was no object," said Adnan. "Put up another one hundred thousand pounds and let’s see if that helps, we all know money talks; someone, somewhere, knows who these men are. The money will talk, eventually.”

"I agree about the money. You see, the other thing, Adnan, is that, in the past, we were always told who had to be killed; we are not detectives, we are just killers and we are in a foreign country, which makes it doubly difficult. We have been patient in the past, we will be patient again, yes?"

"Of course, we are not leaving until the matter comes to a conclusion and that is when we have killed all the men involved in the robbery." Adnan had a look of resolve on his face.

Jeff Collins at CID Rotherhithe, was slightly despondent the extra twenty five thousand pound reward, had not brought in any new names on the Arrow Logistics killing. There was usually talk on the street, but in this instance, not a whisper. They had no clues from the shooting of the police officer at Tower Bridge Road. The only good news was the progress in Malaga, where something could be happening very quickly in the Falcon One surveillance case. Jeff kept wishing he was in Malaga with Karen. They had now formed a good partnership and he was worried sick something could happen to her. Jeff was conscious that he had to make things happen, not wait around doing nothing because, as night follows day, nothing will happen, if you do nothing. That was one of the reasons he was desperate to see Bugsy again, only this time he would have to go to Belmarsh.

CHAPTER 29

Bruce Coyne was enjoying himself; he had a pretty similar schedule most days. He rose late, had a shower, went down to the restaurant and had a good breakfast. He then went back to his room and collected his papers, book, sunglasses, towel and suntan lotion and put everything in his shoulder bag and strolled down to the pool. He got to the pool and then had a very favourite moment. The Germans had already been to the pool at seven a.m. and put their towels on all the sun beds. Although, a number of sun beds were occupied, there were still many with just towels on them. Bruce delighted in removing towels from wherever he wanted to lie and chucked them in the pool. The first time he did it, a fat and belligerent German, came looking for his sun bed and found Bruce lying on it. Cue loads of shouting and then when he saw his towels floating in the pool, he went apoplectic. Bruce just lay there and whenever the German shouted, he smiled, making him shout even louder. Bruce didn't like fucking krauts and delighted in winding them up as much as possible.

Bruce would sunbath and swim until about twelve midday, when he would start on his daily intake of cold beer. At one o clock, he would have a light lunch in the terrace restaurant next to the pool. Then back out to the pool and sunbath till two or three, where upon he would pack up his belongings and head back to his room. He would lie on his bed and fall asleep for a couple of hours, waking at about five pm. He would then sit on his balcony and read for an hour, followed by a couple of beers he kept in the room fridge. At six thirty, he liked to shower again and think about dinner and the evening. The last couple of nights, he had gone down for dinner at seven thirty; there was a sumptuous buffet and as much wine as you could drink. He would go back up to his room at about nine thirty and Consuela would turn up at ten o clock. A quick shag or blow job, the sex was without question functional and it was done without a shred of feeling. He was then ready for sleep at about eleven. He was getting a bit of a tan and felt very healthy in the glorious sunshine. He went to bed that night, thinking he might have a change tomorrow: either go out for lunch or dinner.

Telfer and Scott had been drinking heavily again and both woke up, not feeling too good. They eventually went down to the restaurant and had croissants and lots of coffee. After breakfast, they phoned Richard and told him they were leaving the hotel; would pick up the hire van and make towards the Marconfort Beach Club Hotel. Just before they got to the hotel, they would stop and rendezvous with Richard, for a final meet.

Richard was more than a little annoyed with Telfer and Scott. He'd spoken to Telfer and could tell just on the phone that he was under the weather through drink; and if he was that bad, then Scott was probably even worse. Fucking amateurs, he thought. They shouldn't have even had a drink last night. Anyway, if anything goes wrong, he'll make sure he's well out of it and they are well in it. His pistol had been delivered, a Smith and Wesson SD9 with sixteen 9mm rounds. He always felt more comfortable when he had a weapon, and would not be slow to use it if he was threatened in any way. I just hope those two fucking idiots get their act together or I might end up shooting them as well, he thought. Richard was very calm but knew the whole plan hinged on Coyne going out for either lunch or dinner. He'd had all his meals at his hotel, but Richard was sure it was about time he had a change of scenery.

The day started the same as usual for Karen, Miguel, Max and Alfonse. Miguel picked Karen up from her hotel; they then drove to the Sol Principe Hotel and had a coffee in the bar while Karen caught up with Placido. Alfonse and Max drove down to the Los Jazmines Hotel to pick up on Telfer and Scott. It was the same as yesterday morning, and nothing yet indicated it was going to be a day none of them would ever forget.

Alfonse had gone into the hotel to see if he could see Telfer and Scot. He found them drinking coffee in the restaurant and could see that, as usual, they didn't look in very good shape. He went back out to the car and told Max, who relayed the information to Karen that nothing out of the ordinary was happening.

Falcon came down for breakfast and looked very alert and chipper. Karen and Miguel watched as he ate a very hearty breakfast, washed down with orange juice and coffee.

It was ten thirty and all was quiet. The first to move were Telfer and Scott. They got in there car and headed north on the coast road. Max and Alfonse followed at a safe distance in order not to be detected; they informed Karen that they were moving. They then pulled into the car and van hire company and went into the office. They came out and transferred spades and something else wrapped up from the boot of their car, into the silver van. Telfer then opened the sliding door and smeared masses of grease on all the door hinges; he then opened and shut the door several times. They then got back onto the coast road heading north. It was eleven am.

Falcon left the hotel at eleven am and headed north on the same coast road that Telfer and Scott were on. Max and Karen were in constant communication, updating each other where they were. Max said they could be heading for the Marconfort Beach Club Hotel where Telfer and Scott went the other day.

Telfer and Scott pulled into a petrol station about a mile from the Marconfort Beach Club Hotel. As a typical Spanish petrol station, it also had a café and they both two went in and ordered coffee. Five minutes later, Falcon pulled in and joined Telfer and Scott in the coffee shop.

"You two look like shit," said Richard. "Are you trying to drink Torremolinos dry? Because I can tell you, it's not possible."

"Very funny," said Telfer, thinking: shut the fuck up, wanker.

"Get me a coffee then, Scott."

Scott ordered a latte for Richard.

Richard was looking at the two men with a concerned face.

"Are you two up for this, because if you're not, I'll have my money back?"

“We are fine, get off our backs eh,” said Telfer, angrily. They’d spent hundreds on booze already, so couldn’t pay it back, anyway.

“Good, now we move on. Coyne can recognise me, so I can’t go to the hotel. Jim, you better go, we’ll be here waiting for your call. As soon as you see him, make any move, call us and we will be there in five minutes. Let’s pray he goes out for either lunch or dinner. It’s going to be a long day, but that’s the way it is."

Both police cars were now in the petrol station car park and Karen decided they should move to allay any suspicions of them being followed. They parked round the corner where they were out of view, but could still see the entrance to the café.

They watched and saw Telfer leave the café and take Falcon's car and drive north. Karen told Max and Alfonse to follow them and to report when he stopped. Things were heating up and the adrenalin was starting to flow. Karen was getting excited and worried that she would perform at the same time. Suddenly, Karen’s phone rang. Max reported that Telfer had pulled into the Marconfort Beach Club Hotel.

Telfer got out of the car and slowly strolled to the corner where he could see the pool. He scanned the pool just like he did the last time he was here. He stopped and then retraced his steps to the car.

Richard’s phone rang. “Yes Jim, what’s happening?”

“Coyne’s by the pool as usual, drinking beer.”

“Hmm, well, it looks like he probably isn’t going out for lunch, so we’ll have to pray he’s going out for dinner tonight. Stay there and keep watch.”

“OK, speak later.”

Richard thought that was bad news; he was going to have to wait hours to see if Coyne was going out for dinner or not.

Karen had been on the phone to Jeff in Rotherhithe explaining the situation. Jeff was very confident and told Karen she had nothing to worry about. She had three police officers with her; two of them who were armed.

Karen did not mention that Miguel had secured extra firearms which were fully loaded and in the boot of the car, ready for use at a moment's notice.

Jeff hadn't wanted to worry Karen she was with what appeared to be two professional Spanish Police officers, so he was praying everything would be fine. It sounded to him like something was going down today, God he wished he was there.

The waiting game continued. Coyne followed his usual routine and went back up to his room at two thirty.

Telfer sat in the car park, trying to stop falling asleep.

Scott and Richard were sweating in the café, a mile from the hotel.

Karen and Miguel were doing exactly the same round the corner.

Richard was getting agitated and more stressed by the minute. "Scott, I'm going to get some fresh air, call me if you hear anything."

Richard went outside and began to stroll, taking deep breaths and wiping sweat off his brow. Karen and Miguel saw him leave the café and headed towards them. "Shit!" Karen said. "This could be awkward." Falcon was getting closer and closer. He's going to see me and could recognise me, thought Karen. Just as Falcon was getting to the car, Miguel leaned over, took Karen in his arms and started to kiss her passionately; Karen couldn't do anything but respond.

Falcon glanced in the car and got a one second side view of the woman. Lucky bastard, nookie in the afternoon, very nice, he thought, and strolled on.

After he had passed, Miguel pulled away from Karen, gasping for breath. "Well, I think we got away with that."

"I thought that only happened in the movies. Yes, well done, Miguel. That was a good idea." Her heart had been in her mouth. She also thought she'd actually quite enjoyed it, especially rubbing her breasts on Miguel's manly chest. She asked Miguel to move the car again so Falcon would not see them on the way back.

Time was going so slowly, every minute seemed like hours; surveillance of this type was very difficult. It was now 4.00 p.m.

Falcon got past the car and nearly tripped; the girl, there was something about her. He had a feeling but could not put his finger on it, he just knew something was wrong. He was racking his brain, trying to keep it clear, trying to remember. Then it came to him; the woman in the plane, the fucking woman who was late onto the plane. It was the same fucking woman! Could it be a coincidence? Don't be fucking stupid, he thought. Jesus, they're following me! I've been followed all the time I've been here! The sweat was pouring off him and his breathing was becoming shallow and laboured. He tried to walk as casually as he could back to the café.

"Are you alright, Richard? You look like shit."

"Thanks Scott, nice of you to say so. It's the fucking heat, it's killing me. Get me a cold drink, eh?"

"Sure." Scott went to the counter for a cold coke.

Richard was desperately thinking of what to do. Cancelling the whole thing would probably be the sensible thing to do; just call Telfer, get him back here and go back to the hotels. His brain was working overtime and he was looking at all options. He laughed to himself and decided to do something completely crazy. He phoned Telfer.

"Jim, anything happening?"

"He's in his room. Nothing's happening."

"Jim, I'm feeling really ill, I want you to come back and pick up Scott, and you can then leave my car here and return to the hotel in the van. It'll be better for you to have some company while you're waiting."

"Eh.. yea, OK." Good, Telfer thought. Be nice to have some company.

"Jim's on his way; you can go back with him in the van. I'm feeling like shit and need to rest."

"OK, no prob." Scott was happy. He'd much rather be with Jim than this wanker.

Max and Alfonse reported to Karen that they were following Telfer back to the café.

Richard was acting very casual but he was scanning the road leading to the café. He spotted his car pull into the petrol station. A few seconds later a dark Ford Focus pulled in and parked at the other side, away from Telfer. Telfer walked into the café.

"OK look, you two, grab some food and drinks get back to the hotel and watch Coyne. I would still put money on him going out tonight. You let me know the minute he moves."

"OK, Richard." Telfer and Scott got some cokes and sandwiches and went back out to the car park and got in the van. A minute later, they were pulling back out onto the north road. This was the moment Falcon had been waiting for. He watched closely and smiled to himself as he saw the Ford Focus slip out a few seconds, after the van.

Falcon sat for a minute and then strolled out to the car park and got in his car. He started up and slowly pulled out of the car park onto the road, heading back south. The only thing he remembered about the car with the couple in it was that it was blue. He was constantly looking in his rear view mirror for a blue sedan type model. "Bingo!" he said loudly.

Three cars were behind him; he could see a blue Ford Mondeo. He drove slowly back to the Sol Principe Hotel where he parked and walked casually into reception. As soon as he entered the reception, he ran up the stairs and went to the side of the large panoramic window and looked out. There it was, the blue Ford pulled in and parked on the other side of the road. Two people got out, an English looking woman and a Spanish man. He nodded his head as he watched the two coppers stroll to the hotel entrance.

Telfer and Scott were happy they had some food and drinks and had got away from that Richard git. It was now 6.00 p.m. and if Coyne was going to go out, it would be soon.

Bruce woke up from his afternoon kip. After a quick shower, he grabbed a beer and moved onto the balcony. He looked at the view and was feeling good. Yea, he thought. I think I'll go out for some dinner tonight. The only question is, shall I go on my own or invite Consuela? No, I think I'll go on my own. I could get lucky and meet some woman, you never know. He swigged his beer and went back inside to find something nice to wear.

Telfer and Scott were watching for Coyne, Max and Alfonse were watching them, everybody was hot, sticky and wanted something to happen as soon as possible.

Bruce Coyne finally left his room at seven p.m. and took the lift down to reception. He was asking the receptionist to recommend a good local restaurant and was trying to understand what she was saying and work out the directions. Scott was outside the car stretching his legs. He glanced into the hotel and saw Coyne standing at reception, and he immediately went back to the car and told Telfer it looked like Coyne could be on the move. Telfer called Richard.

"Yes Jim, what's happening?" said Richard.

"He's in reception all dressed up. Looks like he could be going out."

"Well, it's what we've been waiting for, about time as well. I'm sick of this bloody café. Look get him in the van. Tell me where you are, and I'll be there in minutes."

"Aren't you coming now then, Richard?"

"I've paid you a lot of money. All you have to do is get him in the fucking van. Jesus! Surely, you two can do that?"

"Yea, alright, I'll call you."

Telfer turned to Scott. "We're to grab him, phone Richard, and he'll come to us."

"I suppose it makes sense, the cafe's only two minutes away."

Richard quickly tidied himself up and went down to the restaurant. As he walked to his table, he said good evening to as many people as possible. He then sat down right bang in the middle so everyone could see him. He looked around; the English woman was not in sight, but he caught a quick glimpse of the Spanish copper hanging around in the coffee shop.

Miguel had seen Falcon take his seat in the restaurant and reported to Karen.

“Well, Falcon's not going anywhere tonight, that’s for sure.”

“Good,” said Karen. "We can all relax a bit."

Coyne had written down the name of the restaurant that had been recommended. “Restaurante Escalera, Calle de la Cuesta del Tajo.” It was supposed to serve great Spanish food and less than a ten minute walk from the hotel, although you could never tell when their English was really bad.

Coyne headed out of reception and exited the hotel, walking briskly in the direction of the restaurant Escalera. He passed Max coming in the other direction, rushing to the hotel toilet.

Falcon was sitting in the restaurant, drinking a nice Spanish Rioja. He loved his wine and was always surprised by the excellent value of the hotel selection. He was waiting for the call that he knew was coming and was getting ready to say exactly the right words. His fish starter arrived and he tucked in hungrily.

Telfer and Scott pulled out of the car park and slowly followed Coyne. They had gone through the plan a couple of times. It was still light, with a very blue sky. Coyne was strolling along, without a care in the world.

“This is easy, Scott," said Telfer reassuringly. "Don’t worry, he’s an old man and the best thing is, he’s not expecting it. We will catch him completely by surprise.”

Alfonse was shitting himself. Telfer and Scott had driven out of the hotel and still no sign of Max. Alfonse rushed into the hotel and found the men’s toilet. He pushed the entrance door and heard groaning. “Max, is that you?” The groaning got louder and Alfonse opened one of the cubicle doors. Max was sat on the toilet; the stink was horrific. “Max are you alright?”

“My stomach!” he groaned. Alfonse heard a disgustingly long and loud fart and hastily shut the door.

“Max! They’ve gone! Telfer and Scott, they’ve gone! Can you hear me?” Alfonse was shouting and almost crying as he added despairingly: “Max, they have left the hotel! We have lost them!”

Max just about found the energy to shout to Alfonse. "Tell Karen! Do you understand? Tell Karen!"

Alfonse left the toilet and called Karen. "Karen, its Alfonse, Max is sick, Telfer and Scott have left the hotel. We don't know where they are!"

Karen was beside herself. This night of all nights. "Jesus! OK, keep calm. I'll call you back."

Fuck! I can't believe this! She quickly recounted the message to Miguel.

"That idiot Alfonse; he should have followed them. I'm sorry Karen."

"It's not your fault. There's nothing we can do now."

"Send Alfonse out to drive around and see if he can see the van."

"Good idea Miguel."

"Alfonse, leave the hotel, see if you can see the van. Stay local, and tell Max what you're doing."

"OK, Karen, I'm on my way."

Coyne had been walking for about twenty minutes and kept stopping to show people the name of the Restaurant he was trying to find. Little did he know he had twice walked past the side street where it was located.

Scott was driving the van with Telfer in the back, operating the sliding door.

Coyne stopped again and looked round. He saw the van behind him and thought nothing of it. The van moved alongside him and stopped. Coyne looked up to see the driver open the window and speak to him.

"Hello, we're looking for the..." Scott looked at a piece of paper and continued in terrible Spanish. "El Gato Braseria." Can you help at all?"

Coyne laughed. "That's funny"

"Oh, you're English?" Asked Scott, surprised.

"Yea, I'm in the same boat as you. I'm looking for the Restaurant La Escalera." They were now both laughing.

Scott opened the door and jumped out and offered his hand. "I'm Scott."

“Hi, Scott. I’m Bruce.”

“Well, this is a right mess, isn’t it,” said Scott. He moved round so that Coyne moved as well and then had his back to the sliding door.

Telfer opened the sliding side door. It was totally silent. He took one step and hit Coyne on the back of the head with a car jack. Coyne went down like a sack of spuds. Scott and Telfer grabbed him and in two seconds, he was dumped in the back of the van and they drove way.

“That was brilliant, Scott," said Telfer, pleased. "You should have been a fucking actor. Brilliant!

"Is he still alive Jim? You hit him pretty hard.” “Yea, he’s breathing, I can hear him. This is the easiest money I ever made.”

They turned off the coast road and headed inland. “We better phone Richard, I nearly forgot.” said Scott. Before Jim could do that Scott added, “Jim, we don’t need that bastard to finish the job; it only means we’ve got to hang around even longer.”

“Yea, OK,” agreed Jim as he took his phone out to call Richard.

Richard was enjoying his meal and noticed that the Spanish cop kept popping into the coffee shop to check he was still in the restaurant.

His phone rang. He put it to his ear and leaned forward. “Yes, Jim.”

“We have the object and are going to take care of it in a minute. No need for you to get involved, OK?”

Manna from heaven, thought Richard. “OK. At last, I can leave this fucking café. Just make sure it’s all neat and tidy. I’ll see you back in the UK in a few days.” Richard clicked off and called the waiter. “Another bottle of this very good Rioja, please.” He went back to stuffing his face and planned to get back home as soon as possible.

Bruce Coyne slowly woke and could feel a throbbing pain in his head. Shit! What the fuck is going on, he thought. He opened his eyes and looked round. He saw a man standing next to him talking to the driver of a van. He suddenly remembered the van, and the man, Scott. Shit! I’m in trouble. He closed his eyes; he wanted to feel better before the two men became aware he had woken up. He strained to listen to what they were saying.

"When is that prat Richard going to pay us the balance?" asked Scott.

"As soon as we get back, I guess," said Jim.

Coyne was listening intently. Richard. I don't know any Richard. It all then suddenly became clear. Fuck! This is a hit and I'd bet money it's that cunt Richard Philips who has put out the contract. I may not have long, thought Coyne. He looked around and spotted two spades on the floor of the van. This sent a shiver down his back. Christ! These bastards mean to kill and bury me out here in the middle of fucking nowhere! He glanced up at the nearest one; he had something in his hand. Then he gasped. It was a very frightening looking Machete.

Jim turned to look at him. "He's waking."

"Finish him now before he fully wakes up," said Scott.

"We can't do that, Scott, because of the mess, unless you want to spend hours cleaning the van before we return it."

Thank God for that, thought Coyne. He opened his eyes again. The one called Jim pointed the Machete at him. "Don't move and don't speak." He nodded at Coyne. Coyne nodded.

Coyne moved his hands. Bloody hell! They haven't tied me. He couldn't believe that. He moved his feet. They hadn't tied his feet either. These two are fucking amateurs, I may still get out of this, he thought. There's one thing that could save my life;

Have they searched me? Slowly, he moved his two feet together, then lifted his left foot and felt his right ankle above the shoe. He could have cried with relief: the knife was still there, they didn't fucking search me. Oh, thank you God, thank you. He now had hope and he was a lot tougher than they thought.

Coyne rested for a few moments. He had to strike either, while the van was moving, or at the second it stopped. He chose the latter. He would feign injury and appear to be out of it and then strike. He put his head down and groaned.

Telfer turned and was pleased he was still suffering the effects of the whack on the head; it would be easier if he was still groggy.

"Scott, how far are we going?"

"We're miles from anywhere. We can turn off the road whenever you like."

"OK, five minutes should do."

Coyne had five minutes to work himself mentally into a killing state of mind. He looked out the window, it was pitch black that would help. He then felt the van turn off the road and it became very bumpy. He had to get ready. He slipped his hand down to his ankle and took the knife. He felt better with the knife in his hand. It was a pretty normal pen knife but he had sharpened it, so it was a deadly weapon in the right hands.

Coyne felt the van slow down. This was it. He tensed his muscles. The van stopped. He was up like a shot and screamed for all he was worth. He lifted the knife just as Jim turned and sunk it deep into his neck and pulled. Muscle and skin tissue were ripped apart as blood flew in every direction. Jim let out an ear splitting scream that reverberated into the night. Coyne plunged the knife back into Jim's neck, his shoulder and his chest. He could hear the sucking noises as he kept pulling the knife out.

Jim slumped to the floor. Coyne then looked for the driver, he was gone. He grabbed Jim's Machete and leapt out of the van. He heard the sound of running feet and set off in pursuit. Scott had seen the madman stick the knife in Jim's neck and panicked. He opened the door and ran for his life. He must have had a five second lead on Coyne but he was so unfit, he soon started to tire. All the booze they had drunk in the past couple of days was hitting him hard now.

Coyne was shouting. "I'm coming to get you, bastard! I'm gonna cut your fucking bollocks off, you snivelling cunt, you can't hide out here, come to mamma!"

Scott was terrified; the man was completely insane. He was so tired now, he had to stop. He saw a slight rise in the ground and lay down on the side away from where he thought the madman would approach. Coyne was a lot closer than he thought. He had seen Scott move to the right. He slowed down. Any man fighting for his life could be dangerous.

Coyne was moving slowly and as quietly as he could. Scott had shut his eyes and was praying to God to save him. Then it happened. Coyne actually tripped over Scott's body. Scott jumped up but was too late as Coyne swung the machete and connected with Scott's wrist. His hand fell cleanly away from the arm. Scott howled with pain and knew he was going to die. Coyne grabbed him by the arm, pulled him back to the van and threw him to the ground. He then dragged the still moaning Jim out of the van and deposited him next to Scott.

"Fucking Tom and Jerry, eh? Couple of right amateur cunts, you two are unbelievable. Quick question before I cut you up. Who put the contract on me?"

Scott was the only one who could talk, albeit very weakly. "Richard Philips. Do you know him?"

"I know that cunt!"

Coyne then lifted the machete high above his head and brought it down hard onto Scott's right leg. It sliced through the skin and hit the bone with great force, shattering it. Scott howled, almost passing out with the mind numbing and excruciating pain.

"So, listen, you two; I'm leaving now, but don't worry, you won't be alone for long."

Coyne jumped into the van; he took one last look at the two men who were lying crippled moaning on the ground; he almost felt sorry for them. He knew what was coming for them.

"Jim! Can you hear me? Jim!" Scott was shouting and pulling at Jim's arm but all Jim could do was moan. Scott gave up; Jim was beyond help and would soon die. Scott knew also if he didn't get help, then he too could easily die out here. It had been hot during the day but it was now getting very cold. I wonder what that bastard Coyne meant, "You won't be alone for long." Oh God! Wild animals, he thought.

"Jim, we have to move. Jesus! Somebody! Help us please!" Scott was scanning the area but couldn't see a thing through the inky blackness of the night.

"Jim! Please wake up!" Scott started shaking Jim again but then decided it was a waste of time. Jim was finished.

"I must get to the road, it's possible someone would see me," he thought.

Scott tried to move, the pain was terrible. He had to pull with his elbows and drag the broken leg. He soon stopped as he could feel himself nearly passing out. He looked back to see how far he had moved, about fifteen feet and it had nearly killed him. "Fucking hell!" he swore and prayed to God for help. Something suddenly caught his eye. He concentrated and looked hard into the night. Yes, a light, two, and then he realised what they were, a dog's eyes, shining in the night. He scrambled forward again as fast as he could drag himself. Scott was now terrified; he forgot the pain as he knew he was fighting for his life. He kept going as long as he could before, again, he felt like passing out. He looked back to where Jim was. He grimaced and welled up as he saw a circle of bright yellow eyes glinting in the darkness; they were getting near to Jim. He redoubled his efforts to get to the road. He must have lost so much blood by now. He felt a panic. He knew he was leaving a trail of blood for the dogs. Oh, fucking hell! Once they've finished with Jim they just have to follow the blood to find me, he thought wildly. He stopped as he heard growling and quickly looked back. He could make out a pack of, at least, eight or ten dogs snarling and baring their sharp white teeth, circling Jim. Suddenly, one of the dogs rushed forward, grabbed an arm between its fangs and started pulling. Jim slowly lifted his head as the pack attacked in force, biting into arms and legs, pulling and shaking. Jim became fully conscious and gave a blood curdling scream, howling with anguish as he felt a foot being ripped and pulled out of his body.

The dogs tore into his body with such ferocity, that he mercifully passed out.

Scott was still dragging himself away but was near death himself. The blood loss had been huge and he knew he could not go much further. He stopped and looked back again. The dogs had finished with Jim; he could just make out Jims head with some bits of bones, scattered around. The dogs were licking themselves clean. Scott pushed his elbows into the dry hard ground and pulled; he gained another few feet but had to stop. He didn't want to but he looked back again; terror gripped him, the dogs were moving round, sniffing the ground and the air. He quickly started pulling again with his elbows. "Jesus help me," he muttered quietly. Then he heard a noise, a sort of gentle patter; he glanced round, the dogs were loping towards him.

"Oh God, somebody help me help!" Fear seized him and he screamed for help. The wild dogs could now clearly hear and see their next meal. They bounded towards him. Scott was pulling for dear life, but he knew he needed a miracle to survive. He could clearly hear them closing in on him and then it happened. He felt a ring of sharp teeth penetrate his broken ankle.

"Ahhhhhhhh!" he screamed and tried to shake his leg free. The dog was now pulling his leg, trying to decapitate it from his body. The pain was unbearable. Scott was still moving but now the other dogs were upon him. One jumped straight onto his back and dug his teeth into the back of Scott's head. The dog was so heavy, Scott was pinned down and could not move. He had one last thought, he wanted it over as soon as possible. He lifted his head as best he could, exposing his neck. The dog biting his head seemed to understand and let go. Scott could smell the dogs stinking breath. It all seemed to happen in slow motion as the dog clamped his mouth around Scott's neck. He felt the teeth clamp on and into his flesh. The last moment had arrived as the dog tightened his grip even more and suddenly ripped his neck away from the body and head. The head rolled to one side as the pack attacked and tore his body to pieces.

Coyne was exhausted and completely drained, he was covered in blood and gore. He drove the van within a mile of his hotel, dumped it and then walked back. He went into the entrance by the pool. There was hardly anyone around. He got to his room, poured himself a huge whisky, emptied the glass and then cried with happiness he had survived. He now had one thought, and that was Richard Philips. He would deal with Richard when he got back to the UK. He undressed and spent over twenty minutes in the shower.

The van was found the next morning. The mutilated bodies were found later in the day by some English tourists walking their dogs.

Alfonse was left at the Sol Principe hotel to watch Falcon with strict instructions to call Karen if he left the hotel; he was also to follow him and inform the rest of them immediately.

Karen, Max and Miguel went to see the van and then the bodies or what was left of them. The Wild dogs had eaten most of the flesh so they looked a lot worse than when Coyne had left them. Karen was almost physically sick, they were assuming it was Telfer and Scott but until dental checks they couldn't be sure.

Karen called Jeff in London and recounted the story; Jeff almost couldn't believe it. He wanted surveillance kept up on Falcon One right to the time he got on the plane back at Malaga airport. He would be picked up at Heathrow by members of the team in London.

Karen had mixed feelings. She did the best she could. Falcon had spent the entire night at the hotel so he couldn't have been involved in the actual killing of Telfer and Scott. If only Max hadn't been ill, If only Alfonse had followed Telfer and Scott, it could all have ended differently. It was all ifs, buts and maybes.

Falcon left Malaga the next morning. Karen and Max stayed over one extra night, Max to get over his Spanish tummy and Karen, to have a rest.

CHAPTER 30

"Tom, are you back?"

"Yea, hi Tony. I came back a bit early. I got bored"

"You can't beat being in your own country, can you?"

"No, you're right. Tony, what's happening?"

"Can't say too much, you understand, but we're going to visit our mutual friend soon and welcome him back into the fold. I need you to organise picking him up, you comprendez Tom?"

"Yes, I understand exactly, and it will be my pleasure. You'll let me know where the meet is?"

"Yea, I'll tell you later. See you there at eight."

This would need very serious planning; Tony didn't want another fiasco like the gig at Arrow Logistics.

Tony and Tom met at the Ship in Rotherhithe, a good local pub.

Tom was in first, closely followed by Tony and someone he didn't know.

"Hello Tom, how are you? Sorry to be vague on the phone but you know how it is"

"Better to be safe than sorry, I say." Tom looked at the man with Tony.

"Tom, this is Patrick." Tom and Patrick shake hands.

They all sat down and ordered some beers. "Tom, Patrick is going to be helping us out with our little visit. Let's say that he has skills that could prove to be very useful in this type of, err... operation."

"Great, if he's OK with you Tony, he's OK with me." Tom smiled.

Tony spoke again. "We need to discuss many issues, the first being that the courthouse is two miles from Belmarsh, which will take the prison van about eight minute. That does not give us much time, plus there will be heavy security. What do you think, Patrick?"

"Well, you're right that there is very little time, but there is always a way, it is just finding it. Quite often the answer is go in hard with massive firepower and blow everything away."

"What does massive firepower mean exactly?"

"I was thinking of a grenade launcher or maybe an anti-tank weapon to take out the serco van, we have used these before in Ireland and they work a treat."

"You see, I told you Patrick had certain skills," laughed Tony.

Tom was amazed that Tony could be humorous at a time like this but he suspected it was half to cover his nerves and half to impress Patrick.

"Anti-tank gun bloody hell, I assume you can get hold of one of these?" said Tom.

"There's no problem getting one at a price."

"Forget about the money, it's not an issue. I don't care what it costs," said Tony with real conviction. "Tom any idea what security there will be on the day?" he asked.

"I don't think there'll be any extra security; because it's so close to Belmarsh, they tend to think people would have to be mad to try anything. So that is a good advantage for us. Let me give you an idea of the route. The serco van will come out of Belmarsh and turn left into Western Way, that's a long dual carriageway. It follows through to the A206 Plumstead road and continues into the A205 Beresford road. It goes past the New Wine Church, continues on to St Mary Magdalen Church of England Primary School and then goes into the town centre, a quick left turn and the courthouse is in Market Street. The whole journey is about eight minutes."

"Surely, we can't just fire a missile or rocket at the van. Won't it blow the whole thing to shit?" said Tony.

“Well, there are different types of shells. I suggest we fire a low velocity shell at the front cab which should leave the back comparatively undamaged.”

“So, the driver and guard will be killed instantly?” asked Tom.

Patrick smiled. “Instant death. Not a bad way to go, eh?”

“Look, I’m going to leave the detail up to you two," said Tony. "I don’t care what it costs or how many we need to bring in to get it done.” he stared at them both. “Just get it done.”

Tom and Patrick spent hours sorting the detail until the plan was done. All they needed now was the date and the time.

Tom rang Tony. “It’s me. Everything’s sorted. The only thing we need now is the date and time. As a last resort, we could camp out but it would be dangerous.”

“I understand. I’m working on the date and time and will let you know as soon as possible, speak soon.”

Tony made his third call to Bradley in two days. “Terence, it’s me. Have you got anything for me?”

“I’m not a fucking miracle worker, Tony," said Terence irritably. "As soon as I hear anything, I’ll call you.”

“Terence, you know very well I do not like to be disappointed. I want that information and I want it very soon. Is that fucking well clear enough for you?”

“Yes, Tony, I’ll do my best.”

“I’m sure you will, Terence. We will have a drink soon.”

Terence had been a solicitor for years and had met all sorts of vicious killers and maniacs but nobody compared to Tony. As for having a drink soon, not if I can avoid it.

Terence tried the normal channels but no date had been decided yet. He also had a friend in the court offices who would give him the nod as soon as a date was set.

CHAPTER 31

The local Kingswood Church had been booked. The Honeymoon would be in the Seychelles, the reception would be at the famous RAC Golf club in Epsom, and stag and hen nights had been organised. Emma was the happiest woman in the world and the way money was being spent, Peter Miller would be the poorest. Paul offered to pay for everything but Peter insisted on doing his bit. Emma spent twenty thousand on her wedding dress and the bridesmaid's dresses. The reception for two hundred worked out at twenty five thousand including all the wine and champagne, cars, printing and presents and all the bits added another twenty. So, by the end of it all, with some extras, the cost was put at about seventy five thousand pounds. Peter Miller had no idea this was small change to Paul. The clubs were doing exceptionally well, especially the new lap dancing ones.

The only concern Paul had was his brother Tony, who now seemed to be living in a world of his own. His drinking was completely out of control; he was getting more and more violent and flew of the handle at the merest provocation. Paul decided he would have to have very strong words with him before the wedding. He was the best man and Paul didn't want him wrecking the wedding. Paul's joy was seeing Emma embrace the whole wedding thing passionately. She was still not too big with the baby, so wouldn't look too bad walking down the aisle. Paul was so looking forward to being a dad and he absolutely planned to be at the birth. Whenever he was thinking of the future, Tony was always the nagging worry at the back of his mind; he had to sort him out.

The recent birthday celebrations had been great, especially the time spent back at the spotlight club in the wet room. Since then, Lexi had visited with Emma twice in Chelsea Harbour and was now one of her best friends. Paul was at work when she first visited but by all accounts they had a wild sexy day. The second visit was in the evening when Paul was in. They had dinner and the rest of the night was spent making love and generally, having a really good time. Emma said that all the sexual fun would stop until after the birth. Paul totally agreed with that, but it didn't stop them having a good time, still.

Paul had never known Emma shop so much. Weddings seemed to require so much shopping, it was incredible. Emma and her mum went shopping nearly every day. Favourite location was the Westfield Shopping Centre in Shepherds Bush, West London. Paul tried to avoid it as much as possible, but got roped in on occasions. He hadn't been for some time but was now booked for the next Saturday morning at 11.00 am. He wasn't looking forward to it very much.

CHAPTER 32

"Paul, I need to see you urgently." Roddy sounded very worried.

"What's the problem?"

"Don't really want to talk on the phone. Can I come over?"

"Can't it wait till tonight at the club?"

"No, I prefer to see you as soon as possible."

"OK, come straight over, I'll get the coffee on."

Paul was at home having some quiet time with Emma. I wonder what Roddy wants. It must be something to do with money, he thought. The clubs are doing well so I wonder... oh well, we'll see when he gets here.

"Emma, Roddy's coming over."

"Oh, that's nice. I better get dressed then." Emma had recently taken to walking round the apartment naked. Paul didn't mind. It was easier to jump on her.

An hour later, there was a knock at the door.

"Roddy! How are you? Come in, it's bloody freezing out there!"

Emma shouted from the kitchen. "Hi Roddy, coffee!"

"Love some, thanks Emma!"

Paul was slightly concerned that Roddy had turned up with bad news, could be something to do with Tony, he thought.

"Come and sit down."

Emma brought in the coffee and sat down next to Paul. Roddy looked at Paul and then at Emma and back to Paul. Paul got the message.

“Darling, why don’t you go and powder something.”

Emma looks slightly agitated for a second and then smiled. “Who wants to hear all your boring work stuff, anyway,” and she strolled off to her bedroom to look at the new shoes she bought the day before.

“So, Roddy, what’s so important?”

“It’s a bit of a delicate subject...”

Paul interrupted, “Money always is, Roddy, carry on.”

“Look, I’ll come straight to the point. Ryder’s creaming a lot and I mean a lot of money from the three new clubs.”

“How much are we talking about?” Paul had become very serious. Nothing got to him more than people who were well paid, being greedy and dipping their hand in the till. Paul was expecting Roddy to say a few thousand and nearly fell off his seat with what he said next.

“Well, I know for a fact he got ten per cent of the refurbishment cost from Bensons so that was about one hundred and fifty thousand.”

Paul couldn’t believe his ears. “What! Are you sure? That fucking bastard! We give him a good job, he’s well paid, he’s shagging all the girls and now he’s stealing from us. How did you find out?”

“Gary Thompson in the office at Bensons got sacked and wanted to cause some trouble for them. He phoned me up and told me the whole story. Apparently, Ryder demanded the kick back or Bensons wouldn’t have got the job.”

“That fucker Ryder, wait till I get my hands on him.”

“Sorry Paul, that’s not all.”

“Go on then” said Paul impatiently.

“Aside from that, I think he’s taking a percentage from all the suppliers, maybe ten percent, plus cash from takings.”

“Jesus! How much a month is he taking? You’re a clever bloke, Roddy, your best guess.”

“It could easily be seventy five thousand a month.”

Paul stared at Roddy with disbelief. "He's going to regret this, believe me. Jesus! Does he have any idea what Tony will do when he finds out?" Paul did a quick calculation.

"Forget about the refurb money, he's taking nearly a million quid a year. Fucking hell! He'll pay for this!" Paul was so angry he stood up and walked round the room, cursing. He then picked up his phone from the coffee table and presses a fast dial.

"Tony, it's me. I'm at home with Roddy. Bad news. That bastard, Ryder, has been ripping us off."

Paul then held the phone away from his ear as Tony started shouting that Ryder was going to wish he had never been born.

"Seventy five grand a month, could be more," said Paul.

Roddy could hear Tony's screaming of obscenities from Paul's phone, from fully five feet away.

"Tony, listen! Tony! Pick Ryder up tonight. Bring him to the Den at about eight and we'll have a little chat with him."

"Thanks, Roddy."

"I'm sorry I didn't find out earlier Paul."

"Don't blame yourself. That Ryder is a snake, and the best thing to do with a snake is cut its fucking head off."

Roddy said he had a lot to do and left pretty sharpish. Emma came back into the room. She looked at Paul. "Trouble?"

"That shit Ryder's got his grubby little hands in the till!"

"He should have them fucking well cut off then," said Emma, with some menace.

Paul looked at Emma; he was surprised at her venom but knew anything that affected him affected her just as much; they were a real couple. Tony picked Ryder up, telling him they were having a celebration because of the success of the clubs. Ryder loved a party and had no idea of what exactly was happening. They got to the Den and suddenly Ryder found out why he was really there.

"You're just a fucking cunt, aren't you?" Tony was in a terrifying mood and was actually frothing at the mouth. Physically he was a frightening sight, tall muscular but the thing people really didn't like about him was his eyes, they were always shining as though he was permanently on something.

The man was tied to a chair while Tony walked around him. "Did you really think we would not find out? You didn't want to steal a few hundred quid, no, you stole hundreds of thousands! Are you fucking insane? We gave you a good, well paid job, you're shagging all the girls in the club, eat and drink what you want but that's still not enough!" Tony was incensed and pushed his face right up to his, just touching his nose. "Take my fucking money." He drew back and head-butted the man on the bridge of his nose, the two other men in the room heard the crunch of shattering bone and saw blood flying in all directions.

"Jesus!" shouted Tony, looking at his blood splattered suit. "Do you know how much this fucking cost?"

"What the fuck are we going to do with you, eh?" Tony was brushing the blood off his jacket, but was really making it worse. "You're just a complete fucking cunt." He turned to his two heavies and repeated again slowly, "What are we going to do with him?"

One of the heavies, Sid, did a hand motion across his neck, signifying he should have his throat cut. Tony turned back to the man who was shaking uncontrolledly, and to all intents and purposes, was completely out of it. He then managed to mumble something, "Go to fucking ... hell, Tony."

"That's where you're fucking going, you cunt!" shouted Tony. Tony was still stalking round him, thinking of what to do with him. He kept glancing at Sid and Steve for some sort of reassurance he was doing the right thing. Tony really wanted to kill him, cut him up into tiny pieces and make sausages out of him, but what would Paul say? Tony again pushed his face close to the man. "Paul will be here in a minute, and then we'll decide what we're going to do with you".

The battered head lifted as best he could. "Always doing what your brother tells you, can't do anything on your own, can you?" He sniggered and spat a mouthful of blood onto the floor. He laughed as he said, "Either Paul or Marie are always babysitting you; your pathetic, do you know that? Fucking pathetic."

Tony was getting more and more psychotic as he listened to the bastard drone on. Marie was Tony's wife and Tony did not like her being brought into the conversation. "You better shut your fucking mouth. I mean it, shut your fucking mouth!" Tony was screaming at Ryder; saliver was hitting his face, not that he could feel it, with his smashed nose causing so much pain.

Ryder stared hard at Tony and said in a jarring voice, "Nice lady, your Marie. I've been there Tony, very nice it was, a fucking great shag, mind, she's been with all your so called mates. She knows how to dish it out alright."

Tony was shaking his hands in the air and shouting. "Don't say another word, not one word, not one fucking word!"

Ryder just couldn't resist. "Your mother was a fucking whore. It seems to run in the family." That was it, Tony pulled his 357 magnum out of his trouser belt and smashed it over the man's head, knocking him unconscious.

"Shit! Tony! I hope he's not dead," said Sid as he walked towards the prone body lying on the floor, with blood forming a puddle around his head.

"Get the cunt back up!" Where the fuck was Paul? If he doesn't turn up soon, I'll deal with this myself, he thought viciously.

At last Paul arrived. He stuck his head in the door and looked at the blood splattered Ryder and then motioned for Tony to join him outside.

"What are we going to do with that wanker?" Paul looked angry and anxious.

Tony knew exactly what they should do with him. "We carve him up, drop him into the foundations of a new build and cover him with cement, easy."

"You do realise he's Richard Philip's cousin, he might not take kindly to us doing that."

"Who gives a shit what that fucking cunt thinks!" Tony was now losing control.

"Someone has to do the thinking round here and that's me," said Paul calmly.

What would Richard say, would he even find out? He may not even be bothered. Paul knew exactly what to do.

"Richard, its Paul Bolton, yea I'm fine, thanks. Look, bit of a problem."

"What's that Paul?"

"Your cousin Ryder has been robbing us blind, I'm talking big numbers here. If he wasn't your cousin, he'd be dead already. This is a courtesy call. What do you want us to do with him?"

There was silence. Richard was obviously thinking.

"I appreciate the call Paul, thank you, but you're obviously mistaken because I don't have any cousins. Have a nice day." The phone went dead.

Paul went into a separate office and quickly dialled a number. "It's me, some thing's come up. Listen, we are in......." The conversation went on for a couple of minutes. Paul pressed the red button and went back to see Tony.

"Tony, do whatever you want with him but get him out of the club as soon as possible."

Tony's eyes lit up and a huge grin spread across his face. "Oh lovely, I'll sort it, don't worry."

Tony went back into the office and shut the door. Paul went upstairs to see Roddy and find out how they could get their money back from a dead person. Tony then made a couple of calls and everything was set up.

They took Ryder to the Isle of Dogs. There were some building works at Millwall Park which would be perfect. Ryder had come round and kept asking where they were going. Tony, Duke and Sid just ignored him. They pulled into the building site and parked. Ryder didn't like this one bit, and he was scared to death at what they had in mind for him.

"Tony, I'm really sorry. I'll work for nothing, look anything you want I'll pay back all the money and give you every penny I've got."

"Shut the fuck up!" said Sid.

Ryder knew they were going to kill him. He thought of his family and started to sob. "Please Tony, please, I'm not all bad please, Tony."

Tony couldn't stand the noise "Shut your fucking mouth, you cunt!"

They heard the approach of a truck and all turned to look. It was a cement mixer lorry with the huge mixer on the back, turning.

Ryder went white and tried to get over Duke to open the door. Duke gave him a slap and Ryder fell back.

"Tony, this isn't fair, it was only money, please!" Ryder was now openly crying. "Please Tony, I'm only thirty five, please Tony!"

"It may have only been money, Ryder, but it was our fucking money and not yours!"

Tony looked at Sid. "Shut him up!"

Sid took a cudgel out of his coat pocket and hit Ryder over the head. He went limp and the noise stopped.

The cement truck backed up to the foundation works; the cement dispenser swung out over the deep hole with all the steel bars in it and started to pour cement. The hole filled up quickly and Tony told the driver to stop when it was half full. Sid and Duke then carried Ryder and threw him down the hole and onto the cement, making sure he landed face up. They all stood still at the side of the foundations, looking down and waiting.

It took ten minutes before Ryder began to come to. He opened his eyes and looked round. He saw and felt the cement. He tried to move but he was stuck. He looked back up and saw Tony. "Please Tony I've learnt my lesson. Help, help me, anyone, help!" Ryder was screaming.

Tony looked at him and said in a deceptively gentle tone, "Ryder quiet. It's alright. You didn't seriously think we would really go through with this, did you? We just wanted to scare you."

Ryder was sobbing. “Thanks, Tony. Get me out please. I’ll do anything, anything you say from now on.”

“You see, Ryder, we spoke to Richard,” said Tony, staring hard at Ryder.

They’ve scared me, yes, that’s all, thought Ryder. Richard saved me, thank God, and he took a deep breath and slightly relaxed. He looks up expecting to see them getting ready to help him out.

“Trouble was, Richard didn’t want you back,” said Tony slowly and he turned to the cement lorry driver and nodded. The cement started raining down. Ryder was screaming, the noise mixed with that of the cement mixer was ear splitting. Ryder knew he was being buried alive. The cement poured into the hole, gradually covering his body, with bits spilling into his mouth. Ryder frantically spat the cement out but it soon filled his mouth. The time came when the cement was too much; it flowed into Ryder’s mouth and down his throat. It was a hideous death and Duke and Sid made a mental note never to cross Tony.

They got back in the car and drove back into central London to the club.

Tony entered the club, went straight to the bar and had a very large whiskey. Paul joined him

“Hi Tony, all sorted?”

“Of course,” replied Tony as he flicked a small amount of cement off his expensive shoes.

Paul then thought it was good to have Tony around on occasions; his own days of inflicting severe violence on people were well and truly over.

CHAPTER 33

The problem with Ryder had been a distraction and now Tony was able to focus all his attention on the plan to get Bugsy free. Bringing Patrick in from Ireland had been a good idea; he brought with him expertise that Tony could not find locally. The plan was to attack the Serco prison van with a low velocity anti-tank shell; it had to hit the front cab from the side and not head on. Hopefully, only the front cab would be destroyed, giving them the opportunity to get Bugsy out unscathed.

The route the van would take had been assessed and it was felt the best place to attack would be at the roundabout, where the A206 Beresford Road moved into the A205 Grand Depot Road. They would base themselves at the New Wine Church, right on the corner. The beauty of the location was that it was two hundred yards from the river and escape.

It was an audacious plan and if it went wrong, Bugsy could go up with the entire van. It was costing Tony a fortune but he considered it money well spent if it kept him out of the clutches of the law. Patrick had also recommended using the River Thames as the means of escape. Again, this would never have been considered by local organisers. A Searib fully inflatable speed boat was purchased; it was ideal for the purpose. It was used by Special Forces throughout the world so came highly recommended. The plan was simple: hit the prison van, down to the river by car, into a boat waiting by the Ferry terminal across the river into another waiting car and off. If it all went to plan they would be on the other side of the river in ten minutes. There were six in the team, three attacking the prison van, one driver to take the team to the river, one with the boat and one on the other side of the river with the final getaway car. There was a lot that could go wrong but sometimes the most simple of plans can be the best.

Tony was not getting involved. He was leaving it to Patrick and Tom who made a good tight team. Patrick would fire the Bazooka shell at the prison van, Tom and another guy, Barry, would rush the van and release Bugsy. The three of them would then get in a running car and be driven at speed down to the river. Once there, they would jump in the boat and speed across the river. The last leg would be to meet the final car driven by John, on the other side and then make for the safe house in Dagenham, where Jan and Chris were. It would all happen very quickly. If it didn't, it would fail. The final piece of the jigsaw was to find out when Bugsy was leaving Belmarsh.

"Terence, it's me. Have you got any news yet, for Christ's sake?"

"No, but I hope to have later today. I'll call you back at 2.30 p.m."

"Make sure you do."

Good, thought Tony, we should soon have the vital last thing, the day and time.

Terrence had been in to see Bugsy and told him the plan. He seemed pleased and thought it could work. Terrence thought it sounded like a bloody James Bond film and was delighted he wasn't going to be involved. For security reasons, solicitors were informed of court appearances for prisoners from HM Prison Belmarsh only the day before. He was sure the case would be coming up tomorrow, so he should hear very soon. He couldn't wait for the end of the Bugsy situation, he wanted to forget about Tony and move on without any more contact with the criminal element, other than as their legal representation.

"Tony, it's me. Tomorrow, he will leave his current location at 11.00 am"

Tony immediately called Tom and Patrick with the news.

"Well, Tom, are you ready to go?" said Patrick.

"I'm very ready, Bugsy is a personal friend of mine so I'll move heaven and earth to get him out."

"Good. Look Tom, I've been doing all this shit for years, it's all about overwhelming force used quickly. As well as the bazooka, we're using

Uzi machine guns. They're not for show. Anybody gets in the way, we blast them, you understand?"

"I understand, don't worry about me."

"OK, try, and get some sleep tonight and I'll see you in the morning."

The next morning was fresh and a bit chilly. The crew checked in and everybody was on point at ten thirty. Patrick, Tom, Barry and Ted were parked up at the side of the New Wine Church in Woolwich. Ted, the driver, stayed with the car, ready to run them the two hundred yards down to the river. The speedboat was just up the river and would arrive at the prearranged spot at five minutes past eleven. John was sitting in his Mini clubman on Pier Road, on the North side of the river, waiting. Everybody was waiting.

Bugsy was on the move in Belmarsh. He was being taken to the exit door that led to the yard where prisoners were put on vans to go to court. There were two prisoners other than Bugsy going to court. Bugsy hoped they survive the attack. They settled in the van; Bugsy sat right at the back, as far away as possible from the front cab. There was a driver and a guard in the front, the van back doors were security locked. The van pulled away and Bugsy checked his watch, it was exactly eleven o clock. The van moved out of the prison and turned left onto Weston Way.

Bugsy was nervous, very nervous. He pushed himself against the back door and covered his face with his hands, waiting for the explosion. The other prisoners looked at him and wondered what the hell was wrong with him. Bugsy remembered them and turned round. "Get against the back door and pray." They looked at him blankly but then they jumped up and threw themselves against the back door, covering their faces.

The van continued and was nearing the roundabout.

Patrick was ducked down by the side of the car against the wall with the Bazooka held over his shoulder. Tom and Steve were ready on the other side, machine guns in hands.

The seconds ticked away. Then they saw the van pull onto the roundabout. Five seconds, four seconds three, two, one. Suddenly, Tom heard a loud *whoosh* and Patrick fired the Bazooka. It entered the side of the cab in the middle of the driver's door, where it exploded into a massive fireball and the van ground to a shuddering halt. The driver had disappeared. The other guard was almost naked; his clothes had been burnt off his body and he had burnt marks on most part of his body. Tom and Steve ran to the van.

Bugsy knew it was going to happen any second; he was waiting, and then it came, a massive explosion. The tremendous force threw him against the door. The heat was incredible. He felt like his skin was on fire. He touched his hair to check it was not in flames. He lay still and then heard shouting.

Tom and Steve were calling his name. “Bugsy! Get out! Bugsy!”

The near naked guard was wandering close to them. Tom lifted the Uzi and shot him in the chest, almost cutting him in half. He was hit by so many bullets.

“Bugsy!" Tom was still calling his name and he knew he must move if he wanted to escape. He stumbled over the wreckage. He had been blinded by the smoke and began to shout too.

“I’m here! Tom help me! I’m here!” He stumbled out into the fresh air and felt a pair of hands grab him.

“Barry, he’s here! Help me!” Steve grabbed Bugsy’s other arm and they dragged him over to the waiting car. Patrick had the door open and they piled in. Ted already had the engine running. As soon as the door was shut, the car gunned down towards the river. Within a few seconds, they screeched to a halt. The doors opened and they rushed to the pickup point. They felt the water on their feet and looked round.

“Where’s the fucking boat?” asked Patrick frantically. Tom ran two steps to the right, desperately looking for the boat. It was not there. He turned and looked the other way, no fucking boat.

“Patrick! Get back in the car!" said Barry. I can here sirens!"

Patrick heard the police sirens. Shit! Now, we’re in big trouble. He said loudly, “Wait, Tom. Remember what I said!”

Police cars were appearing and officers were shouting, sirens were blaring. Suddenly, shots rang out. Tom threw Bugsy to the floor and started shooting. Patrick, Barry and Ted were firing at the police who were now returning fire, bullets were hitting the car from all directions. It was absolute chaos.

Tom looked back at the river and saw the boat coming in at high speed. "Patrick, the boats here!"

Patrick looked round. "Take Bugsy down. We'll cover you!"

The boat pulled up and turned round. Tom dragged Bugsy to the boat and threw him in. He turned to see Ted take a bullet in the chest. Shit! We've got seconds to get away.

"Patrick! Barry! Let's go!" They both turned and ran for the boat. Bullets were flying everywhere. It would be a miracle if they got away. They reached the boat and Patrick jumped in. Barry fell in as a bullet hit him square in the back of the head. The boat pulled away clear of the shore.

Tom couldn't believe they were safe. "Bugsy, we're safe!" he looked at Bugsy. Jesus he looks like shit but he's alive, that's the main thing.

Tom shouted at the boat driver. "What the fuck happened?"

"Got stopped by the fucking River Police, asking me what I was doing. Fucking imagine that! Today of all days."

The boat sped across the river and quickly landed on the North Woolwich shore where John was waiting.

"Tom! Over here! Hurry!" he shouted, waving his arms. Tom and Patrick helped Bugsy up the bank and got in the car. John put his foot down. They flew down Pier road, got to the junction and turned left into Albert road. They wanted to get as far away from the pier as possible before the law turned up. They all heard the sirens. John had driven the route before and swerved into Drew road heading towards City Airport. He then pulled up behind a lock up and waited. Suddenly two police cars tore past the end of the road, heading towards the pier.

John laughed and pulled back out onto the main road. He turned to the others. "Don't worry, we're going to make it." He slowed down and headed towards the safe house in Dagenham. It would take about forty minutes.

Patrick called Tony. "It's me. All sweet, two didn't make it."

Tony needed to know. "Who"

"Ted and Barry."

Tony was relieved it was not Tom or Bugsy. "Speak soon." and clicked off.

They soon arrive at the safe house in Acre Road. The house backed onto Old Dagenham Park. John drove round the back where they could not been seen. Tom and Patrick carried Bugsy through the back door into the house.

"Where's Jan?" Tom asked one of the guards.

"Upstairs."

"Get her down here."

The guard called her name.

Jan came half way down the stairs and then saw Bugsy. She started to cry but quickly pulled herself together. "Get him up here into one of the bedrooms, quickly!"

They lay Bugsy on a bed. "Tom, you help me everybody else out," said Jan, taking charge.

They stripped the tattered remains of clothes off Bugsy and then looked for wounds.

"I think he's alright," said Tom.

"I can't see anything serious," said Jan. "I'm going to wash him and then I think the best thing is to let him sleep."

Bugsy stirred and looked up. "Where am I?" he spluttered feebly.

"Bugsy, its Jan. You're safe." Jan caressed the side of Bugsy's face.

"Thank God," said Bugsy as a single tear rolled down his cheek. Jan gave him a thorough wash and put him in fresh clothes and then tucked him up in bed. He was fast asleep in seconds.

CHAPTER 34

Jeff got into Rotherhithe Nick even earlier than usual. He was desperate to see Karen. The operation in Malaga had gone to shit; two dead bodies identified as Jim Telfer and Robin Scott, and by all accounts they had met a particularly nasty end, cut to pieces by very sharp knives or machetes and then eaten by wild dogs. Karen had taken it hard. Falcon one was back in the UK, seemingly untouched. They had picked him up at Heathrow and surveillance was back in operation.

Eventually, Karen turned up. Jeff got her a coffee and they sat down in the CID Room.

“Some you win, some you lose Karen, its history. We move on,” said Jeff, consolingly.

“Yea, I know. I’m even more determined than ever to get that bastard Philips. I know he was up to something in Malaga."

Richard Philips had returned from Malaga, assuming that Coyne had been taken care of, and that Telfer and Scott were in Madrid or somewhere, drinking themselves into oblivion. He told Jack everything was taken care of and decided to have a couple of days rest to get over the trip.

“So Jeff, what’s happening with the Arrow Logistics case?” Before another word could be spoken, Michael pushed the door hard and entered the office.

“Just heard the Prison van taking Bugsy Cooper to court was attacked. He got away.”

“Fucking hell!” said Jeff.

“Yea, that’s what I thought,” said Michael.

“Any casualties?” asked Karen.

“The driver and a guard on the van both killed. There was a firefight at the roundabout near the ferry terminal, two officers received gunshot wounds. The hoodlums used a fucking Bazooka and machine guns.”

“Those bastards are ruthless!” exclaimed Karen.

“Jeff, this is between us three. I don’t give a shit what you do, or how you do it. I want those cunts brought to justice.”

Both Jeff and Karen were mildly shocked they had never heard Michael use the C word before.

Jeff and Karen spent an hour going over all the evidence from the robbery at Arrow Logistics and the killing at Tower Bridge Road. There was so much information, it was difficult to see the wood for the trees. Jeff decided to take everything back to basics and take a fresh look to try and pick out the relevant information.

“Karen, let’s look at the simple things we have, I’ll talk, you listen.”

"Firstly, let’s split the two of them. Coombs lived like a monk, so we concentrate on Philips who we know has committed crimes in the past and almost certainly, is still doing so now. We know Philips and Combs are major criminals and are involved in Brothels, pub security, drugs and probably a few other smaller areas we don't know about. We can’t touch them for the pub security business, although I’m one hundred per cent sure, it’s not; it would appear to be all above board. So that leaves us with the brothels and drugs. Drugs, we just don’t know about at all, so it’s prostitution and Brothels; that’s where we have to nail him." He looked at Karen “Is there anything we can get from the Malaga trip?”

“I wish.” Karen looked well pissed off. “He was in the hotel eating dinner and enjoying two bottles of red wine when Telfer and Scott were killed.”

“So, who did kill Telfer and Scott, and why?” asked Jeff.

“Telfer and Scott visited a hotel, the Marconfort Beach Club, and did a recce. We think they recognised someone there and then left. So, let’s assume for a minute that they were looking for a mark and found him.”

“OK, that makes sense," said Jeff thoughtfully. "Philips had a meeting with Telfer and Scott at the Mayflower Pub in Rotherhithe Street just before going out to Malaga. So to all intents and purposes, they were a team."

There was a long pause as they both did some thinking.

"So, think about this," said Jeff. "The three of them go out to hit someone who was staying at the Marconfort Hotel. For whatever reason, Falcon One drops out of the hit, leaving it to Telfer and Scott. They fuck it up and got killed. Falcon comes back here and carries on as normal. So who was the man staying at the Marconfort Hotel, and is he still alive? What happened to the list of foreigners staying at the Marconfort?"

"Well, we had one, and the other was sent back to you," said Karen.

"OK, let's go back over the list. If Falcon was looking to get rid of someone, it could have well been a competitor. So, someone with a business that he and Jack wanted; something similar that could slot in without too much trouble."

"Jeff, let's do that. I've just got a feeling it could lead somewhere, especially as the passport copies show photos as well."

Jeff and Karen checked through the list but could not see anybody they knew. They then asked every local police officer in Rotherhithe to drop into the office and look at the passport copies, to see if they could identify anyone in the photo. Most of the officers came in; none could identify any of the criminals. Jim, the longest serving officer at Rotherhithe, then popped in.

"I hear you CID people are looking for help, as usual," he said.

"Hi Jim, just look through this list of people and see if you know any of them."

Jim sat down and Karen gave him a pile of passport copies.

"Well, that's a good start. I know the first one, Bruce Coyne. He was arrested, gosh, about four years ago for GBH, happened in Stratford. I remember it well."

"What's he doing now Jim, do you know?"

“Everybody knows what Bruce does. He manages the doors on about forty odd local pubs.”

“Fucking bingo! Philips and Coombs have a big pub security business. We need to speak to this man as soon as possible. Karen, put him through the system, let’s get an address.”

Karen put Bruce Coyne into the police national database and it gave an address: 34 Collett Road, Bermondsey.

“Let’s go Karen,” said Jeff as he grabbed his coat and made for the door. “I think Collett Road’s at the back of Bermondsey station.”

They were soon zooming down Lower road and then left into Jamaica road. Five minutes later, they were in Collett Road.

“34,” said Karen, scanning the numbered houses.

Jeff slowed down and then parked outside number 30. They both jumped out of the car and headed towards number 34. They walked up the path and ring the doorbell. It all seemed very quiet. Jeff rang the bell again.

“Stop ringing the bell, for Christ’s sake!” The door opened to reveal a middle aged well-dressed, burly looking man.

Jeff looked at him closely. “Mr Bruce Coyne?”

“I’m guessing, but you two look like coppers, am I right?”

“You're right Mr Coyne. Can we come in please?”

“What do you want?”

“We'd like to have a chat with you about your recent trip to Malaga, in Spain.”

Fuck, thought Coyne. How the hell have they connected me to Malaga and Spain?

“Well, I have just come back from Malaga but why on earth would you be interested in my holiday?”

Karen was looking closely at Coyne. He’s hiding something I’m sure of it, she thought.

“We believe you may be able to help us with our enquiries into two murders that took place in Malaga last week," said Jeff. "Look, we can do this here or down at the station your choice.”

“Please come in, I’ve nothing to hide.” He opened the door wider.

Jeff nearly laughed. In all the phycology classes at Hendon, they taught you that when someone said they had nothing to hide, you could bet your last dollar they were hiding something.

“Thank you, Mr Coyne.”

They walked into the house and Coyne led them into the lounge “Would you like a cup of tea?”

“No, thanks.” said Jeff. “Let’s get straight to it.”

“Fine by me,” said Coyne.

“So, how was your trip, Mr Coyne?”

“Lovely. I had a very nice few days, thank you, and your names?”

“Sorry, I’m DC Jeff Collins and my colleague, DC Karen Foster, CID Rotherhithe.”

“So, your break in Malaga?”

“I had a great time Jeff, what else can I say?”

Remembering what Michael had said about not caring how he got Collins, Jeff decided to try something totally outrageous.

“Bruce, this may come as a surprise to you but I can tell you every single thing you did in Malaga, from what you had for lunch every day at the Marconfort Beach Club Hotel, to shagging Consuela every night for an hour at ten pm, and to the fight with Telfer and Scott in the desert using a machete. You may be surprised to hear that certain aspects of this case fall into, what we shall call it, “National Security.”

Coyne looked shocked. He now knew that he had been followed all the time he was in Malaga.

“From what you say, Jeff, it would seem I need to call a lawyer?”

“I wouldn’t be too hasty Mr Coyne, as I said there are matters of National Security to take into consideration here”

"So, what are you proposing Jeff? I don't understand?"

"Bruce, I'm going out on a limb here. There's only one thing I am interested in and that is locking that bastard Richard Philips up and throwing away the key. Can you help me do that?"

Coyne looked thoughtful for a minute. "Well that's interesting because it would now appear we have something in common, and yes, if we are clever, we could put that snake Richard Philips away for a very long time."

Jeff and Bruce smiled at each other. Karen's not sure but joined in the new feeling of bonhomie radiating from the two men.

"Jeff, I don't know how to say this, but in working with you to ensure Mr Richard Philips gets his due desserts, I could open myself up to, shall we say, certain criminal charges."

"Look Bruce, you and I can go somewhere of your choice; we can stay here if you like. You can check me for wires and then we talk, you and me, and in that circumstance, you can say anything to me, it is not admissible evidence in any prosecution that I or anyone else brings against you, you are safe."

Karen took her leave to make coffee in the kitchen.

"So, I agree then, firstly Richard Philips, Jim Telfer and Robin Scott came out to Malaga while I was there with one intention in mind, and that was to kill me. Philips and Coombs had made me an offer for my business which I had turned down and that was why."

"Well, well, that's pretty much what I thought. Now, let's get down to the real nitty gritty."

Jeff and Bruce spoke for three hours. At the end they shook hands; the deal was done.

CHAPTER 35

The wedding was not long away and the excitement for the big day was building. Emma had got the seamstress to alter the wedding dress a little, just to hide the tiny bump that was now appearing. Emma's family were more than excited, especially Fifi, who was positively bursting with pride and gratitude at being asked to be chief bridesmaid. Peter Miller was looking forward to walking down the aisle and giving his daughter away. Emma's mum had even neglected her flower arranging classes to get the wedding organised, which was unheard of. It was truly probably the best time that the Miller family had ever known. Paul had been welcomed into the fold and Emma's parents now looked upon him as another son.

Nothing in life had prepared Paul for the closeness that came from the Miller family but he loved the feeling of it. As usual, Paul's only problem in life was his brother. Tony had now been banned from the Miller residence as well as Paul's apartment, something to do with the fact that he nearly beat Ian Miller up for suggesting Millwall were a rubbish team. Paul was looking forward to the wedding except the part where Tony had to give his best man's speech. In fact, Paul had been giving serious thought to changing his best man, but that was more difficult than imaginable.

Shopping trips followed shopping trips, which were usually followed by even more shopping trips. Paul had avoided most of them but had been roped in to the next Saturday trip to Westgate, in Shepherds Bush, the favoured destination.

Artan Papadikis was becoming more and more frustrated, nothing was happening and the flushing out of the robbery gang had ground to a standstill. He was even more upset to hear that the man caught at the robbery had escaped from custody. He also knew that Adnan and

Bashkim were getting very fed up sitting around the house doing nothing all the time. Artan's wife Eleni was also fed up cooking and washing clothes for the two visitors who it seemed were never going to leave. There was no answer other than to continue to pray that someone came forward to claim the rewards which now totalled one hundred and seventy five thousand pounds, a huge amount of money. Artan still visited his company every day but his heart was no longer really in it. He left most of the decision making to the other directors and was quite happy for them to get on with it. Artan was tired and as soon as this was over, he decided he would take a very long holiday with Eleni. Maybe a Caribbean, or even a world cruise would be a very welcome change.

Bugsy was recovering at the safe house in Dagenham. Jan had nursed him and there were no long term injuries to contend with, or at least none that anyone could see. Bugsy was a broken man. The thought of life imprisonment, the stint back in Belmarsh and the explosion when the rocket hit the prison van, had shaken him beyond belief. There was also the question of getting his children back from Social Services, which Jan would have to sort at some point. There had been too many killings and with Tony around, that was unlikely to stop. Bugsy was still terrified that Tony would have him killed and had retreated into himself, almost to the point where he didn't speak at all. He had also started nodding his head all the time, which was certainly a worry. Jan felt a long holiday in the sunshine would sort him out and was planning a trip to Spain. She didn't know that the plan had been for Bugsy and the family to relocate to Spain full time. Tom popped in occasionally to see Bugsy and was shocked to see his friend in such a mental state. Patrick had gone back to Ireland. He had told Tom he would be very welcome to visit him any time he liked, but Tom had no plans to rush over. Bugsy had told Tom that he was scared Tony would want to get rid of him permanently, but Tom told Bugsy to relax and that it was never going to happen. It wasn't long before Tom found out how completely insane Tony Bolton really was.

"Tom, how are you?"

"Fine, thanks Tony, and you?"

"You never need to worry about me Tom, I'm always well. Tom, we have a problem we need to sort out, well, actually, two problems to be precise."

Warning bells were ringing in Tom's head, I don't like the sound of this, he thought.

"What problems are those, Tony?"

"Bugsy and Bradley of course, Tom, two problems that have to be sorted, and sorted soon."

Tom was shocked. Tony now wanted to kill Bugsy and Bradley, who Tom knew was a solicitor who did some work for him.

"Are you there Tom?"

"I'm here, Tony."

"Look, Tom, don't go all fucking pansy on me. Bugsy and Bradley can put both of us inside for life. They need to be taken care of, do you fucking well understand Tom?"

The pressure from Tony when you speak with him was colossal. He seemed to get into your head until you have to agree and do what he said.

"I understand, Tony."

"Good. Get a plan together and then we'll talk, and Tom, I want it done soon, yea."

Tom heard the phone click off. He had to sit down. He knew that he couldn't do it anymore. God, please, no more killing, no more blood and gore. Then something else hit him like a hammer. Of course, he thought, as soon as Bugsy and Bradley are taken care of, it would be my turn. Jesus! What to do?

The next day, news broke that a body had been found buried at an old Iron works in North London. The male had been identified as Philip Evans, an unemployed builder from Bermondsey. He had been tortured and murdered. Tom was mortified and aghast. So many thoughts were whiling in his mind. Phil tortured! What the fuck is going on? Surely, not Tony again. I'm not telling Bugsy!

Tom thought long and hard and finally picked up the phone he dialled a number.

Jeff was at Rotherhithe nick when the call came in. The reason it interested him was because Mr Evans lived in Bermondsey. It was too much of a coincidence that bodies were turning up all over the place and each one had connection with the Bermondsey area. Had he been involved in the Arrow Logistics robbery? If so, how the hell did he end up in North London, in a very mutilated state? The post mortem revealed a catalogue of injuries, some of them beyond belief. There was also a mention that the torture used was characteristic of methods used by Greeks and Albanians. This was a most interesting development as the owner of Arrow Logistics was Greek. Jeff decided to pay a visit to Artan Papadikis and see if he could gather any further information.

Karen had called Arrow Logistics and been informed that Mr Papadikis was at home that day. Jeff decided that an unannounced call was in order. Jeff and Karen took an unmarked car and switched on the siren. It cut the travelling time in half and they were soon in North London. Jeff loved the Papadikis house, a big, old rambling mansion with extensive grounds. They rang the doorbell and a maid opened the door for them.

“Hello, we are police officers. We're here to see Mr Papadikis.”

“Please wait a moment while I check to see if he is in.”

Jeff thought she had been well trained. Artan Papadikis then came into view.

“Come in, come in, hello officers. To what do I owe this pleasure?”

“Perhaps we could sit somewhere. There have been developments in the case and I would like to discuss these with you.”

“Of course, please come into the lounge where we will be comfortable. Tea or coffee?”

“Coffee would be great for both of us, thanks.” Artan shouted for Eleni to make some coffee.

“So, what are these developments please?”

“A body was found recently, about five miles from here, a Mr Philip Evans. He had been tortured and murdered.”

Jeff paused and waited. He continued. “I believe he may have had some involvement in the robbery at your company.”

“I’m deeply shocked. I don’t know what to say.” Artan was really shocked, he never thought the body would appear so quickly. Suddenly, Artan heard voices and the door opened. Adnan and Bashkim walked into the lounge. They saw Jeff and Karen and stopped talking immediately.

“I’m sorry, we didn’t mean to disturb you,” said Adnan and turned around to leave. Jeff saw in front of him two vicious looking men who might well be capable of the Evans murder. He jumped up from his chair and went towards Adnan.

He stuck his hand out. “Hello, I’m Jeff and my colleague is Karen.” Adnan shook hands, Jeff then shook hands with Bashkim. “And who do I have the pleasure of addressing?” asked Jeff. Adnan could see Artan out of the corner of his eye telling him through his eyes to be careful.

“I am Arber and this is Behar.”

“So, you are here on holiday, visiting with Mr Papadikis?” Jeff wanted to know more.

“That’s right,” said Adnan looking at Artan.

“They are my relations here for a few days” said Artan. He looked at Adnan and Bashkim “These are police officers from the world famous Scotland Yard. They have come to give me an update on the robbery.”

Before Artan could say another word, Karen asked Adnan, “And what do you two gentlemen do back in Albania?”

“We own a supermarket.”

“Really. That’s very interesting.” Karen and Jeff knew they were lying; they knew Karen and Jeff knew they were lying.

“We must leave you to it. Good to meet you.” Adnan and Bashkim left the lounge.

“So, how did Arber get that scar it looks terrible?” Jeff was suspicious of the nasty scar on Adan’s face.

“Yes, a terrible accident many years ago.”

Jeff was absolutely sure that Artan and his two associates were mixed up in the killing of Evans. Maybe it had something to do with the culture, that they needed to exact revenge for the killing of his brother, Timius. Jeff decided to send a message to Mr Papadikis.

“Mr Papadikis, is there anything you can tell us about the death of Mr Evans at the Iron works?”

Artan put on a show. “How can you ask me that? I have no idea what you are talking about.”

“Mr Papadikis, I just want you to understand that in this country, the police do the investigating of crimes. If it was to be found that you or your colleagues are involved in anything that you shouldn’t be, you will be held to account by the law, is that clear?”

“It is very clear officer, but I can assure you that we are not involved in err.., how you said it, anything we shouldn’t be, and yes, that's it.”

“Good, we will take our leave then. Thank you for your assistance.”

“Guilty as hell," said Karen, as soon as they were back in the car. "That guy with the scar sent a shiver down my spine. I wouldn’t want to meet him on a dark night.”

“I agree, they're up to mischief and I strongly believe those three are responsible for the torture and killing of Philip Evans.”

“So what do we do next?”

“Bloody good question Karen, what do we do next?”

Artan Papadikis was still getting over the visit from the two police officers. His phone rang, he did not recognise the number. “Yes, Hello.”

“Doesn’t matter who I am. Listen, I am going to give you the name of the shooter in the armed robbery at your company, but first I want the money. I’ll text you the account details and as soon as payment is made, you’ll get the name."

“I’m delighted to hear from you, but how do I know you are genuine and will not run off with the money?”

“Trust me, you dealing with this bastard will make me very happy”

Artan listened to the voice closely. He detected real hate. He had to take the risk. "OK, send me the details."

Five minutes later, Artan received a text message with the account details, a bank in Guernsey.

Artan phoned his contact at the Greek Bank and it was done, one hundred thousand pounds was wired to Guernsey.

Artan was sitting on the sofa in his lounge, Adnan and Bashkim were sitting opposite him.

The mobile started to vibrate, indicating a text message.

Artan's hand was shaking as he pressed the icon and then pressed for the message. It read: Tony Bolton, Bermondsey.

Artan looked up at Adnan and Bashkim. "Soon you will be able to go home, my friends."

The first thing Artan had to do was to find out who this Tony Bolton was. They were always taught in Special Forces: if you are able to, know your enemy as much as possible.

Adnan and Bashkim were over the moon. Take care of one more stupid English man and they could go home to their beloved Albania.

They found Tony Bolton through a Greek friend at the post office. He lived in the expensive end of Grange road, Bermondsey. The first thing they did was drive down to Bermondsey and drive past the property. It was a relatively new property, detached, with probably four or five bedrooms, double fronted, so it was a sizable plot. At first glance, it didn't seem to have any burglar alarms. They stopped the car further down the road; they assumed that Tony Bolton would be at work so Adnan walked back up the road to walk past the house and get a better view. Adnan was walking slowly and was nearly at the house. He suddenly heard a car and a huge Jaguar pulled up right in front of the house. Artan was watching all this in the rear view mirror of the car. Three big men got out of the car and started looking around, then the front door opened and a man came out. He too was big and muscular and looked like he could handle himself. The man walked towards the car and almost bumped into Adnan. They looked at each other for half a second and Tony clocked the scar. One of Tony's guards gave Adnan a push to get him out of the way. Adnan walked on. The car then roared off up the road.

Five seconds later, Artan stopped right next to Adnan. "Quick get in! We've got to see where they are going!"

Artan drove very carefully some distance behind the Jaguar, Adnan spoke.

"This man is dangerous," said Adnan. "Believe, me I have seen his eyes. He also has bodyguards, who I am sure are armed. This will not be as easy as the last one, we must be very careful."

Artan almost lost them on numerous occasions but soon the Jaguar was slowing down outside a club in Soho. The bodyguards got out and checked the front of the club, then one of them nodded at Tony who was sitting in the back. He got out and walked between two of the guards into the club.

Artan drove past the entrance noticing the name, "The Den." He turned to Adnan and Bashkim. "What animals live in a Den?" Adnan spoke first

"Lions," said Adnan.

"And Wolves," added Baskim. All three went quiet. Adnan and Bashkim just looked at each other as though to say, we better be very careful with this man.

"Hello Tony, how's things?"

"Yea, alright thanks, Paul."

Paul could not for the life of him understand why Tony now insisted on going everywhere with three or four bodyguards. He never used to be like this. Mind you, Tony is now on a different planet, most of the time.

Tony went to the bar and had a large whiskey.

"That stuff will kill you," warned Paul.

Tony just looked at him and then disappeared to the back of the club, followed by his team of bodyguards.

Artan, Adnan and Bashkim returned to North London and settled down in the house for a crisis talk.

“So, Adnan, how are we going to take this man?” asked Artan.

“Very carefully,” said Adnan, looking at Artan with concern.

“You have dealt with all sorts, Adnan but you look worried, why?”

“I have a bad feeling about this man that he is not all human.”

“What! Are you going crazy?”

“I’m telling you what I see, Artan.”

Artan turned to Bashkim and opened his hands. “Bashkim, do you have any idea what Adnan is talking about?”

“Yes, we must be more than careful. This man has the senses of an animal. He can smell and see danger coming long before it gets close to him.”

Artan was now getting worried. He shook his head. “Bloody hell! I’m not going to believe all this mumbo jumbo! He’s a man! We will kill him!”

“Bashkim, I want you to go back to the Soho club tonight and see what time Bolton leaves. Follow him home and see who stays overnight at the house. Do not take any risks, is that clear? Just observation.”

“OK, just observation”

Artan spent the afternoon on calls to his office. Adnan and Bashkim sharpened knives and cleaned the Uzi machine guns.

They had an early dinner and Bashkim departed for Soho.

Adnan had an uneasy feeling. He couldn't put his finger on it but there was something telling him to take every precaution. He wished he had gone with Bashkim.

Bashkim got to the Den and waited out of view.

It was a very long night. The Bolton man finally left the club at two o clock in the morning. He had three bodyguards with him and headed towards Bermondsey.

“Roddy, have you seen Tony?” asked Paul.

“You just missed him literally, one minute ago."

"Shit! I told him I wanted him to sign some documents for tomorrow."

Paul looked around. "Daniel, can you do me a big favour?"

"Sure, what is it?"

"Take one of the pool cars and shoot after Tony with these." Paul gave Daniel a folder of papers. "Get him to sign them and then bring them back. Get a move on, he's just left."

"I'm already gone."

Daniel knew he would soon catch Tony because he didn't like being driven too fast, unlike Daniel, who put his foot to the floor.

Daniel roared down Shaftesbury Avenue and into Charing Cross Road. He was glancing around and saw Tony's Jag pulling away from a Kentucky. Daniel laughed; Tony and his Kentucky Fried Chicken. Daniel slowed down and noticed a silver Mercedes pull out from a parking spot a little short distance behind Tony. Daniel was not sure but there was something funny about that car. He slowed down even more and watched the Mercedes. He seemed to be tailing Tony. Perhaps, it's more back up, he thought. Nah, let's see what happens. Daniel finally decided that the Mercedes was definitely following Tony. He got on his mobile.

"Tony, its Daniel from the club."

"Yes Daniel, what can I do for you?" Tony was relaxed for a change.

"Well, Tony you forgot to sign some documents at the club for Paul, he knew you wouldn't want to come back so he sent me after you."

"So, you are behind me and have the documents with you?"

"That's correct, Tony"

"Well, in that case we'll stop. I'll sign them and then you can bugger off."

Daniel got in quick before Tony asked the driver to stop. "No, Tony don't stop!"

"Don't fucking tell me what to do?" Daniel interrupted him.

“Sorry Tony. Listen carefully. I was chasing to catch you up and noticed something.”

Tony was now very alert. “What’s happening Daniel?”

“There is a car following you, it’s a silver Mercedes registration NTO5AVD”

Tony was now fully alert and thinking fast. Who the fuck is following me and what do they want? He sat up, alert. “Weapons out but keep them hidden." The bodyguards took out hand pistols. One of them opened a secret compartment behind the back seat and took out two machine guns.

“Sid, drive perfectly normally back to my house,” he said to the driver. He then turned to Ian who was sitting in the front passenger seat. “Ian, watch the silver Mercedes NTO5. Don’t let it out of your sight, he’s following us. If he comes up fast, warn Sid, and Sid, you take fucking evasive action.”

If this bastard was going to hit us, he would have done it by now, thought Tony. So he wants to see where I’m going and who I'm with; he’s just on surveillance. “Listen up, everybody, this is what we’re going to do.”

Bashkim was alert, as they were now heading down the New Kent Road, very close to Grange road. He concentrated and watched the Jaguar closely. The Jaguar moved down Grange road and then stopped outside the house. Bolton got out of the car with one of the bodyguards and entered the house. The Jaguar roared off up the road. Bashkim turned and parked in a side road but still with a view of the front of the house. Lights came on in the house. Much later, all the downstairs lights went off and the upstairs ones come on. Bashkim watched until the upstairs lights went off. Everybody was apparently now in bed, asleep, he thought. He looked at his watch; it was now three a.m. Jesus! I’m tired, time to go.

Bashkim pulled back out into Grange Road and headed back into central London. What he didn't see was the two cars that were following him.

As soon as Tony got in the house, he went straight out the back door and started walking towards Abbey Street, round the corner. There, he met the Jaguar crew and Daniel. They moved the cars so they could just see the Mercedes. Tony wanted to know who this man was, and who he was working for; then he would teach them a lesson none of them would ever forget.

Artan and Adnan were having a whisky in the lounge. The mobile rang. "Hello Bashkim everything alright?"

"Yea, fine I'll be back in thirty minutes."

"We'll have a whiskey waiting for you."

"Sounds good. See you in a minute."

Adnan was relieved Bashkim was on his way back and all was well.

Bashkim was getting closer and closer and eventually pulled into the driveway. He got out of the car and headed towards the front door. It opened and Adnan welcomed him back "Mire se vini mbrapa ju Mire" (Welcome back. Are you alright?)

"Fine, but a bit tired. Whiskey sounds good." Adnan put his arm round Bashkim's shoulder and they went into the house. The house was not full; the kids were away, Eleni was in bed, Artan was in the lounge where they joined him.

Tony and his crew were parked round the corner, a one minute's walk from the house. Daniel stayed with the cars while Tony, Ian and Sid walked quietly to the house. They were at the side and could see the three men in the lounge, drinking and laughing. They won't be laughing in a minute, thought Tony. Tony was leading and they made their way to the back of the property. Tony tried the backdoor handle. Unbelievably, it turned and the door opened. He was totally focussed and turned to the other two and put his finger to his lips. They moved into the kitchen and could now clearly hear the men laughing. They moved along a corridor and saw the lounge door. Tony stopped, looked at Ian and Sid and nodded at them. Tony gripped his machine gun, took two steps and he was in the lounge doorway aiming his gun at the two men, why only two?

Artan and Bashkim expected to see Adnan back from the bathroom but instead, they saw a harbinger of death. They were both momentarily in shock. How did this monster get in here? They both jumped up and reached for their guns, but they stood no chance. Tony aimed his gun and fired. Artan and Bashkim took several shots to the body and face. Bits of flesh and blood flew onto the wall. Tony kept firing, the bodies were shaking and falling to pieces, with the ferocity of the bullets.

Adnan was doing up his flies in the toilet when he heard a machine gun fire in the lounge are. What the fuck is that? He thought. He was not armed but still rushed to the lounge to see what was happening. He took one look and saw Artan and Baskim dead, riddled with bullet holes. Blood and guts everywhere. The man with the eyes has come hunting and made a killing. Tony saw Adnan and started shooting but Adnan had already gone. He rushed through the hall, opened the front door and ran for dear life. The three armed men ran after him. He could hear them shouting. It was very early in the morning and Adnan decided to start screaming. Adnan shouted as loud as he could." Police! Police! Help!" Lights started going on in all the neighbouring houses. Tony stopped. Shit! They've got to get away, get back to the cars. He shouted. They sprinted to the cars jumped in and were away. Tony was cursing. One of the bastards got away.

Adnan could hardly breathe. He was hiding in the back-yard of the house next door. He thought of Eleni. Thank God, she would have survived the massacre. How did he find us? Of course, they must have noticed Bashkim and followed him back. He could hear police sirens. Soon, three police cars were in the drive. He decided to go back to the house. Adnan approached and was stopped by an officer.

"Who are you sir?"

"I am visiting the family and escaped from the gunmen."

"You better come with me, sir." The officer led Adnan back into the house and took him to the dining room. Adnan could imagine why they were not going to the Lounge. He saw Eleni.

"Thank God, you're safe." He rushed to comfort her.

She screamed at him. "You and that Bashkim brought death to my house! Artan is dead! You killed him!" She collapsed onto a chair, crying and wailing.

“Do you know who is responsible for this attack?” The officer was looking at Adnan.

“I have absolutely no idea officer, no idea at all." No one is going to take this lion from me, he thought. I will hunt it, I will find it and I will kill it.

The house was sealed off for forensic examination. Eleni and Adnan were taken to a local hotel. A police officer kept guard outside their rooms.

Tony got home and was happy. They got two of the bastards. But he was really pissed that they missed one. Pity I didn’t get a good look at that bastard so I could recognise him for next time, he thought. There was always the possibility that the remaining one could still come for him. I better increase security even more, he thought. The next time Tony went to the club, he had six bodyguards round him, at all times. Paul just could not believe what he was seeing. Later that day, Paul was watching the news and saw that two men had been killed by machine gun fire in North London. Paul was thinking: people get killed, suddenly Tony has more bodyguards than Barack Obama. Something's not right and I need to find out what that is.

"Hi, it’s Paul. Did you hear about North London, two killed……Yes, we go ahead?"

Jeff and Karen at Rotherhithe, were in shock. They had just been sitting having tea with Mr Papadikis and his friend who they’d now found out was called Bashkim. Now, they heard that they'd been killed, with multiple gunshot wounds from a machine gun.

“You know what, Karen, we’ve got so many dead bodies, and it’s difficult to know where to start. The only good news is, Coyne has committed on the Falcon case.”

CHAPTER 36

Emma was really excited by the shopping expedition. Paul and Fifi were coming with her, which was a real bonus. Westfield shopping centre was just incredible. There were thousands of shops and when you got tired and hungry, loads of really good restaurants. Emma had gone down to Kingswood on the Friday and stayed over. She and Fifi took the train up to London Bridge, then onto the Northern line to Bank, changed onto the central line and straight to Shepherds Bush; two minutes and you were in heaven.

Paul dropped into the club for half an hour and was then going to drive over to Westfield. When he got to the club, he was surprised to see Tony there, he was even more surprised when he found out that Tony had actually slept the night at the club and demanded that two of his bodyguards do the same. When Tony saw Paul, he was very pleased. He asked what he was doing and Paul said he was going shopping with Emma at Westfield. Shock, horror for Paul: Tony asked to join them. Paul didn't think Emma would be overjoyed at Tony turning up but he had promised to behave. Paul also limited the number of bodyguards to Duke and one other, David. They ordered in some croissants and had some coffee and then set off for Westfield.

Paul was driving and they were all in one car. None of them noticed the motor bike following them.

The house in Totteridge had been professionally cleaned. The floor had new carpets and wall paper, replaced. Adnan and Eleni moved back in and tried to carry on. Eleni wanted Adnan to move out as soon as possible and he had promised to be gone in a couple of days. He had sat down and considered his next move. He was now alone up against a ruthless killer and his guards. What he could not accept was that, he left without killing the man called Tony Bolton, who had killed Artan,

Bashkim and Timius and goodness knows how many more. But he knew he could pick up Bolton any time he wanted at the Den club. He could even bomb the club, but he didn't really want to kill hundreds of innocent bystanders. There was also the problem of following him. They would be looking out for cars, so a motorbike would be a good alternative and with a helmet on, he could not be identified. He bought a small bike and disguised it as a pizza delivery bike. Perfect, he thought. The timing and opportunity were a different kettle of fish. He had no idea of Bolton's itinery except that he was driven from home to the club and from the club back home. Bolton had also increased his security to five or six bodyguards, so hitting him on the journey, or at either location, was out of the question. So, Adnan decided to keep up permanent surveillance, until an opportunity presented itself. That Saturday morning, as Paul drove away from the Den club, Adnan followed on his bike. It was a relatively short ride to the Westfield Shopping Centre.

Emma and Fifi arrived first and made for Carluccios, for the first coffee of the day. They would have lunch at Jaimie's Italian, one of Emma's favourite Westfield restaurants.

Emma saw Paul coming in and then she saw that nutcase, Tony and his bodyguards.

"Paul, how are you darling." Emma kissed Paul and whispered in his ear, "What is he doing here?"

"I know, sorry, but he's promised to behave. Buy lunch and get Fifi a nice present."

"Hmm, well let's hope he behave. Tony nice to see you."

"Emma! It's always a pleasure to see you and your lovely sister, Fifi."

Fifi hated Tony and just ignored him. It would be a miracle if she spoke to him even once all day.

"So, coffees all round," said Tony, smiling.

They all got their coffees and sat at a table away from the entrance. Tony made sure he sat facing the entrance, so he could see everybody who came and went. Tony had told Duke and Dave to stay very close and to watch anybody who came anywhere near them.

Coffees finished, they moved out and started serious shopping. They walked as a group, or in ones and twos, popping into shops as they strolled along. Paul wanted to buy a new suit, so he was looking forward to visiting the Armani shop.

“Tony, I’m going to buy you a new suit today to celebrate.”

“Celebrate what, Paul?”

“We don’t need a reason Tony, let’s just celebrate life.”

“Hmm, OK.” Tony took a swig of whisky from his small hip flask.

Paul and Emma were holding hands and generally acting like kids on their first date.

“Tony, where’s my present then?” asked Fifi.

"Well, what do you want?” Tony knew the only reason Fifi was speaking to him was to get the present he promised.

Adnan followed Tony to the Westfield shopping centre. He parked his bike and followed at a discreet distance. He had had to take off his motorcycle helmet as you were not allowed to wear them in the shopping centre. He carried his Uzi in a holdall. He could not get too close as it was possible he could be recognised. He continued to follow the group, looking for an opportunity to strike.

The group continued to stroll round the shops and then Paul saw the Armani shop.

“Emma, I can see my new suit. Tony, how do you fancy a new Armani suit?”

Duke and Dave were scanning the area ahead and behind, for threats. The place was beginning to get very busy, making life very difficult for them.

Paul went into the Armani shop. Tony was swigging out of his hip flask again.

“Tony, you said you were going to buy me a present.” Fifi was smiling and sucking up to Tony.

Emma was looking in a shop window at a beautiful coat.

Adnan knew there would not be a perfect opportunity, so he must take any chance he could get. He saw Tony drinking out of his hip flask again. One of the men had gone into a shop. It was the time.

Fifi was looking round and saw Adnan. She whispered to Tony, "Cor, Tony, there's a man over there with a huge scar on his face."

As soon as she said scar, Tony remembered outside his house. He reacted and grabbed Fifi and dragged her in front of him. Half a second later, bullets were flying into the group, hitting people without discretion. There was pandemonium. People were screaming and running in all directions. The gunman was screaming out the names of Artan, Bashkim and Timius. Adnan was firing in every direction, desperately trying to make sure he hit Tony. Emma was running towards Fifi, screaming, "Fifi! Fifi!" She went down as the first bullet slammed into her leg.

Paul heard the machine gun fire and rushed out of the door of the shop. Outside, he saw chaos; people screaming and running in every direction. His eyes frantically searched to see where Emma was. He saw, to his horror, Emma lying on the ground, a few feet away. He was screaming her name as he rushed towards her. Duke also ran towards her whilst firing at where he thought the bullets were coming from. He dived to try to cover her, but was too late. Bullets thudded into Emma's chest and shoulder. Tony and Dave were returning fire but nobody could really see who was firing, and from where. Duke received a shot in the arm and one in the leg. Adnan was now running away. He had dropped the Uzi and was making for the exit with hundreds of others. Dave was lying prone on the floor, not moving; a river of blood was pouring from multiple wounds to his head.

Tony looked at Fifi, half her head had been blown away. He dropped her and moved away quickly. Everything went quiet. Heavily armed police officers in swat type gear, were rushing past the casualties, scanning for gunmen. Paul called to them.

"We need ambulances please! Now, hurry!" People were now coming to the aid of casualties. There must have been about twenty adults and children with bullet wounds.

Paul had found Emma and was crying and cradling her in his arms. “Emma! Don’t go Emma! You can’t leave me now! Emma please!" He was sure she had gone but continued to cry, scream and beg God to help her. He held her tightly. "My baby!" He screamed. He had lost her and the baby. He couldn't believe this had happened. He looked around for Tony; he was lying on the floor near Fifi.

Paul looked back down at Emma and saw her hands twitching. “She’s alive! Somebody help me! She’s alive here! Somebody help me!”

Fast car Paramedics were arriving. Paul looked up. “Over here! Over here! She’s pregnant! Please help, quickly!"

A Paramedic rushed towards Paul. He crouched down next to Emma who was now lying on her back on the floor. Paul was crying and his breathing was getting laboured. “Help her please.” He could hardly speak. His breathing was getting shallower and more laboured. He tried to say her name but couldn't because he could now hardly breathe.

The Paramedic handed Paul a paper bag. “Put this over your mouth and breathe in and out into the bag.” The Paramedic went back to work on Emma.

Ambulance men with trollies were now in the centre. The Paramedic called to one of them. “Here, quickly, she’s hanging on!” The ambulance crew quickly lifted Emma onto the trolley and started running towards the exit.

Paul was running next to the trolley, shouting as loud as he could, “Clear the way! Clear the way!”

They finally went through the glass doors and Paul saw a line of ambulances. They rushed to the nearest one, yanked open the back door and pushed the trolley into place. The Paramedic and Paul jumped into the back and the ambulance roared off with sirens blazing and lights flashing. The Paramedic started connecting a drip into Emma’s arm. One of the crew was trying to stem the massive flow of blood from the chest wound. Paul was still blubbing and talking. “Please help her, let her live please, Emma you can do it, don’t give up! I love you!"

It was a short journey to Hammersmith Hospital and they were soon pulling into the Accident and Emergency department. Paul jumped off the back of the ambulance. Staff were waiting. A major accident announcement had been made and staff were moving quickly in all directions. Emma was wheeled into the Accident and Emergency and taken straight through to a cubicle, where a team of doctors and nurses were waiting. The senior doctor took charge. Paul was standing back, praying they could do something. Nurses were setting up blood transfusion and adrenalin tubes. Paul was terrified as he listened to all the medical diagnosis being used to describe Emma's condition.

"Severe Ballistic Trauma."

"Severe tissue damage."

"Wounds to the chest, shoulder and leg"

"Definite Lung damage and other organs"

"Seal the chest to stop blood loss."

"Stabilise and straight into Theatre."

"Quickly, to have any hope of saving her."

"Fucking hell!" said Paul as they wheeled Emma out, heading towards theatre surgery. Paul sat on a spare chair before he fell down. He looked around, more trollies were being rushed in with casualties. He thought of Fifi. He had seen her terrible injuries. She must be gone, he thought. And what about Duke, Tony and Dave? Paul sat, crying with his hands over his face. He felt a hand on his shoulder and a gentle voice whispered close to his ear, "Come with me please." He stumbled up and the woman held his arm as she guided him away from the blood, guts and carnage.

Paul was taken to a special room for families of casualties. He sat down. The helper brought a cup of hot sugared tea which he tried to sip.

The helper then took his hand. "I'll come back and see you shortly."

"There are other members of my family and friends; I need to know how they are." The helper assured him she would come back soon and take their names.

Paul was still in shock. He was trying to think of the past few minutes' terrible events. What happened? Why the hell did someone start shooting at us in a shopping centre? It's something to do with Tony. I'll make him suffer for this. Oh God! I've got to phone Peter and his wife! How can I do that? He looked for his mobile, it was still in his pocket. He took it out and pressed the contact list. He was dreading having to call Emma's parents. How could he explain to them the terrible fate of their two daughters? God, please save Emma. Fifis gone, but please, save Emma. He pressed the button.

"Hello, Peter speaking."

"Peter, its Paul." He broke down crying and gasping.

"Paul! For God's sake! What is it, what's happened?"

"Shooting at Westfield shopping centre. A madman, he shot Emma and Fifi."

"Oh God! Are they alive? Please tell me they're alive!"

"Emma's in theatre, she's very badly injured; its touch and go." Paul didn't want to say anymore.

"And Fifi, Paul how is she?"

"She's dead Peter, dead!" Paul was now on the floor, his legs had given way under him.

Paul could hear Peter telling his wife. She was screaming in the background. Peter came back on the phone.

"Paul, where are you?"

"Hammersmith Hospital."

"OK, I'm on my way!" The line went dead.

The hospital helper came back and helped Paul into a chair.

"Now, shall we make that list," she said gently. Paul gave her the names and she left the room. Over the next forty minutes the room filled up with crying distraught relatives and friends of those lying in blood and guts, fighting for their lives. Paul tried to comfort one or two but could not cope himself.

The helper eventually returned with the list. "Let's sit in the corner for a minute." she led Paul to a corner of the room.

"It is not all bad news, Paul. Tony Bolton is being treated for shock. Edward styles who you know as Duke is in surgery; he has two gunshot wounds, one in the leg and one in the arm. He'll be fine. Dave Roberts, I'm sorry he didn't make it, multiple gunshot wounds."

Paul looked at her and took her arm. "Tell me the worst."

"The young girl Fifi Miller ..., I'm sorry Paul."

Paul started sobbing. "Her mum and dad will be here soon." He looked at her. "Any news from theatre? Emma."

"I'll see what I can find out. Keep positive."

Paul was fretting and praying. What he didn't know was that Emma had already gone. In the theatre, the surgeon had taken one look and knew it was hopeless. Emma had suffered catastrophic injuries from bullets that hit her in the chest, shoulder and leg. She had suffered over fifty per cent blood loss; the chest injury had destroyed one lung and so much tissue, it was impossible to save her.

Peter and Mary Miller arrived. Mary was inconsolable, she couldn't stop crying. Peter was just about holding himself together.

"Any news Paul?"

"Not yet Peter, I'm so sorry."

"It's not your fault, Paul. A lunatic running amok with a gun, it's just really bad luck."

"How long since you had any news about Emma?"

"She's been in there about an hour. I don't know what's happening."

Twenty minutes later, the hospital helper came back into the room. She walked towards Paul. Paul looked at her and noticed the grim expression on her face. It was bad news.

"No please don't tell me!" sobbed Paul. Mary was looking at the lady and then let out a hideous scream. The lady put her arm round Mary and look helplessly at Paul and Peter. "I'm so sorry, Emma didn't make it."

Peter, Paul and Mary were crying. It was the end of the world as far as they were concerned. Ian Miller turned up to take Peter and Mary home. He looked at Paul. He didn't say anything, but Paul could feel the hate, the look that said you're to blame for all this. Paul still could not grasp what was happening. They went shopping and everybody got shot. It's just insane, he thought.

Someone entered the room, Paul looked up, it was Tony. He came over and hugged Paul. Trust Tony to escape unhurt, thought Paul.

"Paul, are you alright? I'm so sorry."

"No. I need to get out of here. I need a drink."

Tony agreed. "Let's go." He took Paul's arm and led him out of the room. Paul stopped. "I've got to say thank you to someone." He looked round for the helper and saw her coming round the corner. Paul went to her and hugged her. "Thank you."

She looked into his eyes. "Time heals everything. Good luck, my dear."

Tony drove Paul to the club. They hit the bar the second they walked in. Two huge glasses of whisky. Paul knocked it back in one. He then heard his mobile ringing and answered it. "Paul." He recognised the voice instantly.

"I'm so sorry. If you need anything, call me."

"Thanks," and Paul and hung up.

The drinking went on for hours until Paul could drink no more and he collapsed in one of the office chairs and slept. He slept for a couple of hours but the demons woke him and plagued him, blaming him for the deaths of Emma and Fifi. He hoped he would wake up and realise it had all been a bad dream. Paul woke up at eleven o clock the next morning.

He went straight to the bar and drank another huge glass of whiskey, shut his eyes and went back to sleep. He did that for four days, drinking every night, sleeping and drinking. He was lost in a world of alcohol. He tried to numb the pain, but it wouldn't go away.

Adnan had joined the crowd heading for the nearest exit. As he approached it, he could hear shouting. He glanced back and saw armed police swarming the area. He quickly pushed through the door and headed for the car park. Once there, he found his Pizza motorbike climbed on and started her up. He headed towards the exit which was some way off. Shit! He thought. He could see the police had set up a stop sign at the exit, checking every car that was leaving. He couldn't risk trying to get through. He had to leave through somewhere else. He slowed right down and searched for another exit. Then he saw it, a damaged fence on one side of the car park. He drove slowly towards the fence, trying not to attract attention. His undoing was the disguise he had chosen. A police officer was scanning the car park and saw the pizza delivery bike.

He turned to one of his colleagues. "Tom, fancy a pizza?" He turned back just as Adnan was approaching the fence. The officer stopped and watched and then shouted, pointing. "He's escaping with the motorbike!" All eyes turned to the bike. Something was wrong. Adnan got through the fence and went to full speed, away from the car park. Two motorcycle policeman leapt on their bikes and were in pursuit in seconds.

The officer at the car park was on his radio. "Westfield shootings. A suspect just left car park on a motorbike, disguised as a pizza delivery vehicle. He's on the A3220 west cross route, heading west. Two police motorcycles are in pursuit."

"Thank you. MP Tango Oscar, we will patch in."

"All units! Two MP units in pursuit of motorcycle on the A3220, going west. Confirm positions."

The met control room immediately scrambled a helicopter to assist in the pursuit.

Adnan was driving hard and fast down the A3220 zipping in between cars and Lorries. He has seen the police motorcycles behind him and was trying to shake them off. He knew the longer the chase the more police units would be involved. He came to the roundabout junction with Holland Park Avenue, but didn't slow down. He careered round the roundabout, touching a blue Mazda that skidded sideways into the path of a coca cola lorry. The lorry crashed and bottles were scattered all over the road. He was across the roundabout and speeding down Holland Road at 90mph, and past the Kensington Suite Hotel. He was looking for a turning, saw it and swung into it, turning left into Addison Road. He slammed on the breaks, did a sharp right and headed into Warwick Road. He looked in the side rear mirror, no sign as yet, of the police motorcycles. He was desperate to get to the M4 and head to Heathrow.

The two motorcycles were still behind him but were held up at the roundabout. A police car had joined the motorcycles and was following down Addison Road, in hot pursuit. Another police car was doing 110mph over the Hammersmith flyover, heading to cut him off. He could now see the turning for the A4 Cromwell Road. He slowed down slightly, traffic was moving fast along the A4. No point having an accident, he thought. He zipped straight into the fast lane and increased his speed to 110mph. Some bastard was doing 60mph in front of him. He cut inside and accelerated to 120mph. The driver of the car looked at him in disbelief. Adnan's motorbike scraped the middle barrier and he started to lose control. He slid across into the middle lane and hit a BMW. A container lorry behind the BMW couldn't brake in time and slammed into the back of him. Cars were scattering in all lanes, looking for safety, ending up causing more chaos. Adnan looked in his mirror and was pleased that that should slow them down a bit. He then heard a noise he had been dreading. The helicopter was fifty feet in the air, just to his right. He looked up to see a man pointing at him and signalling for him to stop. He increased his speed to 125mph. He heard a police siren but it was not behind him. He was looking for it as it passed him in the opposite direction, doing at least 110mph. In no time he was up over the Hammersmith flyover. He glanced in his mirrors, he could see the bikes and a car behind him, albeit a fair distance away.

He was now on the Great West Road heading fast towards the M4, his head down and at high speed. He was in the fast lane and soon hit the M4. He could still hear the helicopter and realised that his efforts were futile. There was no way he could escape and was thinking of his next course of action. He made a decision but it seemed almost too late as he slammed on the brakes and belted down the slip road to the Chiswick High Street Roundabout, straight out onto the roundabout, at full speed and round to the third exit. He was almost there. He turned sharply right into Gunnersbury Avenue. I could be safe here, he thought. He rode to the end of the road and parked outside Gunnersbury Tube Station. He took his Pizza jacket off and flung it in on the floor. He ran towards the entrance. He was about to go in, and stopped. He looked up to see the helicopter and the copper looking at him through the window. He smiled, waved and was gone. He hoped the police would think he would ride into central London and get lost. He did the opposite and went to Richmond. He exited Richmond tube and grabbed a taxi. “Twickenham Guest House, Chertsey Road, please.”

“Yea, no problem. How’s your day been, then?”

Adnan took a deep breath. “Bit hectic, actually.” Adnan laughed to himself. If only you fucking well knew, he thought.

CHAPTER 37

Jeff and Karen were dumbfounded. More killings and another connection with Bermondsey. The shootings at Westfield were all over the news; seven killed and eleven injured. It was a terrible assault, whilst people were going about their everyday business of shopping. Jeff had made enquiries; most of the shoppers were from out of town. One of the dead was Dave Roberts and one injured, Edward Styles, were residents of Bermondsey. Witness statements were also taken from brothers Anthony and Paul Bolton, again a connection to Bermondsey, with Anthony living in Grange Road. Someone running amok at Westfield with an Uzi sub machine gun. It smacked of a bungled hit, rather than a random maniac. There was also a flimsy identification from police officers at the scene and film from the helicopter. Interestingly enough, there was mention that he looked a bit Greek. Jeff had immediately informed Scotland Yard that the killer could be an Albanian named Arben, and gave the address in North London. Armed officers visited the address, but only found a woman named Eleni Papadikis in the house. An alert was put out to all airports and ports to look for an individual Albanian, wanted in connection with multiple murders.

Raptor was still in progress but surveillance on Jack Coombs and the Brothel in Peckham had been pulled. Manpower was needed elsewhere, to counter the terrorist threat from Muslim extremists.

Paul Bolton was tough, he had to be. Peter and Mary Miller had told him they never wanted to see or hear from him, ever again. He had even been banned from the funeral. This set him off drinking again, but he knew he had to pull himself together eventually, and that day came. That lady at Hammersmith Hospital had said time healed everything. You may heal but you never forget.

Paul decided to pop in and see how Duke was getting on in Hospital and to thank him for trying to save Emma. Paul had seen him dive to cover her and a second earlier, he might have been in time.

Duke was still in Hammersmith and it was two weeks after the shootings. Paul bought some magazines in the main reception shop and made his way to the Christopher Booth ward.

He found Duke's bed. "Duke, how are you?"

"Hello Paul, I didn't expect to see you."

"Just popped into see you." Truth was, being back at the hospital was really an ordeal for Paul and he had had to sit down and collect his thoughts before seeing Duke.

"Duke, I saw how you tried to save Emma." Paul was nearly in tears at the thought of his Emma.

"I'm just so sorry I couldn't do more." Duke looked at Paul with pity in his eyes.

Paul bucked up. "You did your best, that's all anyone can do. When are you getting out?"

"They say about two weeks."

"Look, when you come out, you will work for me and only me, OK?"

"Yea, if you say so, Paul. What about Tony?"

"He's got no say in it. OK?"

"Paul, is Tony working?"

"That's a strange question, Duke. Why do you ask?"

"I just wondered if everything was alright between you."

Duke realised that Paul had not seen Tony pull Fifi in front of him to save himself.

"Duke if you've got something to say, you better say it now."

Duke had to say something. "The shooting. Fifi might have been alright but Tony pulled her in front of himself to protect him."

"What! Fucking what?! Are you saying he deliberately pulled Fifi in front of him so she would take the bullets and not him?"

"That's exactly what I am saying. He has also been involved in some jobs recently that have gone seriously wrong."

"Such as?" Paul was getting mad now. His fucking brother!

"The job in Plaistow."

"The armed robbery where someone was killed?" asked Paul.

"That's right. I heard there could be a connection."

"What? From that to Westfield?"

"Yea, that's right."

"So, Tony killed Emma and Fifi?"

"I can't comment on that. Look, please, don't mention my name Paul, he'll kill me."

"Don't worry. I haven't even been here."

Inside Paul was raging. Tony was responsible for all this and he'll have to pay.

"Duke, get better soon. I've got things to do."

Paul went back to the club and had a long hard think about what to do. He made a call.

"It's me, I'm ready when you are.

CHAPTER 38

Jeff and Karen were very happy they were on their way to the Frog in the Old Kent Road. They had two armed officers with them, just in case.

"So, it's about time then," said Karen

"Yes, he's been running around causing mayhem for much too long. Look Karen, I want you to read him his rights."

"Are you sure? I thought you would pull rank on that."

"No, I want him to see that to me, he's just another criminal, nothing more nothing less."

"I'll be delighted, of course."

"This will look good on your file, you know."

"Well, I hope so," said Karen smiling

They pulled up around the corner from the Frog. One of the armed officers went to the back of the pub. Jeff, Karen and the other armed officer entered through the front door. Jeff led the way into the bar and looked for the door marked private. They went through and climbed the stairs. Jeff came to the door he was looking for. He didn't bother knocking and just opened the door and walked in.

Jack Coombs and Richard Philips were sitting near the window, having coffee. Richard immediately got up and walked towards Jeff. "What the fuck are you doing? Don't you usually knock? Jack, call security."

"Don't bother, Jack." Jeff turned back to Philips. "Long time no see, Richard."

"You're a fucking copper, what do you want?"

“Karen.” Jeff looked at Karen. Karen took her handcuffs off her belt and approached Philips. “Turn round, please.”

“What the fuck are you doing?” He refused to turn.

Jeff and the other officer approached Philips and turned him round. Karen expertly cuffed him and turned him back.

“Mr Richard Philips, I am arresting you for the murders of Mr James Telfer, Mr Robin Scott and Mr Adrian Thompson (Monty). You do not have to say anything, but if you do...”

Philips was dumbfounded. Murder of Telfer and Scott; what the fuck is she talking about?

Martin looked at Jeff. "There's no way you can pin me with those murders! I didn’t do it!”

Jeff was enjoying this. “That’s funny Mr Philips, we have an eye witness who swears it was you and will testify in court to that effect.”

Philips was thinking how can they have a fucking witness. He laughed. “I don’t think so. You're bull shitting. Take off the cuffs.” He held out his hands. Jeff said it slowly

“Eye witness by the name of Bruce Coyne.”

The colour drained from Philips' face. He was confused; Coyne was dead. Telfer and Scott went to Madrid. I’m being fucking stitched up here.

“You bastards, you won’t get away with this.”

Jeff leaned close to him. “I already fucking have. Now who’s the cunt?” he turned to the officer. "Take him away."

“Mr Coombs, how are you?”

“Very well, thank you officer.”

Jeff leaned close. “We’ll be back for you.”

“I doubt very much if we will ever see each other again, officer; you see, I am retiring to spend time in my garden.”

Jeff just looked at him. Yea, you're probably right, he thought.

He turned to Karen. "Let's go."

Jeff sat in the car on the way back to the nick, thinking to himself; well, Michael did say do whatever you had to, which was exactly what we did. Coyne will testify, and with the knife which was used on poor old Monty sent to us with fingerprints and DNA all over it, Philips was truly fucked. I wonder who sent us that knife.

Tom was at Heathrow to see off his friend Bugsy to Spain. He had given him the hundred grand he got from Artan Papadikis. Bugsy was going out to buy a villa for him and his family. Jan was half way through getting the two girls back from Social Services and as soon as that was completed, she would go out there to begin a new life. Bugsy had decided crime did not pay and he was going straight.

Tony was now completely psychotic. He was taking hundreds of tablets every day because he didn't want to sleep in case the killer from Westfield came after him. He knew it was the man from the house in North London. He never went anywhere without his favourite Magnum, now tucked into a shoulder holster. He was also drinking more than ever. Paul thought he could drop dead any second from an overdose or heart attack; he had even considered having him sectioned.

It was a Friday night, Paul had asked Tony to join him for a meal to talk about the business. They left the club and headed to the Royal Lancaster Hotel, in the Bayswater Road.

"How are you, Tony?"

"I'm OK." Paul glanced at Tony. As usual, he couldn't sit still. He kept looking at all the cars on either side, imagining the killer was going to suddenly appear, guns blazing. He kept reaching inside his jacket to check that his gun was there.

"Tony, relax. We're going to have a quiet dinner and a couple of beers."

They reached the hotel and took valet parking. They went through the main entrance and headed to the Island Grill on the second floor. Paul brought Emma here once and he made sure they sat at the same table.

"Relax Tony, and enjoy the great views of Hyde Park. What do you want to drink?"

“Whisky, large.”

“OK. Do you want some wine with your meal?”

“No, just keep the whiskeys coming.” Tony was looking around, checking to see who was sitting where and whether they looked like crazed gunmen.

“Tony, relax. Your guys are outside. Everything is cool, enjoy yourself.” Paul looked at his watch.

“Easy for you to say Paul, you haven’t got a madman after you.”

“What would you like to eat?” Paul passed the menu to Tony.

“You order for me,” he said giving him back the menu.

Paul was looking at the menu but he didn't need to; he ordered the same meal Emma had, whenever they visited. The waiter arrived to take their order.

“We’ll have smoked salmon to start, followed by Gressingham Duck and the special trifle for dessert."

“Any wine, sir?”

"Yes, a bottle of your Prosecco Casa Saint Orsola Brut, please.”

Paul’s mind was wandering. Emma loved that Prosecco so much, he had to control his emotions as he could feel the tears coming. He looked at his watch again.

“So, what do you think our next move with the business should be?”

Tony didn't even hear him. He was in a world of his own.

They finished the meal, had a glass of port and slowly made their way to the lifts.

They reached the ground floor and Paul turned right out of the lift. Tony was next to him. They took a few steps and Paul slowed down and looked at his watch. As they approached an open door, they heard voices.

“Ladies and Gentleman, I would like to introduce tonight’s speaker. We are very fortunate to have with us, one of the most experienced League Referees in the country, Mr Cyril Jones, from Hatfield!”

Tony heard the name and repeated it to himself. Cyril Jones from Hatfield. His eyes widened. He reached for his pistol and started shouting.

"He's here! It's him! He's come to kill me!" Tony levelled the gun at the stage and ran down between the rows of chairs. Half way towards the stage, he started shooting. Cyril Jones got hit in the leg and the stomach. The third shot to the forehead killed him instantly.

Pandemonium erupted as people started rushing for the door. Tony stood over Cyril Jones, his one thought was, "Where has the scar gone?"

Police arrived two minutes later and Tony was taken away. Paul melted into the background as did the bodyguards, and left the hotel.

Paul made a call. "It's done. I'll see you tomorrow."

Jeff and Karen were having a fag outside the back door at the nick in Rotherhithe.

Jim opened the door. "You won't believe this, but Tony Bolton from Bermondsey has just been arrested for shooting a Football League Referee at the Royal Lancaster Hotel."

Jeff opened the piece of paper he was holding in his hand. It said: The man you are after for the Arrow Logistics job and killing the copper down the Old Kent Road is Tony Bolton. Get him for me, from A. Jeff knew who it was from and he suspected he was more than likely already back in Albania.

Paul was driving down London Road. He pulled onto the last roundabout and looked for the fourth exit. He took it and looked for the Miami Hotel and Conference Centre. He saw it half way down the road, approached and entered the car park. He'd been thinking of Emma and sweet little Fifi. He still cried whenever he thought of them. He went every month to their graves. They were buried together at the local church at Kingswood.

He entered the hotel and asked the concierge for the coffee lounge. The concierge escorted Paul to the door. Paul stopped and breathed in deeply. I AM THE BEST, THE GREATEST, NO ONE COMPARES TO ME. He walked in and saw his new business partner.

“Jack, how are you?”

“Very well Paul; more importantly, how are you?”

“Good, Very good indeed, thank you.”

“I hope you didn’t mind coming down. As a matter of interest, this is one of our hotels and it’s very local for me. They also do a very good steak and a lovely trifle for dessert.”

“Sounds wonderful and trifle is my favourite.” Paul took a serviette and wiped a tear from his eye.

“It’s all worked out then,” said Jack.

“Yea, it's all worked out.”

They shook hands and Paul opened a new chapter in his life.

THE END

The Author

Chris Ward lives in Epsom Surrey with wife Helen and two of their seven children!

He has been commercial director of several Food Manufacturing Companies and currently runs a Food Marketing business.

Hobbies include West Bromwich Albion, Reading, Naval History, Food & Wine.

Visit Chris online at:

Facebook: http://facebook.com/BermondseyTrifle

Twitter: http://twitter.com/BermondseyT

The second Book in the Trilogy

"BERMONDSEY PROSECCO"

Out in

September 2014.

"BERMONDSEY PROSECCO"

What happens to Paul Bolton? Can he ever find love again after Emma?

Jack Coombs retires to tend his roses, but life's not that simple, is it?

Tony is stuck in Broadmoor with a load of other lunatics.

Richard Philips is banged up in Prison with a life sentence.

DCs Jeff Swan and Karen Foster continue to hunt down criminals and take on a gang of ruthless people traffickers.

There's more violence, love, passion and action aplenty to keep you on the edge of your seat!

ACTION, ACTION AND MORE ACTION !

A MUST READ !

6865348R00158

Printed in Germany
by Amazon Distribution
GmbH, Leipzig